A 'COP FOR CRIMIN.

D1484953

PAINT
— THE —
DEAD

JACK GATLAND

————————

Published by Hooded Man Media
Cover photo by Paul Thomas Gooney

First Edition: May 2022

PRAISE FOR JACK GATLAND

'This is one of those books that will keep you up past your bedtime, as each chapter lures you into reading just one more.'

'This book was excellent! A great plot which kept you guessing until the end.'

'Couldn't put it down, fast paced with twists and turns.'

'The story was captivating, good plot, twists you never saw and really likeable characters. Can't wait for the next one!'

'I got sucked into this book from the very first page, thoroughly enjoyed it, can't wait for the next one.'

'Totally addictive. Thoroughly recommend.'

'Moves at a fast pace and carries you along with it.'

'Just couldn't put this book down, from the first page to the last one it kept you wondering what would happen next.'

There's a new Detective Inspector in town...

Before Ellie Reckless, there was DI Declan Walsh!

Read an EXCLUSIVE PREQUEL, completely free to anyone who joins the Jack Gatland VIP Reader's Club!

Join at www.subscribepage.com/jackgatland

Also by Jack Gatland

For Mum, who inspired me to write.

For Tracy, who inspires me to write.

CONTENTS

1

ROOFTOP VIEW

To some people, the skyline of the city of London at night was like a cluster of sparkling jewels, each shining brightly as they boasted their existence out to the world; each a window, an office still lit up, people still working, going about their lives, and unaware, for the moment, of the world outside. Some windows might even have people staring out at their *own* skylines, but with the lights on, they were more likely to be checking their own reflections in the full-length mirrors that the windows became after the sunset.

For Ellie Reckless, the skyline was something she'd looked at every day. It was an old friend, although tonight, it seemed to have had a bit of a *falling out* with her.

'As fun as this is and all that, can we move on?' she asked politely, a hint of tiredness in her voice. 'I've got a dinner date.'

Ellie was in her mid-to-late-thirties, her dark brown, almost-black hair shoulder length and curly, with the look of a style that had started the day in a bunch, but at some point had just given up the whole idea. She was wearing a cheap navy suit, and a pastel open-necked and collared blouse, both of which were badly clashing with the grey *Converse* trainers she wore on her feet. They weren't the Chuck Taylor 'high top' style that was still popular; they were the 'ox' style of low ankle trainers, favoured by Ellie purely because it meant she could kick them off when she got home, and didn't have to fiddle drunkenly with the laces before collapsing into her bed.

Not that she was expecting to be doing that tonight, she thought to herself as she played a smile for the audience. *Right now she'd be happy if she managed a hospital bed rather than the morgue.*

Her audience comprised what could only be described as a bag of muscles that had squashed into a tight-fitting grey suit, with a shaven, flushed head plonked on top; this was Josh, and he was the one who had a gun aimed at her. Ellie, however, knew that although Josh was the one with the weapon, he wasn't the one that was going to be a problem.

The problem was the runt of a man that was currently leaning against an air conditioning unit, watching her with the weakest attempt of a *sneer*.

Walker.

A skinny, balding, middle-aged *dickhead* in a shiny three-piece suit, obviously bought off the peg from one of those super-cheap market shops that claimed to be *Italian menswear*, Walker was a man who believed that he was *better* than his station in life.

'Oh, you do, do you?' he asked mockingly, the slight sneer now resting comfortably on his lips. 'That's a shame, because Josh here was gonna shoot you in the face.'

Ellie tutted, shaking her head.

'Christ, how did I find myself in the middle of a bloody amateur hour?' she asked herself, perhaps a little too loudly.

'You have a problem with being shot in the face?' Walker enquired, a little surprised by the response.

Ellie shrugged.

'It's just stupid, that's all,' she replied. 'I mean, we're on a rooftop. Why don't you just throw me off? That way, you don't have to explain the bullet when forensics finds it, and you can just claim that I fell.'

Walker looked at Josh, who didn't look back, eyes and weapon still trained on Ellie as she continued.

'I'm guessing you're both pretty bad at this, because maybe you've not had much experience before?' she asked, looking at Josh. 'Am I right?'

Josh shrugged noncommittally at this, a motion that irritated Walker immensely. But before he could reply, he realised Ellie was looking at him now, a smile forming on her lips.

'Look, Mister Walker, I get why you're pissed at me,' she said calmly. 'I came to steal your Lamborghini.'

'Damn right I got a problem with you about that,' Walker hissed.

Ellie held a hand up to stop him.

'But, you see, I'm doing this on behalf of my client, Big Slim, who *you* stole the Lamborghini from.'

It was Walker's turn to shrug now.

'If he's got a problem with that, then he should go to the police,' he replied.

Ellie nodded, as if agreeing.

'But then he'd have to explain to them how he got it in the first place,' she stated calmly, still watching Walker, even though Josh was the one with the gun. 'And we both know that's not gonna happen.'

Walker considered Ellie for a long moment, as if measuring her up.

'You know, I've heard of you,' he eventually said. 'Ellie Reckless, the bitch that works for favours.'

'Sometimes,' Ellie replied calmly.

'Working for cash is better,' Walker offered.

'Depends on the favour,' Ellie smiled again.

Walker moved closer to Ellie now, a quick movement that encroached on her personal space, forcing her to step backwards, moving closer to the edge of the building.

'You might make the suits shit themselves, but you don't mean nothing to me,' he hissed. 'You're nothing but a corrupt ex-cop, and we got tons of them on the books.'

Ellie bristled at this.

'I'm not corrupt,' she whispered.

Walker laughed at her answer.

'Of course you are,' he mocked. 'Nobody gets kicked off the force for being a Girl Scout, *ex-* Detective Inspector Reckless.'

He smiled.

'As I said, I've heard of you.'

'If you had, you'd know that I quit the force,' Ellie's back was against the edge of the building now.

'Jumped before you were pushed, more like,' Walker replied. 'Still, you've made a big splash in what, under a year since you lost your job? Lot of favours owed to you in that time, so I hear.'

He spat to the ground.

'Like that'll mean anything.'

'Your point?' Ellie frowned at this. In response, Walker chuckled.

'You ask a criminal to owe you, to repay this favour... do you honestly think they'll actually *do* it? That Big Slim will give you something you ask for, once his Lambo is back in his garage?' Walker laughed. 'Christ, no. Why would they?'

'Because they know if they don't, I'll burn a bigger favour to remove them,' Ellie's voice was cold and dead. 'I've done it before, and people know it. And as much as they probably want to screw me over—and yes, I know there's no *honour among thieves*—they're too scared of what would happen if they *refuse*.'

She shrugged.

'Also, they *want* me on their side,' she added. 'I can do things, find things, solve problems better than any of their other guys, and my favours are usually cheaper in the long run.'

Walker considered this for a moment, before smiling widely, as if looking like a brilliant idea had suddenly come into his head.

'Josh, mate. Don't waste a bullet. Throw Miss Reckless over the edge, will you?'

Josh, placing away the gun carefully, started towards Ellie, who raised up her hands.

'Wait!' she protested. 'Don't I get a last phone call at least?'

Josh stopped, looking at Walker.

'Calling the cops?' Walker asked.

Ellie spat to the side.

'Please,' she scoffed. 'They'd want tickets to watch. You can toss me off the building in a moment, but don't insult me.'

Walker watched Ellie now, as if trying to work out whether this was some kind of plan. Then, relenting, he stepped back, motioning for Ellie to pull out her phone.

'You call anyone I don't like, or try anything stupid...' he muttered, leaving the ending empty, the warning obvious. Ellie flashed him a grin as a reply, moving through her contacts list.

'We're not up here by chance, are we?' she asked. 'I mean, you have offices in the building, right?'

'So what?' Walker looked at Josh now, confused.

Ellie tapped a contact, letting it dial.

'I was just confirming that you distributed for Johnny Lucas,' she replied.

Walker didn't like the way this conversation was going.

'And what if I do?'

Ellie held up a finger to silence him as her call connected.

'Johnny? It's Ellie,' she said into the mouthpiece. 'Ellie Reckless. Sorry to call so late.'

She held a hand over the mouthpiece as she looked at Walker.

'I think he was asleep,' she whispered. 'He's not happy. Maybe it's Jackie, he's a miserable bastard at the best of times. Nah, that personality's gone now, hasn't he?'

'Wait,' Walker looked nervous now. 'You're calling Johnny Lucas?'

But Ellie had already returned to the phone.

'Those favours you owe me?' she asked conversationally. 'When I saved your arse recently? I'm calling one in. You know a "Walker" that works for you?'

She stopped, listening, looking back at the now scared, weary-looking man.

'He asks what's your first name?'

'Bill,' Walker replied automatically.

Ellie gave a cheerful thumbs up.

'Bill, or maybe William,' she said into the phone. 'Yeah, that's the one. Terrible shiny suits.'

As she continued, she looked directly at Walker.

'I want him removed from your organisation,' she said. 'No, I don't care how, I just want it done immediately. Do that, and you only owe me *one* favour.'

A moment later, she looked down at the phone as the call disconnected, before looking back at Walker, an almost apologetic expression on her face, as if she'd heard something bad, and didn't know how to explain it.

'He didn't even argue,' she said. 'That's how little you matter to him.'

'What did you just do?' Walker spat, his face pale now.

Ellie moved away from the wall as Josh, realising what was happening already pulled out his gun in preparation, Walker now the one stepping back as she encroached on *his* space.

'I'm the cop for criminals, the one that takes cases for favours,' Ellie replied softly. 'You already know that. But the thing is, these favours? They're set before I take on the case. If I work for a favour, then that favour can be called in at any *time*, about any *thing*, and at any *size*. If it's within your remit, you *have* to do it. And as I've already said, you *don't* want to see what happens if you refuse. You understand?'

Nervously, Walker licked his lips as he nodded.

'Basically, if you take the deal, then you pretty much have something big and bad you need sorted. And your boss, Mister Lucas? A little while back, he had something big and bad that he needed, well, to be sorted. You may have heard of it. And I did it for a favour.'

Walker was continuing to back away; he'd heard the rumours of how Johnny Lucas had stopped a recent gangland coup on his territory, and had also heard whispers of Reckless' involvement, but Ellie hadn't finished just yet.

'Now I take these cases, because I want these favours. I'm banking them, you see, chits from the biggest and most brutal out there. I have a plan for them, too. But sometimes? Sometimes you just need to burn one to remove an irritation.'

She looked over at Josh now.

'There'll be a job opportunity opening up soon, mate. Might want to check for a text.'

Josh nodded, pulling out his phone, watching it intently.

'What are you doing?' Walker wailed to his bodyguard, still not understanding the situation he was now in.

'He's wondering if he'll be the one that gives you the severance package,' Ellie replied. 'The one thing he *won't* be doing is tossing me off this building, because he doesn't yet know what other favours I have set up, ones that go into action after my death, aimed at whoever kills me.'

Walker was hopping from foot to foot now, nervous, angry, almost hysterical. Reaching into his jacket, he pulled out his own gun; a chrome-plated Glock 19.

'I'll give you bloody severance—' he started, but he didn't finish the sentence, as before he could fully extend the gun, Ellie had moved in, now within his reach, grabbing the wrist that held the Glock and twisting, pocketing the Glock into her own jacket as it fell from his pain-filled hand to the sound of a yelp from Walker as she twisted harder, snapping something loudly within the wrist, punctuated by a louder scream.

'Wrong move,' she hissed as, still holding onto the now-broken wrist, she used the momentum to spin Walker around, slamming his head hard into the side of the metal air conditioning unit.

As Walker staggered back, blood streaming from his nose, Ellie grabbed him once more, pulling out a car remote from his pocket before sending him stumbling towards Josh, crumpling to the floor in front of his onetime bodyguard, now staring down at him as if unsure what to do.

'He's all yours, mate,' Ellie said with a weary smile, already walking off towards the rooftop door, while Josh glanced at his phone, still waiting for a message.

'I'll get you for this, Reckless!' Walker, for the moment still untouched by his bodyguard, shouted out angrily.

At the door, Ellie looked back and grinned.

'Good for you. Always stay positive,' she encouraged, before leaving the two men alone on the roof.

THE BUILDING WAS PART OF A HALF-BUILT SCIENCE PARK JUST south of the Thames, to the right of North Greenwich and the O2 Arena. And although those two areas were a hive of tourist activity, this area still felt like the *old* London that the new buildings had tried to replace. As Ellie left the dark brick building and walked across the car park, she could almost hear the theme tune of the Eighties movie *The Long Good Friday* playing, and expected to see Bob Hoskins turn up in his "flash mo-tarr".

Instead, ahead of her was an army-green 1992 Land Rover Defender, complete with khaki material roof and spare wheel on the bonnet, parked up next to a hideous yellow Lamborghini. In front of it, leaning against the bonnet and in her own olive-coloured German Army coat and blue jeans, her curly blonde hair pulled back into a better ponytail than Ellie had managed, currently poking out from under a grey *New York Mets* baseball cap, was a woman, a wide grin on her face.

'Took your time,' she said mockingly.

Ellie smiled. Tinker Jones would have finished this repo job in a matter of moments, and wouldn't have blown a favour on it, Ellie was sure. But, at the same time, Tinker Jones would have racked up a body count that would have had every police force in the district looking for her.

'Here, do something with this,' Ellie said as she approached, passing Tinker the shiny Glock that she'd taken from Walker. 'You know I hate the bloody things.'

She stopped, grabbing Tinker's arm where, around her sleeve, were the telltale signs of blood.

'What's this?' she asked. 'You were only supposed to drive me here, not kick off a fight.'

Tinker shrugged.

'I didn't start it,' she explained. 'Some "locals" wanted me to leave.'

'You should be more careful,' Ellie admonished.

Tinker laughed.

'What about you?' she asked. 'I noted you didn't call me in.'

'Didn't want the body count,' Ellie shrugged.

As if accepting this answer, Tinker nodded to the car.

'You get them?'

Ellie pulled out the remote, waggling it at Tinker.

'Want to take it back to Big Slim?' she asked with a slight smile.

'Christ no,' Tinker laughed. 'I wouldn't be seen dead in that bloody thing.'

Ellie sighed.

'I'll do it then,' she replied. 'Take off for the night and I'll see you tomorrow.'

'Grab some dinner first?' Tinker suggested. 'There's a great street van by the Greenwich Yacht Club. We could leave a kebab in the boot of the lambo, see how long Slim takes to realise.'

Ellie shook her head, glancing at her watch.

'No time,' she replied. 'I want an early night because I've got brunch with the ex tomorrow. Although you're welcome to come along to that, if you want?'

'Brunch with Nathan?' Tinker shuddered. 'That's not a meal, that's an execution squad. I'll pass.'

Ellie nodded, fully understanding what Tinker meant. Which was a shame, because if Tinker had gone, then Nathan might have been on better behaviour.

Who was she kidding? Nathan was always going to be a prick.

'Although I never thought you'd be a brunch kind of person,' Tinker smiled.

'Tomorrow, Caesar's, noon,' Ellie ignored the jibe, pressing a button on the remote and watching one of the Lamborghini doors open slowly.

'We could move it to the *Ritz*?' Tinker suggested innocently. 'We could have little sandwiches with the crusts cut off. I mean, it sounds like you're into that sort of thing now. I hear *Claridges* does an amazing lunch deal.'

In the distance, from the top of a building, they heard a gunshot.

'That sounds ominous,' Tinker whispered, reaching into her jacket instinctively. 'How did you get out again?'

Ellie looked up at the building.

'Burned a favour,' she said. 'Had Walker fired.'

'Did you mean *literally?*' Tinker raised an eyebrow as Ellie shook her head.

'Josh the bodyguard? He's not dumb,' she replied, climbing into the car. 'If he wanted him dead, he could have thrown him off the edge and saved a bullet.'

'And how would he know that?' Tinker climbed up into the Defender's driver's seat.

'Because I told him,' Ellie finished as she closed the driver's door, revved the Lamborghini engine, and sped off into the night.

2

HIGH ROLLERS

IT WAS CLOSE TO MIDNIGHT WHEN DANNY FLYNN AND HIS trophy wife Chantelle eventually left the golf club's black-tie charity event, and while driving home in their champagne-coloured Bentley, their driver Ricardo's eyes darting from the road to the rear-view mirror, it was about three minutes after their exit when they started to argue.

Danny was in his mid-thirties and was the archetypal 'Essex wide boy'; that was to say, he looked far more comfortable in a bright red *Adidas* tracksuit or a *Fred Perry* polo shirt than he did in his current attire, that of a dinner suit and bow tie—and his constant fiddling at his dress shoes betrayed the fact that he was far happier in a pair of slip-on knitted *Nike* trainers.

His hair was jet black, not bottle dyed but hereditary, cut into a trendy, razor-faded style that really didn't work on his egg-shaped head, and his nose and chin seemed to be from a head slightly larger than his own, giving him a face that was slightly caricaturist on first meeting.

He was slim, bordering on skinny—although rather than

lean, he was what people called "fat skinny", where although slim, he still had a protruding beer belly, and he was currently adding to this cartoonish appearance with a red-faced and furious expression, as he argued with his wife.

'You didn't have to show your tits at him,' he muttered half sulkily, folding his arms in a defensive gesture and glaring out of the window as the country road passed by.

Amused by the outburst, Chantelle chuckled. The polar opposite to Danny, Chantelle was stunning, self-believed-sexy in the confident way that *The Only Way is Essex* stars seemed to nail so well (a show she'd even been a part of when it started, until the producers learned she'd knocked a couple of years off her age and dropped her), and dripping with jewels, complementing the emerald-green and incredibly low-cut evening dress that she wore.

She had tied her strawberry blonde hair up to show off an extravagant pearl necklace, but now her hair was loose and over her right shoulder as she snapped back at Danny, her green eyes flashing with anger.

'You said *be nice to them*,' she replied haughtily. 'I was being nice.'

'I said be nice, not flash your nipples,' Danny countered, glancing at the front of the car and noting that Ricardo was watching the fight through the rear-view mirror. Danny didn't like Ricardo; he'd been Chantelle's hire after Wilson, the old chauffeur, had retired, a year or so back. Wilson had been part of the family for years; he'd been Danny's dad's chauffeur before he died a few years back, and being hideously camp, and only interested in teenage boys, Wilson had never been any kind of threat to Danny's manhood.

Ricardo, however, was *different*.

He was Italian, young and muscled, sandy-haired and working double, or even triple-duty as the mechanic and handyman around the mansion, where he seemed to take every opportunity to show off his gym-earned muscled physique and luscious brown tan, almost as if mocking Danny's scrawny frame and flabby stomach. Ricardo's *abs* had abs, while Danny's six-pack was a party box of Fosters cans. Danny had even considered getting a personal trainer, one of those guys that helped actors prepare for superhero movies, all weight-gains and macro-nutrients, but he just didn't have the time.

No, he had the time, he just couldn't be bothered.

Ricardo, noting Danny's furious expression, focused his attention back on the road.

Damn right you watch the road, Danny thought to himself. *Who's got the money out of the pair of us? Not you, you Italian ponce.*

'They weren't looking at my tits,' Chantelle continued, still arguing, and still flushed with anger, bringing Danny back into the conversation.

'*Everyone* was looking at your tits!' Danny exclaimed angrily. 'And they bloody well should be, I paid enough for them!'

They were approaching Danny and Chantelle's house now, a seven-bedroom detached building with side "coach house" for his driver, a house he called his *mansion*, even though it wasn't technically one. It was on the edge of Chipping Norton; far enough out not to be classified as part of the "Chipping Norton set", while close enough to pay the exorbitant house and council tax prices. Danny hated the place and wanted to move back to Epping and his home roots, but Chantelle had fallen in love with it three years back after they'd been to a party at *Soho Farmhouse*, just down the road, and what his princess wanted, she got.

For just under two and a half million bloody quid.

Of course, she also wanted a *membership* there, and so far that little gift had eluded him; that bunch of elitist pricks.

As the argument fizzled out, both Danny and Chantelle crossed their arms and ignored each other for the rest of the journey. Ricardo, however, looked back at Danny as he slowed the Bentley down, about a hundred yards from the driveway to the house.

'Mister Flynn?' he asked.

Danny looked back at him, glancing through the front windscreen, and noticing for the first time the small collection of blue flashing lights far down the road, all likely to be parked outside his residence.

'Shit,' he whispered, pulling down the centre rest of the back seat and rummaging through his pockets, starting to empty them into the gap behind. A small blade, a little baggie of cocaine, a wad of banknotes clipped into a silver money-clip, a small bag of pills and another knife, all sliding into the hidden hole, as Ricardo drove as slowly as he could towards the house.

'What are you doing?' Chantelle, still in argument mode, hadn't noticed the police yet. Danny pointed at the lights, drawing her attention to the oncoming legal issues they were about to have.

'They're raiding the house,' he hissed. 'Take the necklace off!'

'Nana gave it to me!' Chantelle protested.

'And they'll take it away from you if we don't hide it,' Danny snapped back. 'They're probably "confiscating" anything that isn't nailed down, and it'll be a bastard to get back once they have it, yeah? So get your arse into gear!'

Reluctantly and with great remorse, Chantelle pulled off the old necklace, passing it to Danny.

'Not to me, put it in the back,' he said, throwing the necklace carelessly in with the other items, and pushing the centre-rest back up moments before the car drove through the open wrought-iron gates, and pulled up next to a police officer, his fluorescent jacket glowing in the headlights as he waved them to a stop.

'Can I help you?' he asked Ricardo, peering through the passenger window as Danny pressed a button, lowering his back seat passenger side window.

'I should ask you the same thing, mate,' he replied through it. 'That's my driveway you're stomping around.'

The police officer leaned closer, trying to look into the vehicle.

'Mister Flynn?'

'That's right.'

'And who's in the car with you?' the police officer asked.

Danny half-climbed out of the window, mainly to block the officer's view.

'My wife, my driver, and Mickey sodding Mouse. What's it to you?' he snapped angrily, looking around. The front door was open, and officers were walking in and out of the house.

Shit.

Nonplussed by the response, the police officer nodded, turning from the car and calling up the driveway.

'*Sarge!*'

Danny glanced nervously at Chantelle as a burly black man in another fluorescent jacket and peaked cap walked over from the side garage entrance, nodding at the officer as he passed.

'Claims he's Mister Flynn, sir,' the officer said, as if Danny was lying. On this, Danny had to bite his tongue, silently counting to ten. The last thing he wanted to do was piss the police off any further, especially before he found out why he'd pissed them off enough to raid his house in the *first* place.

'Daniel Flynn?' The Sergeant asked.

'Look, what's going on?' Danny ignored the question, deciding to brazen it out. 'You can't go into my house without a warrant, mate. Get your plod pals out before I sue your arses.'

The Sergeant looked back at the house for a moment before walking to the car's window, slightly crouching so that he could speak to Danny face to face.

'I think there's been a misunderstanding here, Mister Flynn,' he continued. 'We're here because of an anonymous phone call from someone on the street. It looks like there's been a break in.'

Danny felt his stomach gurgle and his bowels turned to water. The Sergeant, not noticing Danny's pale expression, continued, now reading from his notebook.

'Two men, in a red car. One of your neighbours probably saw it, but didn't want to get involved, or give their name,' he said. 'Now, if you'd like to come with me, we need to know exactly what was taken.'

Nodding quietly, Danny looked over at Chantelle, now glowering at him.

'Oh look,' she hissed. 'I could have kept Nana's necklace on.'

'Not the time, Chantelle,' Danny shook his head,

climbing out of the car, his head spinning. He was Danny bloody Flynn. His dad was an old-school villain, and whether or not he had the physical build to instill fear in men, he'd grown up with violence as his nursemaid. Anyone who dared break in to his house must have known this.

So who the hell was stupid enough to attempt it?

———

THE HOUSE ITSELF WAS FILLED WITH POLICE AND FORENSICS officers; Danny guessed that the call about the burglary had been a blessing from on high for them, as it gave them all a chance to have a right old proper poke around the Flynn residence, to see what nasty little secrets could be uncovered quietly, things to help them nail the *rotten little bastard* once and for all.

Well, the joke's on you, he thought to himself as he waited for an officer to move out of the doorway. *I don't shit where I sleep, rozzers.*

The Sergeant was still talking as they entered.

'Call came in about nine pm,' he explained. 'Two men, apparently, in and out through the back. You'll have a better idea of what they've taken than we can work out, but they don't seem to have gone for the usuals. TV, laptops, all left behind.'

Danny was already ahead of the Sergeant as he tried to work out which bastards had done this. Chipping Norton wasn't exactly close to his usual stomping ground; Birmingham had recently undergone a bit of a change in regime after Macca Byrne tried to kill his dad and got them all arrested in the process, and London was mainly split between Johnny Lucas in the East, having recently shed his 'evil twin brother' persona, the Seven Sisters in the North, currently going through their own issues with the now blind Mama Delcourt fighting all rivals, the Triad had lost one of their own and were re-consolidating, and Simpson in the south of—

Oh shit. Was this Nicky Simpson?

Danny almost wanted to look behind him, in case Simpson himself was standing there. He knew it was stupid to think that; Danny was a nobody in the grand scheme of things, and had been ever since his dad died. In a way, Danny preferred that. He played the gangster here and there, and his finger was in a lot of dodgy little pies, but at the same time he wasn't anywhere near the league of the bag of bastards he'd just considered.

However, Simpson had a reason to do this.

Slowly, as the Sergeant continued to walk Chantelle around the house, pointing out places where the burglars might have been, while ostentatiously giving his own officers time to keep rooting through the premises, Danny slipped behind, moving into the living room.

It was open plan, leading into a kitchen to the south, painted cream and with white leather sofas against two of the walls, a white shagpile rug in the middle. To the west was a black IKEA unit with a massive, sixty-five inch 4K HD television, connected to a surround sound system that cost more than the leather suite. These two electrical items alone were worth over five grand, yet they hadn't been touched. In fact, nothing in the room seemed to have been moved at all.

This wasn't an opportunistic theft, this was made-to-order. But what could it be?

The Sergeant was returning into the room with Chantelle.

'I'm sorry, Mrs Flynn—'

'Call me Chantelle.'

The Sergeant flushed a little.

'I'm sorry, *Chantelle*, but it looks like they raided your jewellery box,' he explained. 'We'll need a list of anything that was inside it.'

'Of course,' Chantelle was subdued now, as if realising how lucky she'd been to have worn her Nana's jewellery that night.

'Please, have a look around, see if there's anything else missing,' the Sergeant continued, looking back at Danny. 'And if you could come down to the station and make a statement later, it'd be appreciated.'

'Yeah, of course. And now we're here, get your plod out of my house, yeah?' Danny replied, his confrontational tone papering over his fear and confusion as to what was going on here.

The Sergeant nodded, mumbling that of course he would, and called his officers, emptying them out of the house, leaving Chantelle and Danny alone in the living room.

'*Call me Chantelle*,' Danny mocked, irritated.

'Not now, Danny, for Christ's sake,' Chantelle snapped, looking around the room. 'Who did this? Who'd dare do this?'

She glanced back at Danny, eyeing him up.

'Yeah, a lot of people, I suppose,' she replied. 'You're not exactly Vito Corleone. More Fredo.'

'Maybe it was Ricardo?' Danny asked almost automatically, ignoring the jibe. Chantelle shook her head at this.

'He's putting the car into the garage, now the police have got out of his way,' she replied. 'He was with us all night.'

'No, he was in the car,' Danny glared out of the window,

watching his car enter the garage. 'He could have come back, done this, and then returned.'

'Don't be a prick, Danny,' Chantelle sighed. 'Just because he makes you feel insecure, don't mean he's one of your pikey thieving crowd.'

Danny nodded, only half-listening as he now stared at the wall facing him, in particular at a large rectangular mark on the wall above one of the white leather sofas, a slightly lighter discolouration of the paint now revealed by the missing painting-shaped-item that had previously covered it.

Chantelle, obviously still thrown by her jewellery, hadn't noticed the absence, but Danny had.

The bastards. The utter, utter bastards.

He couldn't tell the police; they'd ask where he got it. He couldn't tell anyone.

It was nothing more than a copy. He'd always said that. *Even if it wasn't.*

'They took the bloody *painting!*' he half shouted in anger, the raised voice bringing the Sergeant back into the doorway to the house, still open, a concerned expression on his face.

'Problem?' he asked.

Danny and Chantelle both turned to face the Sergeant, twin images of innocence on their expressions.

'Nope,' they both replied calmly, smiling.

'Well then,' the Sergeant nodded, leaving the room for a second time, Chantelle following him, heading upstairs to check her stolen jewels, leaving Danny alone.

Taking one last, furious and frustrated look at the empty spot on the wall, Danny pulled his phone out. Then, realising that he didn't have the number to hand, he walked to a side cabinet, pulling out a drawer and rummaging through the small pile of business cards within.

Finding the one he wanted, he eventually pulled it out, tapping the number into his phone. Pressing connect, he discarded the business card back into the drawer, closing it as the call connected.

'It's me,' he said. 'Yeah, I know it's late. No, I'm not arrested. Look, I need you to put me in touch with someone.'

He looked back at the space on the wall and visibly swallowed. He didn't want to do this, but he had no other option.

'I need you to put me in touch with Ellie Reckless,' he ordered.

There was a frantic whispering down the line, as the person on the other end tried to inform Danny that *this was a bad idea,* and *there were other options* and *why the hell did he want Ellie Reckless of all people, anyway?*

Danny waited patiently for them to finish before continuing.

'Because someone's nicked the bloody painting, and calling the so-called *cop for criminals* looks like my only option,' he replied. 'Currently, I'm utterly screwed, and she's my only option. So find her, or whoever she works for, and get me a meeting first thing tomorrow.'

This done, he disconnected the call, staring around the room, as if hoping that this had been only a prank, that someone had taken it down and hidden it.

They hadn't, and it wasn't in the room.

Danny Flynn sighed.

That bloody painting was going to get him out of a massive hole, one that he only had a matter of days to climb out of.

That they had taken it tonight was too convenient to be chance. Someone was deliberately targeting Danny, trying to ensure that he couldn't pay his debts.

Unfortunately, his salvation was now in the hands of a crooked ex-copper.

Slumping into one of the expensive white leather sofas, Danny Flynn placed his hands over his face and silently *screamed*.

3
_____

OLD DEBTS

IT WAS THE FOLLOWING MORNING WHEN DANNY FLYNN MET Ellie Reckless.

The *Finders Corporation* was a chrome-and-glass building in the middle of the City of London, a location that gave a completely different impression of the company for the public than the underworld of London believed, considering their knowledge of Ellie Reckless and the clientele she seemed to focus on. But, as Danny and Chantelle pulled up alongside the building, Danny telling Ricardo to wait outside, he had to double-take as he approached, as he felt like he was walking into a high-level solicitors, rather than a strange, off-the-books "criminal assistance" organisation.

Inside, it looked like an Apple store and Wall Street had married and had babies. Open-plan offices with glass-walled boardrooms passed by as the receptionist, whose name was apparently Sara, walked them to the back offices, and the boardroom they'd be meeting in that morning.

'So, what do you know about the Finders Corporation?' she asked, a little too peppy for Danny's liking.

'You find things,' Danny replied, half-sarcastically

'Well, that's part of what we do,' Sara admitted. 'Primarily, we're an insurance investigator.'

As they continued down the corridor, Danny felt more exposed than he had expected. There were full-length windows everywhere, and even though he could see they weren't, Danny had the distinct impression that everyone was watching him and his wife as they walked through the building.

'So what does an insurance investigator do?' Chantelle asked, yawning. 'Sorry. Didn't sleep well last night.'

'The police do their best to find stolen items, but they're sometimes a little slow, and their success rate is extremely low,' Sara continued. 'We're faster, and we're on a seventy percent success rate this week.'

'What was it last week?' Danny muttered, but Sara didn't seem to hear him, as Chantelle, her face giving the impression of a bulldog chewing a thistle, spoke over her husband.

'How much do you charge?'

'Depends on the insurance company hiring us,' Sara explained. 'Usually it's about ten percent.'

'That don't sound much,' Chantelle looked to Danny, who shrugged.

'Depends on the thing they find, I suppose,' he said. 'I mean, ten percent of a million is a hundred grand.'

'Exactly,' Sara smiled. 'We're very much into the *high-end* scale.'

'And if it's not an insurance company asking?' Danny asked nervously as they walked to the door of a boardroom. 'I mean, if it's something a little more *personal?*'

Sara opened the door.

'Then you negotiate,' she smiled. 'In here.'

In the boardroom, sitting at the table as they entered, was a man in his early forties. His dirty-blond hair was cut short and parted to the right, with the temples peppered with a slight dusting of grey. He wore a dark blue suit over a pale blue shirt, and unlike the others Danny had seen, this man wore no tie. As he rose to shake his hand, Danny also couldn't help but notice that the man wore a very expensive looking gold Rolex on his wrist.

'This is Robert Lewis,' Sara explained. 'He deals with the more off-the-books cases.'

'Thanks, Sara,' Robert nodded. And, as Danny and Chantelle sat, Sara left the room, closing the door behind her.

'Water?' Robert asked. Danny and Chantelle shook their heads.

'Coffee? Tea?'

Again, Danny shook his head, glancing nervously around the room, looking into the corners of the walls.

'Take a coffee, you look like shit,' Chantelle muttered, before returning to Robert. 'It was a stressful night. He took a tablet, knocked him out, but he tossed and turned all bloody night. I managed maybe two hours.'

'So, can I get you a coffee?'

Chantelle nodded as Danny kept glancing around the room.

'There are no cameras in here, Mister Flynn, if that's what you're looking for,' Robert smiled. At this, Danny relaxed a little, snatching a glance at Chantelle for reassurance before speaking.

'So, this is like a confessional, right?' he asked nervously. 'Solicitor-client privilege and all that?'

Robert nodded.

'Not quite the same, as I'm not your solicitor, but once you become a client, all these rules apply. Nothing you say here today will be repeated outside these walls, unless with your permission. Only the people working on your case will *know* about your case.'

'And if it's not your usual type of case?' Chantelle added.

At this Robert smiled, a knowing one, almost as if amused at the naivete of the question.

'We have no "usual" type of case,' he replied as Chantelle reddened, cursing her idiocy. 'But we do have unusual investigators.'

Danny smiled.

'You mean Ellie Reckless,' he said.

'Among others,' Robert looked up, out of the boardroom window, and it looked to Danny like he was searching for the other investigators, expecting them to arrive now.

Danny, however, folded his arms and leaned back.

'I want Ellie Reckless,' he stated.

'She's currently on another case,' Robert was apologetic, but firm. 'Miss Reckless is more junior than some of our other investigators—'

'Yeah, but she gets the job done though, right?' Danny replied. 'I heard about Lucas and what she did for him. And a few other people she's sorted out. Word moves quickly; she's fast and I need fast. And I'll pay whatever it costs.'

'If you know of Miss Reckless's reputation, then you'll know that she doesn't work that way,' Robert fidgeted as he spoke.

Danny frowned.

'How does it work, then?' he asked.

Robert shifted in his seat, as if this was a conversation that was uncomfortable for him.

'You want something done legally? We charge a percentage of the item's worth,' he explained.

'Yeah, the woman told us that,' Chantelle interjected. 'Ten percent, right?'

'That's correct, and on legal matters Miss Reckless and her team takes a cut of the fee we gain, but illegally? Miss Reckless works for favours. In fact, she's the only person here who takes off-the-books cases like this.'

Robert sighed.

'Personally, we'd like her to stop, but we made a deal when she started,' he almost apologised.

Danny leant forwards.

'What are you saying, illegal?' he demanded.

In response, Robert leaned back, watching Danny for a long moment.

'Are you saying this problem of yours *isn't* involving any illegality?' he asked. 'I understood it was a stolen item, one that you don't want to report to the police. But if this isn't the case, then we can happily—'

'Just get on with it,' Danny hissed. 'Do the bloody sales pitch.'

Without replying, and reaching to the chair beside him, Robert pulled out a sheaf of papers, placing them onto the desk, sliding them over to Danny.

'As I said then, when elements of a less-legal situation are involved, Miss Reckless works on her own payment scale; that of a favour owed,' he explained, tapping the top sheet. 'We make nothing from these, and this is classed as a perk of her employment, such as it is. If you're agreeable, just sign here,'

Danny stared down at the papers.

'How *big* a favour are we talking?' he asked suspiciously.

In response, Robert chuckled.

'Last week, it was a lift home for a woman down on her luck. Last night, it was the removal of a drug dealer,' he replied. 'We never know what goes through Ellie's mind on a daily basis.'

Again, he looked out of the full-length window. As Danny followed the gaze, he saw a woman, slim with dark, curly hair enter through the doorway, walking into a room on the other side of the corridor.

'On that note,' Robert rose. 'Give me a moment to get you your coffee. Please feel free to peruse the papers, and if you need more time to decide, we can always reschedule for next week.'

Now alone, as Robert left the boardroom, closing the door behind him, Chantelle looked at the papers on the table.

'What do you think?' she asked.

Danny sighed, running his hands through his hair as he stared up at the ceiling.

'I think I'm screwed,' he muttered.

WITH DANNY AND CHANTELLE LEFT TO THEIR OWN DEVICES IN the boardroom, Robert walked over to Ellie, pulling a chocolate bar out of a vending machine in the break room.

'I thought we were catching up last night?' he asked, taking a coffee pod from a box and placing it into a machine. Already opening the wrapper, Ellie rose from the vending machine, turning to face him as she bit into it.

'Sorry, I had to drop the car to Big Slim,' she replied

through half-eaten chocolate. 'And then he made me stay for a drink, and as he's a client, I had to stay for one or two...'

Robert nodded as if this was usual for him.

'And it went okay?'

'Sure,' Ellie smiled. 'Piece of cake.'

'You sure about that?' Robert continued, his voice still relaxed, but his eyes now narrowing, and Ellie's expression fell.

Rumbled.

'When did Tinker call?' she asked, knowing she'd been grassed up.

Robert smiled.

'Around when you faced a drug lord on a roof who wanted to shoot you in the face,' he replied. 'Is he dead? Tinker said she heard a gunshot.'

'People can be clumsy,' Ellie tried to bat away the question. But as Robert stayed quiet, Ellie relented.

'Local A&E had a man admitted with a wound to the leg last night, so I think he'll get away with a limp and unemployment,' she smiled. 'I've heard a lot of bad things about Walker, Robbie. That's why I asked Tink to stay downstairs, in case there was trouble.'

'Surely you needed her *beside* you, if there was trouble?'

Ellie smiled.

'Having her there beside me would have made damn sure there *was* trouble. But yeah, he started being a problem, I knew he was into some bad shit, and he needed to be removed.'

'That's the police's job,' Robert leant in, lowering his voice. 'And no matter what you seem to believe, Ellie, *you're not the police anymore.*'

This struck a nerve, and Ellie's face hardened as Robert continued.

'And more than that, you burned a favour from Johnny Lucas,' Robert continued. 'You need all you can get if you're going to—'

'I know,' Ellie interrupted. 'I had two, I can still use the one that remains.'

'And if you need a second?'

'Then I'll save his arse again.'

There was a moment of silence in the break room.

Eventually, Robert sighed, stretched his shoulders and nodded.

'Fine,' he finished, pulling a now-filled coffee cup from the machine. 'Come on then, you're late.'

'I'm on a case,' Ellie replied. 'We're close to getting Marcus Somerville, either today or tomorrow. You—'

'You'll want this one,' Robert interrupted. 'Trust me.'

'You're taking me off a paying case?' Ellie clicked the top of her mouth with her tongue. 'Or are we working them both?

Robert simply smiled.

'Depends on how much you want Ramsey to shout at you,' he said.

Sighing audibly, and fitting the remains of the chocolate bar into her mouth, chewing furiously, Ellie followed Robert out.

DANNY LOOKED UP AS ROBERT BROUGHT THE DARK-HAIRED woman into the boardroom, passing over the cup of coffee.

'Is this her?' he asked.

'Mister Flynn, meet Miss Reckless,' Robert said.

Ellie nodded to Danny, sitting down beside Robert, facing Danny and Chantelle across the boardroom table. She was chewing on something, holding up a hand to hold Danny from asking questions until she swallowed.

'Sorry about that,' she said. 'Breakfast of champions.'

Danny glanced at Chantelle, noting she, too, had the same confused expression that he had.

'I expected something different,' he replied.

'And between us, Danny? Can I call you Danny? I couldn't give two shits what you expected,' Ellie smiled.

'Now listen here—'

'No, you listen,' Ellie rose now. 'I'm tired, I have a hangover and I really don't need shite from Arthur Flynn's mini-me.'

She smiled at Danny's expression.

'Yeah, I knew your dad,' she replied. 'Nicked him a couple of times too, when I started in Mile End. Small time, but knew when to keep his calm and stop shooting his mouth off. From what I hear about you, you're the complete opposite.'

She looked over at Chantelle now.

'You know, all mouth and no trousers. How am I doing?'

Chantelle glared.

'Is this how you deal with all your clients?' she hissed, before sipping at the coffee and grimacing.

Ellie sat back down, shrugging.

'He's not my client,' she tapped the paperwork. 'I don't see a signature. Do you?'

Before Chantelle could reply, Ellie leant closer.

'Loved you in *TOWIE*, by the way,' she said. 'You were the best actor out of all of them.'

'It's reality TV,' Chantelle snapped irritably while flushing at the compliment. 'We don't act. We play ourselves.'

'Exactly,' Ellie grinned knowingly as she looked back at Danny. 'So, Danny-boy, oh Danny-boy, what exactly do you need fixed that would bring you into my domain?'

Danny shifted awkwardly in his chair.

'I need your help,' he muttered reluctantly.

'The kind of help someone pays for, or the kind that leaves them owing a favour?' Ellie leaned back in her chair, as if enjoying Danny's discomfort. 'I'm guessing Robbie's—'

'Robert.'

'—*Robert's* explanation of my payment terms is why you've delayed in signing?'

'What does a favour mean?' Chantelle tapped at the papers again. 'It's still confusing.'

Ellie turned to her.

'One favour, given without question or argument at a time or place of my choosing,' she replied. 'If I find whatever you lost, or sort whatever problem you have, that is.'

She looked back at Danny.

'If I solve your case, you owe me whatever I ask for, but know it'll always be within your remit and something you can afford. I'm not demanding houses or jewels, and most of the time these favours are burned to further other cases.'

Danny nodded.

'I heard about Callahan, and how he lost everything,' he said. 'I also heard that was you.'

'I couldn't possibly comment,' Ellie leaned back in the chair. 'I can say, however, that Callahan owed me, decided *not* to honour this, and the same night his private files were leaked to the press. I never saw the files, and I didn't know he had kiddie porn on them.'

She shook her head sadly.

'Such a terrible coincidence.'

'Didn't you also have a favour owed around then by a hacker group connected to *Anonymous*?' Robert asked in mock curiosity.

'I did, but I called it in,' Ellie smiled, and the implication of the statement was ominous. Danny wasn't stupid; he knew that Callahan lost everything the day after he bragged he was going to tell Ellie Reckless where to go.

And now Danny knew how it happened.

'Who do you work with?' he asked, and Ellie sighed.

'Why don't you sign the papers and then tell me what they stole from you?' she asked. 'It's effectively a non-disclosure agreement for Finders to have on file, and a confirmation of our agreement. I think you understand now what happens if you renege on the deal. And, to be brutally honest, I can't decide my team until I know the case. And I can't do anything until you sign.'

As Danny looked down at the papers, she rolled a pen across.

'And remember, you came to me,' she smiled sweetly.

Picking up the pen, Danny signed the contract with a great deal of reluctance. Ellie understood why Danny was annoyed; it was horrid to be forced to owe someone else, especially someone like Ellie Reckless.

She didn't care though, as she knew that Danny Flynn owing her, would definitely get her closer to the goal.

Danny took a moment to gather his composure before replying, leaning in as if worried that anyone outside might hear.

'I had a painting stolen,' he said. 'Police had a call, but nothing more than an alert that someone with a red car was at my house. Then this morning, they called me to say another witness had seen a black car open the gates, and allow a red car in.'

'Any idea who the witness was?'

'No, they wouldn't tell me,' Danny replied. 'And as the police are looking for some jewels rather than the painting, I don't think they'll work too hard.'

Ellie nodded, noting this down.

'So this painting,' she said, looking back up. 'Tell me about it.'

Danny shifted uncomfortably in his seat for a moment.

'How much do you know about the *Gardner Heist?*' he eventually asked.

It was another twenty minutes before Danny finished his story, nodded to Chantelle, and left. After giving them a moment to leave and then checking her watch, Ellie rose from the chair, following Robert out of the room as he headed for his own office.

'I need to get going,' she said, turning towards the way out. 'I have a nightmare brunch to get to. Get someone to put me a pack together about this, will you? I know Ramsey will be all over it, but Tinker's not that artistically inclined.'

Robert, however, turned to face her, blocking her way.

'Hold on, Ellie,' he said. 'There's something we need to talk about.'

Ellie sighed.

'Look, Robbie. If you're going to lecture me again—'

'Actually, I kind of need a favour,' Robert admitted sheepishly. 'Bryan Noyce.'

Ellie stopped, staring at Robert as she replied.

'You seem to have it wrong,' she whispered. '*My* favours are the ones connected to Bryan, not yours—'

She halted her words as she saw through the door opposite the boardroom, realising that Robert had positioned himself exactly in the right spot to allow the view.

There, sitting at a desk, was a skinny, bookish fifteen-year-old boy.

A boy she recognised from photos in a wallet.

'Why's Casey Noyce in the office?' she asked, feeling the room spin a little. Memories of Bryan laughing as he showed pictures of his son came to mind, Bryan's voice, from varying times, echoing in her head.

You'll love him Ellie. He's got your sense of humour.

I know I said it'd be a clean break, but Casey's everything to me. I need to keep joint custody.

I'm sorry, Ellie. I can't do this. I'll lose my son.

Shaking herself back to the moment, Ellie backed away from Robert.

'No.'

'You don't know what I'm asking.'

'Yeah I do,' Ellie snapped. 'You want me to bring him into my gang of misfit toys.'

Robert looked into the room, watching Casey for a moment.

'He's getting into trouble,' he whispered. 'He needs a positive role model.'

'Because that's totally me,' Ellie snapped back.

'I promised his mother I'd do something to help, and you owe me,' Robert argued. 'She doesn't know, Ellie. Neither of them do.'

'You're nothing to do with his mother.'

'Be serious, Ellie! I became connected the moment I defended you in court, for his father's *murder*,' Robert hissed.

Silently, acknowledging this, Ellie nodded.

Leaning into the room, Robert tapped on the door to gain Casey's attention.

'Casey?' he said once the teen looked up. 'This is Ellie Reckless. You're going to be working with her.'

Ellie forced a smile, but inside, all she could think was how much he looked like his father.

His dead father. Who she'd got killed.

Run, you stupid bitch. Get out of here before you do something you'll really regret.

'Great,' Casey replied to Robert's question, with the face of a teenage boy that really wasn't happy about it.

Get out. You don't need this.

Yes, you do, a stronger voice finished the conversation. Ellie owed whatever this was to the boy; she couldn't bring his father back, but perhaps she could sate some of the guilt she had by helping somehow.

'What sort of things do you like doing?' she asked.

Casey shrugged.

'Stuff,' he replied.

'What sort of stuff?' Ellie persisted.

'*Stuff* stuff,' Casey returned to his Nintendo Switch as Ellie looked back at Robert.

'Oh, he's a keeper,' she mocked.

'Casey's a hacker,' Robert explained. 'Or whatever they call themselves these days. Got caught breaking into a police server.'

'Why?' Ellie asked, looking back at Casey, who glanced up, as if daring her to stare him in the eye.

'I was looking for proof my dad was set up before he

died,' he replied, and Ellie had to lean against the door before she stumbled; the room was spinning slightly again.

Robert tapped Ellie on the shoulder.

'I know how you love lost causes,' he smiled.

Ellie looked at her watch, and then at the teenage boy.

'Come on,' she said.

Reluctantly and with great visible effort, Casey packed away his things and joined her as she exited the corridor.

4

BRUNCH TIME

Emerging out of the Finders Corporation building and now standing on the Farringdon pavement, Ellie looked back through the door, as if checking to see whether Robert had followed them, suspicious of her intentions, before turning to face Casey.

'Look, I'm sure you're a good kid, but I've got a team,' she said, pulling a wad of twenty-pound notes out of her pocket. Pulling off five of the notes, she offered them to Casey. 'Take this, go home and if Mister Lewins asks, you're working for me remotely, okay?'

Casey nodded, but still didn't take the money.

'He told me you'd try this,' he replied.

Damn you Robbie, you know me too well.

'Oh, and what else did he say?' Ellie asked, too curious to stop herself.

'He also said that if there was anyone out there that could prove my dad's innocence, even after his death, that it'd be you.'

Ellie stared silently at Casey, unable to speak as the enormity of what he had said smacked her right between the eyes.

The kid doesn't know about you and Bryan, the voice in her head explained. *If he did, he wouldn't be saying things like that about you. He'd be trying to gouge your eyes out.*

'Look, kid—'

'Casey.'

'Look Casey, I audition my crew,' Ellie backtracked. 'I don't take walk-ins. But I'll do what I can to look into your dad's case, okay?'

Casey nodded, taking the handful of money and, after a moment of consideration, staring down at them, placed them into his pocket before walking off.

And, with a frown, Ellie walked after him.

'Hey,' she said, grabbing at his arm, stopping him. 'That stuff about me proving your dad's innocence and all that? Robbie *didn't* say that, did he.'

It was a statement more than a question, and in response, Casey smiled.

'No,' he admitted. 'He said you were an arrogant drunk, but you were all right, and a bloody good detective. And I remember my dad talking about you before he died. You worked with him, didn't you?'

Ellie nodded, trying to hide on her face the blade of pain and sorrow that suddenly pierced her heart.

'He was an informant for me,' she replied; not quite a lie, but definitely not the truth. 'We were close. But I didn't realise how deep he was into, well, the *people* he was informing on. Eventually someone found out he was talking—'

'How?'

Ellie shook her head.

'I don't know,' she said. 'All I can tell you is the courts insinuated it was someone in the police, close to the investigation. And I'm still looking for them.'

Casey bit at his lip as he nodded.

'What will you do when you find them?'

'Honestly? I'm not sure.'

Ellie looked away, so Casey wouldn't see her conflicted expression. On one side, she knew that finding the actual mole, the person who gave up Bryan Noyce to his killers would give her a shot at taking down the man she believed ordered the killing, Nicky Simpson. Also, clearing her name would give her closure, as well as a chance at returning to the police force.

Maybe a small, provincial post, a little village up north that did good cheeses, or somewhere in Northumberland.

There were a lot of pretty castles up there. Lots of dog walking spots.

But at the same time, she knew this was a dream; the force, even if she proved she was innocent, wouldn't let her back. She was damaged goods. And even if she cleared her name of Bryan's murder, they still knew her as the *cop for criminals*. She'd always be seen as dirty, no matter what she did. Her old team was doing very well at keeping those rumours going.

Besides, if she was honest, she didn't want to go back. The money at Finders; from the legitimate jobs, was good. Certainly better than a Detective Inspector's salary.

But more importantly, she didn't want to go back because if she did, she wouldn't be able to do what she *wanted* to do once she cleared her name and laid the smoking gun at Nicky Simpson's feet.

An eye for an eye, you smug bastard. Get your affairs in order and kiss your sick dad goodbye, because I'm going to bloody well bury you when I'm finished. In the ground, a stone above your head.

Casey was watching her, and Ellie realised she'd drifted off, staring vacant eyed across the road. Now back in the moment, she patted him on the shoulder.

'Your father was a brave man, Casey,' she finished. 'And I want you to know that I'm still looking to get justice for his death.'

'You got fired because of it, didn't you?' Casey probed and internally, Ellie groaned. The information was out there; the case against her, stating she killed Bryan Noyce, was public knowledge. Anyone with a computer could find it, and if Casey was a hacker, according to Robert, he knew everything.

'Okay, kid, what do you know?' she asked, sighing. 'One time only, whatever you need.'

Casey considered the offer and nodded.

'I know he died, that you were blamed, but the jury found you innocent,' he replied. 'I can't get into police reports or anything, so it's only what I find on news servers and chat rooms.'

'I'm guessing a lot of it isn't flattering,' Ellie faked a smile.

'You'd be surprised,' Casey shrugged. 'The world is full of conspiracy theorists. Half the pages think you're a patsy for some kind of new world order.'

'Nothing like that. We had an argument,' Ellie started. 'It got physical.'

'What was the argument about?'

I'm sorry, Ellie. I can't do this. I'll lose my son.

'I—I pushed him too hard,' Ellie lied; well, more a half-truth. The words were correct, the scenario not so much. 'We were close, but I needed him to make a commitment.'

'About being your informant?'

'Yeah,' *another lie.* Ellie had punched Bryan in the face; they'd been drunk, he'd just broken up with her. She'd been sick of her new role as *the other woman* and had given him an ultimatum; his answer, however, wasn't the one she wanted. 'That's pretty much it—'

'*Are* you innocent?' Casey stared at Ellie. 'Did you kill my dad?'

'No!' Ellie exclaimed. 'We fought, I struck him, he had a nosebleed. He got those now and then. Some of it got on my sleeve as I held his head back. The police used this to claim I was involved in his—in his shooting.'

Casey stared at the pavement.

'He was having an affair, you know,' he whispered. 'I hacked into his credit card bills. He was going for dinners, staying in hotels. Double rooms, room service for two.'

He looked up, examining Ellie's face.

'Did you know about this?'

Ellie wanted to lie, but something stopped her.

'... yeah,' she said. 'In a way, the fight we had? Was because of that.'

'I never told mum,' Casey carried on. 'It would have killed her.'

'If it helps, I can promise you that when he died, he'd already ended it with—with the woman,' Ellie almost choked on the words, but kept her face impassive.

Casey nodded, keeping his eyes on Ellie's.

'Thanks,' he said. 'For being honest, treating me like a grown-up.'

Ellie forced another smile, while inside she felt twisted and torn up. What she'd said was only honest from a certain point of view. One day, Casey would find out the truth.

She couldn't do that to him.

'I still don't take walk-ins,' she repeated.

'You will when I audition,' Casey grinned now, and in the way that teenagers did, all of his concerns and woes were gone once more. And, before Ellie could protest at this, Casey Noyce threw his skateboard to the floor, skating off into the street, avoiding a cab and disappearing from view.

Ellie watched him disappear, a slight smile on her lips.

Force of nature, she thought. *Just like your bloody dad.*

Looking at her watch, Ellie cursed.

She was late for brunch.

As it was, even though Ellie was fifteen minutes late for the brunch meeting, she was still the first to arrive, left to nurse a small glass of scotch at a table for two while she waited irritably for her brunch companion.

Eventually, Ellie noticed a man enter through the doors and glare daggers across the restaurant at her. After a few words with the door manager, he stomped over to the table, slumping in the opposite chair, and giving her an ice-cold look. In his late thirties, his thinning hair cut short, likely doing more to reveal his balding crown than if he'd kept it long, with his glasses chunky and black rimmed, the man wore a white polo shirt, top button done up under a blue jacket. Ellie knew he'd secured the top button just to annoy her, but with the glasses, hair and clothes, he looked like Brains from *Thunderbirds*, if they had evicted him during a midlife crisis.

Which, in a way, he had been.

'Nathan,' Ellie nodded.

Nathan Marks looked around, caught the attention of a waiter, and pointed to the table.

'Vodka on the rocks and the bill. She isn't staying long.'

Ellie groaned, leaning back in the chair and staring up at the ceiling.

'Brunch isn't happening?' she asked innocently. 'Oh, I'm crushed. See this? Actual tears.'

'Don't get smart with me, Elisa,' Nathan hissed icily, and Ellie bristled as she returned her attention to him. 'You lost that right a long time ago.'

'Look, I get you're angry with me—' Ellie started, but Nathan half-rose in response to this, stopping himself in the nick of time, settling back in the chair as he straightened.

'Angry?' he hissed. 'Why would I be angry? Everything's great in my life! Oh, apart from the fact that my ex-wife was kicked off the force, was accused of being a criminal-controlled murdering *bitch*, and I'm the laughing stock of the City.'

'I did nothing illegal back when we were together,' Ellie snapped back, but was answered with a sharp, harsh laugh.

'*Back when we were together*,' Nathan mocked. 'That speaks volumes. Tell that to the court. And the newspapers. Do you know the shit I went through daily because of you?'

'No, I must have missed all that as *they systematically destroyed my career in front of my eyes*,' Ellie replied, fighting back the urge to lean across and slam Nathan's smug, punch-able face into the table. 'You know, the accusations you didn't lift a finger to help me with. But hey, sorry people are *laughing*. That must be life destroying for you. Maybe you could tell the press about it again? Like you did in that tell-all *The Sun* paid you for?'

'I had every right to give my side of the story,' Nathan muttered.

'There wasn't a side of the story for you to have!' Ellie exclaimed in exasperation. 'You and me? We were dead long before this happened.'

The waiter turned up, glass on his tray.

Nathan took the vodka, downing it in one and slamming the glass on the table.

'Better you'd died,' he hissed, taking the bill off the serving tray and tossing it at Ellie. 'Here, you can pay.'

'Christ's sake, Nathan, what the hell's made you so much of a prick today?' Ellie snapped, finally reaching the end of her patience. 'Well, more of a prick than usual, anyway?'

There was a moment of silence as Nathan pondered her question.

'You know what happened earlier this week?' he continued. 'I was almost mugged.'

'Are you alright?' Ellie sat forward, concerned, but stopped as Nathan raised a hand to halt her.

'Don't give me your fake concern,' he growled. 'Save it for the people who give a shit.'

'Fine, so what happened?'

'Some lowlife scum caught me in an alley, a couple of nights back,' Nathan shook his head. 'Thought I was going to get stabbed up for a phone and twenty quid. You know why I wasn't? Because one of them saw my face.'

Ellie felt her stomach flip-flop. She knew where this was going.

'He looks at me, and then he says *leave this one. He's Ellie Reckless's ex.*'

Ellie went to reply, but Nathan still hadn't finished.

'That they knew you, and feared what *you'd* do to them, more than what *I'd* do? Tells me all I need to know—'

'*Enough.*'

Ellie had hit her limit now, and slammed her fist down on the table.

Nathan, caught in mid-rant, stopped.

'Is this because they mentioned me?' Ellie half-rose in the chair now, towering over her ex-husband. 'Or because your ex-wife was more of a threat to them than *you?*'

Sitting back down, the anger leaving her system replaced with resignation, disgust and pity, Ellie shook her head.

'Must have really hit your manhood. And how did they know your face, anyway?' she smiled, as if realising the answer. 'Oh, yeah, it'll be all those interviews you gave after the case, when you decided to repeatedly stab me in the back for quick cash.'

Nathan stayed in his chair, staring at her.

'Piss off, Ellie,' he eventually said in response. 'Why did you even want this meeting?'

Ellie nodded at this. *Finally, they were at the point.*

'I want custody of Millie,' Ellie replied. 'You don't give a shit about her and she cries all day while you're at work.'

Nathan shook his head.

'What, so you have me watched now?' he whispered. 'Did *you* send the muggers?'

'No, you sanctimonious prick, if I'd done that, they would have finished the job,' Ellie snapped. 'I want Millie, Nathan. You have a week to decide whether you want to contest this.'

'She's my dog.'

'Come on! You didn't want her, you didn't name her, and you never cared for her,' Ellie replied. 'Why hold her over me?'

'You're right,' Nathan shrugged. 'But I'll have her put down before I—'

The slap was wholly expected, but at the same time a complete surprise to Nathan, as he held his reddening cheek in shock.

'Next time you *joke* about putting *my* dog to sleep, remember who you're pissing off,' she hissed. 'I want Millie in my apartment within a week. Or I'll find some muggers who aren't scared of what I'd do to *finish the job on you*. Your hit pieces in the paper did more damage to my police career than the bloody court case.'

Nathan watched Ellie for a long moment, rubbing his cheek.

'Piss off,' was what he eventually said before leaving.

Ellie went to reply, but noticed someone at her side; the waiter, card machine in his hand, had witnessed the entire exchange.

'He loves me really,' Ellie said.

'He's a dickhead,' the waiter replied. 'You could do better.'

'Oh, I am,' she smiled as she passed her card to the waiter, who scanned it.

And then scanned it again.

And again.

'I'm sorry, but your card's been declined,' he said apologetically. 'It's not being authorised.'

'That's impossible, it's a new one,' Ellie said as she took the card reader. 'Have you tried swiping—'

She stopped, however, as she saw the words on the digital display.

HOWS THIS FOR AN AUDITION? Y/N

Ellie pressed Y, and the screen suddenly changed to TRANSACTION APPROVED.

She passed it back to the waiter who, after looking surprised at this, passed the card back to Ellie and tore off the receipt, giving this to her as well, before leaving her alone at the table.

Holding the receipt, Ellie pulled out her phone, dialling a number.

'Tink? It's me,' she said when it answered. 'I know I said we're meeting at twelve, but I need you to bring someone else along. His name is Casey Noyce. Yes, that's right, *his* son. Speak to Robert; I know you love doing that. I'm sure he has the number.'

This done, she sat back and took a long, last sip of the scotch.

It was time to go to work.

5

HAIL CAESAR'S

It was just after noon when Casey arrived at *Caesar's Diner*, a small breakfast café amid the City of London, and just south of Farringdon Station. He was in a hoodie and jeans, a backpack over his shoulder, and as he arrived at the door, he flipped up the skateboard he'd arrived on, holding it in his left hand as he faced Tinker, currently waiting outside the café.

'You're late,' she said.

Casey glanced at his watch; it was less than a minute past the hour.

'It may have escaped your notice,' he explained, 'but I'm too young to drive.'

Tinker grinned.

'Yeah, you'll fit in perfectly,' she said as she opened the door, allowing Casey in.

To enter the inside of Caesar's was to enter a fifties diner; the floor was a checkerboard black and white design, the walls tiled white. There were tables in the middle and along the side were large, opulent red-leather booths, easily wide enough for six or seven people to sit and eat in. On the wall were fifties advertising posters for milkshakes, burgers and soft drinks, and on each table was a small jukebox, where for a 20p piece you could change the fifties song to *another* fifties song. It was a typical city diner; its clientele were often rich, hungry and nostalgic.

Its clientele also included Ellie Reckless, who sat at the back of one booth, waiting.

'Love what you did with the place,' Casey said as he plonked himself down on the booth's seat, sliding along so that Tinker could sit next to him. 'Is it company lunch time? Are the boardrooms all booked?'

Ellie smiled.

'You're starting your first day, so I'll let you get all this out of your system,' she said. 'I meet here because I like the food, it's not rammed full of people, and I always manage to get this booth.'

'Also, some people we meet might not be considered boardroom suitable,' Tinker added, as the door to Caesar's Diner opened, and a man entered; a furious man in his late sixties, dressed in a three-piece pinstripe suit over a white Eton shirt and burgundy striped tie, his grey, almost white hair cut short, a moustache his only facial hair and a silver tipped walking cane in his hand. He looked like the CEO of one of the nearby buildings, but the moment he spoke, this facade disappeared.

'You bitch,' he hissed at Ellie, his accent, a peculiar mix of upper-class and East End barrow boy plain to hear, as he approached, almost as if for a singular moment, a pretence had been dropped.

'Ramsey—' Ellie started, but the man, now known to Casey as *Ramsey,* hadn't finished.

'Three days I staked out that hotel,' he hissed. 'Three boring days of sitting in the lobby half-reading the *Racing Post* while watching everyone walk by, unable to even make a bet. And you withdraw me for this?'

'You don't even know what *this* is,' Ellie replied irritably. 'This could be something completely different.'

'It's another favour, isn't it?' Ramsey asked, looking over at Tinker when Ellie refused to reply. 'See? I'm psychic.'

He turned, as if considering leaving the diner, but then reluctantly sat on the other side of the booth, glaring at Ellie.

'Ellie Reckless,' he hissed. 'The copper for criminals.'

He stopped, finally realising that Casey was in the booth with them.

'And who may I ask are you?' he asked.

Ellie went to reply, but Casey was already leaning forward, curious.

'Now the woman in the army coat I get, but *you* don't seem the sort that would join her gang,' he said, indicating Ellie as he spoke.

Ramsey bristled at this.

'Gang?' he replied. 'Dear boy, I am definitely not in any gang.'

'What about the tie?' Casey pointed at Ramsey's striped burgundy tie.

'An old school tie is not a gang,' Ramsey protested.

Casey shrugged, leaning back.

'Sorta is though,' he replied, his tone and posture showing he was winning the argument. At this, Ramsey glared at Tinker.

'I didn't realise it was bring your children to work day,' he muttered.

Tinker nodded at Ellie.

'Not my idea,' she said.

'Casey is here partly as a favour for Robbie, but also because he's a pretty good hacker, and ever since Lou left, we've needed one,' Ellie sighed. 'He's here on a trial basis.'

'I also didn't realise we were resorting to recruits from kindergarten now,' Ramsey muttered. 'I have suits older than this child.'

'Casey Noyce, meet Ramsey Allen and Tinker Jones,' Ellie said, noting Ramsey's surprised expression when he learned Casey's surname. 'Tinker is a, well, she's a—'

'I'm her solution provider,' Tinker smiled.

'And how does that work?' Casey asked, genuinely curious.

Tinker shrugged.

'Usually very violently,' she suggested.

Ellie nodded, looking at Ramsey now.

'Ramsey Allen's our retrieval specialist,' she explained.

'That's a fancy way of saying 'thief,' Tinker added with a smile, as Ramsey leaned back on his red leather seat, folding his arms.

'Now, now, Tinkerbelle, don't start,' he proclaimed.

'Call me that again and I'll break your jaw,' Tinker hissed, her body language subtly altering, as if preparing to attack.

Ramsey, however, didn't even flinch at this.

'Threaten me again,' he replied calmly, 'and I'll stop clapping my hands and believing in fairies.'

As Tinker and Ramsey glared at each other across the diner's table, Ellie looked at Casey.

'Well done,' she said, a hint of resignation in her voice. 'I think you've suddenly become the most grown-up person at the table.'

'Is your name really Tinkerbelle?' Casey asked.

'It is!' Ramsey exclaimed in delight. 'Her parents just loved Peter Pan.'

Ignoring Ramsey, Tinker nodded.

'Tinkerbelle Jones, but everyone calls me Tink or Tinker,' she said. 'Except for Ramsey here, who calls me "no, please, not in the face".'

Ramsey grinned as he looked back at the counter and waved for someone to come over.

'Is it too much to assume lunch is on you?' he asked sarcastically. 'Or are you still full from your *brunch?*'

Ellie glanced at Tinker, who shook her head.

'Nuh-uh,' she replied. 'I didn't tell him.'

Ramsey grinned, happy that his little one-upmanship had worked on this occasion.

'I have a few people out there, you know,' he smugly replied. 'I know more than you realise.'

Ellie nodded.

'Then you'll also know that it was a complete waste of time,' she said. 'Nathan's a prick and I didn't have anything to eat.'

'I assume you had something to drink, though,' Ramsey muttered as he looked down at a menu that had now been placed in front of him. 'There's *always* time for something to drink in the world of Elisa Reckless.'

Before Ellie could reply to this, Tinker placed a hand over the menu, obscuring Ramsey's view.

'You've been coming here for months,' she said. 'How can you not know what you want?'

Ramsey batted her hand away.

'I'm working my way through the list,' he said, looking at the waitress, a young woman in a fifties diner uniform. 'I'll have the sixty-two, Sandra.'

'With a tea?'

'Of course.'

Sandra the waitress looked up at the others as she wrote the order down. 'And the rest of you?'

'We'll be ordering in a minute,' Ellie smiled. 'Ramsey's just being a dick right now.'

'So it's a normal weekday then,' Sandra the waitress winked at Ramsey and walked away.

Ellie grinned.

'Looks like someone else hasn't fallen for your charms, either.'

Ramsey decided not to bite at this, instead turning to face her.

'So who's the client?' he asked. Tinker, also not in the loop, turned to face Ellie, who seemed surprised at this.

'Robbie didn't tell you?'

Tinker shook her head.

'I've always been *need to know*,' she smiled. Ellie nodded at this and turned back to Ramsey.

'Danny Flynn,' she said.

There was a moment of silence before Ramsey half-rose out of his seat in anger.

'*Good God, Ellie, he's a nobody!*' he exclaimed loudly. '*A second generation Essex bully at best!* And you withdrew me from a high paying assignment for *him*? I ought to walk away right now!'

Ellie said nothing as she waited for his anger to calm. And then, when he had quietened enough, a little red-faced from anger and embarrassment at his outrage, and sitting back down, she continued.

'He's a nobody who owes five million pounds to Simpson, payable this week,' she said.

'How?' Ramsey narrowed his eyes.

Ellie shrugged, taking a 20p piece and placing it into one of the small silver jukeboxes on the table, tapping in a number. After a moment, the *Righteous Brothers' Unchained Melody* played.

'Land deal went wrong, a little while back,' she explained. 'Price plummeted, Danny got caught on the wrong side.'

'What, the wrong side of Simpson?' Tinker shook her head. 'That's not a man to owe money to.'

'He owed two and a half million, but Nicky had a double-return clause; basically "last money in, first money out". Danny probably thought he'd make ten times that and signed happily.'

Ramsey nodded at this, agreeing with Tinker, but then his expression darkened as the realisation took over.

'This isn't about Danny Flynn owing you,' he muttered. 'It's about Nicholas Simpson being harassed by you.'

'Who's Nicholas Simpson?' Now it was Casey who spoke, out of the loop and confused at the names. 'You mentioned him earlier.'

Ramsey turned to face him.

'You've heard of Simpson's Health Clubs?' he asked.

'Course I have,' Casey replied. Ramsey didn't answer, he just leant back in the seat, waiting for Casey to get to the answer on his own.

Which he did a moment later.

'Wait, you mean *Nicky* Simpson?' he exclaimed. 'That's who you were talking about earlier?'

'I missed this earlier conversation,' Ramsey enquired innocently; a little *too* innocently. 'What was Ellie saying about him to you, exactly?'

'Nothing to do with you,' Ellie replied icily, as Casey rocked in his seat, continuing.

'I follow his Instagram. Guy gives sick HIIT sessions.'

'Hit sessions?' now it was Ramsey's turn to look confused.

Tinker leant in.

'High Impact Interval Training,' she replied. 'The guy's a household name for it. *The nation's personal trainer,* he likes to call himself.'

'That's not the Simpson I know of,' Ramsey argued. 'The one I know is a criminal, like his father and his grandfather before him.'

He looked at Ellie, who had the slightest hint of a smirk on her lips.

'I've reformed,' he haughtily replied. 'Doesn't mean I have amnesia.'

Ellie, accepting this, looked back at Casey.

'Nicky Simpson is a household name these days, with his *YouTube* page and his books. What people don't know is that Nicky's *granddad,* Paddy Simpson, used to be an accountant for the Richardson Brothers back in the sixties. Made a lot of under the counter money. And, when they went down for thirty-odd years, he stepped into their shoes. Then, in the nineties, Nicky's dad Max took these connections and worked with the Essex mob. You know about the *Land Rover killings*? Pat Tate and all that? Max Simpson probably pulled the trigger, before taking over everything south of the Thames from dad at the turn of the millennium.'

'Unfortunately, Max now has Parkinsons,' Tinker added. 'So around eight years back Nicky stepped up and took over the family business, bankrolled by land left to him by Paddy.'

Casey paled slightly at this, a queasiness that didn't fade

as Ramsey's all-day breakfast arrived, which he attacked with great enthusiasm.

'Nicky Simpson's a gangsta?' Casey half whispered, as if his childhood dreams had been crushed.

'Officially? No,' Tinker passed Ramsey some ketchup. 'Unofficially though...'

'Like father, like son,' Ramsey said, his mouth half full as he spoke. 'Grandfather, father, son, even.'

Deciding to move the conversation on, Ellie leant closer.

'Anyway,' she said, returning everyone's attention to her again. 'Danny has a five million pound debt. And last night, the painting that he was selling to *pay* the debt was stolen.'

'He had a painting worth five million?' This new piece of news impressed Tinker. Ellie smiled, reaching into a messenger bag beside her, currently on the red leather seat.

'And the rest,' she said, rummaging in it. 'Ramsey, before you fill your mouth again, tell us about the *Gardner Heist*.'

Ramsey wiped his mouth with a napkin as he placed the cutlery down, considering this.

'March nineteen-ninety,' he started, his posture straightening as he moved into an unconscious lecturer position. 'Two men dressed as police officers enter the *Isabella Stewart Gardner Museum* in Boston, and then walk out with five hundred million dollars' worth of art. Rembrandts, Manets, a Vermeer, some statues... '

He stopped, staring at Ellie in horror.

'No...'

Ellie nodded as she pulled out a file from the bag, placing it on the table. She opened it up, flipping through the papers until she found a singular photo, passing it across the table to Ramsey.

'Last night, somebody stole this from Danny Flynn,' she said.

Ramsey stared in utter shock at the image.

'Vermeer's *'The Concert'*,' he whispered. 'Last estimated at over *two hundred and fifty million dollars*.'

He looked back at Ellie in almost despair.

'And Danny Flynn had it on his wall?'

Ellie shrugged.

'Apparently, his dad gave it to him before he died,' she replied.

'My father gave me a watch,' Ramsey muttered, staring at the photo. 'His gave him a Vermeer. *The* Vermeer. Bastard.'

'Now, do you understand why I've taken this?' Ellie asked. 'Big theft, big case, big reward.'

'For you, maybe,' Ramsey, still staring at the photo as if scared to take his eyes away from it, nodded. 'Still doesn't pay my bookie's tab.'

'What happens if Danny can't sell it?' Tinker asked.

'Nicky Simpson is probably very annoyed.'

'No, I'm serious,' Tinker insisted. 'Danny owes Nicky five million. Without this painting, Danny can't pay. I can't see Nicky going "okay, I'll give you longer" or anything. There has to be a backup. Something so bad for Danny that he'd come to you, to us, for a solution.'

'It's no secret that Danny has business contacts Nicholas wants,' Ramsey considered this. 'His father worked a lot in Boston when he was starting out, gathered a lot of goodwill from the families there.'

He pointed at the photo.

'Hence the fact he's apparently involved in a Boston art theft.'

'And Nicky wants to branch out,' Ellie nodded. 'Danny's

business might be small fry compared to Simpson, but he still works a lot with Boston, which opens the US for him. Someone like Nicky, using the same services, could double, triple his income. That's worth more than a painting.'

'So this could be part of a hostile takeover?' Tinker replied. 'Nicky wants the business, finds a debt owed, and adds pressure?'

'Only if the painting isn't sold,' Ellie leaned back. 'Which means Simpson has skin in this game.'

There was a moment of silence, only *Unchained Melody* playing in the background as the group considered the ramifications.

'Who do you know that could fence something like this?' Ellie continued. This finally stopped Ramsey staring at the photo, and he leaned back in his seat, staring up at the ceiling, his meal and the photo momentarily forgotten.

'This is seriously high end art, Elisa,' he said, his eyes unfocused as he thought aloud. 'We're not looking at something as public as *eBay* here, it's going to be dark web, underground auction houses, that sort of thing. But a painting this hot? They're usually stolen to order. Someone would learn of its existence and push for a retrieval.'

'And who would be on top of that list? Someone who could get people into Chipping Norton and steal the painting?' Ellie watched Ramsey now; although he was a miserable, complaining bastard, now and then he showed his genuine experience. Ramsey had been a damned good thief back in the day, a modern-day *Raffles* or *Lupin*, the archetypical 'gentleman thief' of myth. He only went for high-end items, and had only retired from thieving when he was arrested by a young Detective Sergeant Ellie Reckless, freshly moved to the Met Police unit that had been hunting him, under a Detective Inspector Monroe, a dour Scot who'd continually failed to nail him for anything.

He'd always been impressed by that, and Ellie had made sure he never forgot it.

Eventually, Ramsey looked back at her.

'I don't honestly know, but I could speak to someone who might. Sebastien LaFleur,' he said. 'Runs a questionable studio and gallery in Hoxton. He's highly sought after as a consultant with these high-end art works, and would be the first call for anything this large. You may remember we used him last year when he helped us with the Turner forgery?'

'Oh, you mean that creepy little octogenarian with a thing for teenage girls?' Ellie nodded.

'He's only seventy, and they were his apprentices,' Ramsey protested.

'Sure they were,' Ellie smiled sweetly. 'Okay, find out if he knows anything, or can tip us in the right direction. After lunch, of course.'

Ramsey stared at the photo and then at his half-eaten meal, and Ellie grinned. The thought of finding or even seeing this particular Vermeer was making the aged ex-thief want to start immediately.

However, bacon won out, and he returned to his lunch.

'So, what do you want me to do?' Casey asked. Ellie considered this, and then slid a menu across the table, stopping it in front of him.

'Have some lunch, and make sure it's filling,' she said. 'I have a hunch you might miss dinner.'

'I'm still not happy about this,' Ramsey muttered. 'I accept it's an intriguing case, but we still make nothing from this. All we get is one of your favours. And you still won't tell us what they're for.'

Ellie nodded.

'I get that, and I'm aware I took you off the Somerville case for this,' she said. 'So, we'll work both together. We've almost finished it, and then you'll make your cut.'

'And half of yours,' Ramsey replied, his eyes glinting at the chance of some haggling.

'Ten percent.'

'Forty.'

'Five percent.'

Ramsey frowned.

'You're going the wrong way,' he said. 'You're going down, not up.'

Ellie smiled.

'I know damn well you'll make some kind of side hustle off the Vermeer, so don't go playing the poor old man card,' she said. 'I'll give you ten percent of my Somerville cut. And five to Tinker, too. But that's it.'

'And the answer to why you want the favours?' Ramsey pushed a little harder now. However, Sandra interrupted this as she walked back up to the booth.

'Have you decided yet?' she asked. 'It's just that Dino wants you out if you're only buying coffees.'

'Yeah, we're ready to order,' Ellie said, grateful for the distraction. And, as the team ordered a variety of lunch items and drinks, Ramsey taking the opportunity to add seconds to his order, Ellie turned her attention to the case.

Ramsey had been right. This wasn't about gaining a favour from Danny Flynn.

This was, and had been from the start, all about gaining Nicky Simpson's attention. And that, she knew without a doubt, would be exactly what happened the moment they found the painting.

All Ellie needed now, though, was a solid lead. Either the burglars, the arranger or the buyer would do.

The question was, who would they find first? And more importantly, while they were hunting for the stolen painting, *what would Nicky Simpson be doing?*

6

ART CLASS

SEBASTIAN LAFLEUR LIVED IN A SMALL ARTISTIC COMMUNITY IN Hoxton, in East London. That is, he had an office and studio there; nobody ever knew where Sebastian LaFleur really lived. Or what his actual name was, either. All that was known about the artist and forger was behind a nondescript door on the ground floor of a 'creative space'; an open plan area that had once been a warehouse, and was now filled with small offices, with screen printers, comic artists and illustrators, and modern art welders inside.

Tinker sniffed the air.

'I smell burning,' she said.

Ramsey breathed in as well, shaking his head.

'You smell welding,' he replied. 'There are a lot of artists that specialise in metal sculptures here.'

'I smell *burning*,' Tinker insisted as she folded her arms, facing Ramsey. 'In particular, paper. It's a distinctive smell, and I know it well.'

'Does it smell like burned toast?' Ramsey, already boring of this conversation, asked.

'Why would it be toast?'

'Just making sure you're not having a stroke,' Ramsey shrugged.

Tinker flipped Ramsey the middle finger and turned back to the door, her trained eye examining the hinges, the density of the material, the angle of the corridor behind her—

'You're not kicking the damned thing in, you know,' Ramsey half-chuckled. 'I can see the calculations running through your head.'

'Just making sure I'm prepared,' Tinker was now following the edge of the doorframe with her eyes.

'Prepared, yes, certainly,' Ramsey nodded, still not taking this seriously. 'You know, Tinks, there are three types of people. The kind who see a glass half-full, the kind that see a glass half-empty, and those that smack the glass onto the floor, allowing it to break, making sure it's never seen.'

'There's one other,' Tinker looked back at Ramsey now. 'The kind that makes sure they know every single move before it happens, and keeps the glass from being touched in the first place.'

She grinned.

'Then it's always full, isn't it?'

Ramsey sighed, straightening his tie.

'So, how well do you know this guy?' finishing her examination, Tinker stepped closer to the door, awaiting Ramsey's response before knocking. Ramsey thought about the answer for a moment.

'Our paths have crossed once or twice, and we have worked together on occasions,' he replied eventually

'Stole together, you mean?'

'Working doesn't have to mean thieving to a thief,'

Ramsey sniffed. 'Just like, for you, for example, working doesn't have to mean beating someone senseless.'

'Yeah, but it's more fun when it does,' Tinker cracked her knuckles. 'So, this *working together* you did. Before or after you screwed him over?'

'It was more of a mutual back-stabbing,' Ramsey started before pausing. 'Hold on, how did you know I screwed him over in any way?'

Tinker banged on the door.

'You screw everyone over,' she said, stepping back. 'It's in your nature. You're like a well-dressed scorpion.'

'I can't argue with that,' Ramsey adjusted his tie. 'I am indeed very well dressed.'

'Scorpion.'

'What?'

'A well-dressed *scorpion*,' Tinker looked back at him. 'The point of what I said wasn't that you're stylish, Ramsey. It's that I don't trust you, won't turn my back on you, and every time we work together, I expect you to stab me in the throat with your very stylish tie pin.'

'I would never do that,' Ramsey replied, horrified. 'It might bend it.'

Tinker was about to respond to this when the door made a noise, the sound of bolts being slid back at the top and bottom of the other side of it, the echoing clatter of a lock being turned sounding before the door slowly swung inwards, revealing a woman, no more than her mid-twenties.

She wore a white tee-shirt, wild, bottle-green hair and a pair of welding goggles up on her forehead. She was also wearing a brown leather apron, her hands covered in what looked like soot. In the background, Tinker could hear music, some kind of rock album playing softly.

'Yeah?' she asked.

Ramsey half stepped back, as if scared that some of the residue would land on his suit, but Tinker turned to face the woman, giving her most winning smile in the process.

'We're looking for Sebastian LaFleur,' she said.

'You police?'

'Do we look like police?' the question affronted Ramsey.

The woman glared at him.

'Style police, maybe,' she said, looking back at Tinker. 'So what do you and the haunted shop mannequin want with him?'

'To talk,' Tinker replied. 'Is he here?'

'I bloody hope not,' the woman seemed to relax a little, the door opening a little wider as she straightened. 'He died six months back. He owe you money? He usually owes people money when they come. I don't have any, so don't start asking for it.'

Ramsey stepped closer at this.

'He was an old friend, and I didn't know he'd passed on,' he stated formally. 'We were hoping to ask a favour of him.'

'Well, you're shit out of luck there,' the woman scratched at the strap of her welding goggles. 'But maybe I can help. You'd better come in.'

The door was opened wider, and the woman stepped back, allowing Tinker and Ramsey to enter the artist's studio.

It was large, one floor but with high ceilings, the walls painted white a long time ago, but now yellowing with a mixture of age and nicotine. There were black soot marks everywhere, and the floor was a swathe of cracking concrete and burn marks.

Against the back wall, where a barred window could also be seen, was a workshop table and shelving unit, double deep and filled with what looked like rolled lengths of canvas. Beside this was a metal incinerator bin. There was a back door that led to the toilet, the cistern visible through it, beside which was a cloth-covered canvas. In the middle, dominating the space, was a large ironwork statue, shaped like an angel and created from what looked to be the metal parts of rifles and pistols.

The woman locked the door behind them, and Tinker noticed for the first time that her right wrist was in a cast, and looked a few weeks old.

'That looks painful,' she said, pointing at it. The woman shrugged, as if almost unaware that she even had it.

'Snowboarding accident about four weeks back,' she said. 'Comes off next week. I forget it's even there.'

Tinker looked at the statue.

'Must be hard to weld with it,' she replied.

The woman held the cast up, turning it.

'Biggest problem's that I'm right handed, you know?' she said. 'Slows me down a ton. But welding's a damn sight easier than trying to draw with it. My pencil work is shit right now. I draw like a five-year-old.'

Ramsey had walked over to the desk now, but stopped, looking back.

'Sorry, but who are you exactly?' he asked.

'I could ask the same of you,' the woman snapped back.

'I'm Tinker, that's Ramsey,' Tinker quickly interjected. 'Now we're all friends here, maybe you can tell us?'

The woman looked as if she was going to argue this, but then relented.

'I'm Natalie,' she replied. 'I'm, that is, I *was* his apprentice. Started in January.'

She looked around the studio.

'Now it's just me.'

'Big place for one person,' Tinker commented. 'How will you afford it?'

'Dunno,' Natalie shrugged. 'I have awhile to work it out, though, Seb would pay the rent when he had windfalls—'

'When he sold a forgery, you mean,' Ramsey interrupted, gaining a glare from Natalie in reply.

'When he had his *windfalls*,' she repeated, emphasising the word, 'he would pay in bulk, We're currently a year in credit here. He paid eighteen months' worth before he...'

She trailed off, looking away.

'How did Sebastian die?' Ramsey was over by the desk now, picking up a photo frame that had been placed at the back of it angling it to the light of the barred window so he could see it properly. 'I mean, I always saw him as the kind of man who would die in bed, but someone else's one, you understand what I'm—'

'Car accident on the M40,' Natalie interrupted. 'Slammed into one of those car carrier things heading east, just north of Oxford. Died instantly, so they said. But whether that was just told to me to make me feel better, I don't know.'

Ramsey nodded at this, resisting the urge to grimace at the brutality of the situation.

'My condolences.'

'His friends were all at his funeral,' Natalie continued suspiciously. 'I'm guessing, as you thought he was still alive, that you weren't there, so, not really a friend?'

'We were more work acquaintances, and only then when the work was required,' Ramsey admitted.

'I guessed,' the hint of sarcasm in Natalie's voice was not unnoticed.

Seeing Ramsey's obvious discomfort, Tinker walked over to the statue.

'Are these real guns?' she asked, leaning in closer for a better look. 'That one there looks like a nine-millimetre Grand Power K100.'

'Probably is,' Natalie replied, nonplussed. 'Well, a replica, I mean. All of them are. I bought a box load a while back for this art installation. No idea what the names are, but a gun's a gun, right? I actually have one of them in a drawer as a night-time deterrent. I do a lot of all-nighters, as welding is loud and the other studios get annoyed, and I find having even a fake in my hand makes the crazies stay away.'

Tinker stepped back, taking in the whole statue, and Ramsey stifled a laugh as he saw her expression to the hand-wave statement about guns being guns, desperately wanting to start her TED talk on *guns and how they're all different, you naïve bitch*, while keeping to the softly softly approach she was trying to use.

'What's it supposed to be?' she asked as she looked up at the statue. 'I mean, I get that it's some kind of angel, but what's the message?'

'It's a protest against the industry of war,' Natalie glanced at Ramsey as he picked up another photo frame, looking down at it. 'Be careful with that, old man.'

'I'm not that doddery,' Ramsey snapped back irritably. 'I can hold a photo frame without dropping it.'

He punctuated this by almost dropping the frame, recovering himself just in time, as Tinker rolled her eyes.

'Who's the chap with Seb in this picture?' he asked, showing the frame to Natalie. 'He looks familiar, but I can't work out where from.'

The photo was of a black-tie event, in the centre of which

was Sebastian LaFleur, in a black tuxedo and bow tie, his thinning white hair slicked down into a parting. Next to him, and smiling widely, was a middle-aged black man with short greying hair and a goatee. He, too, was in a black tuxedo, but he wore a black tie rather than bow tie in the photo, Sebastian's arm visible around his shoulder, his wrist glinting with something silver; either a watch or a bracelet. Just entering the shot was a woman caught in conversation with someone off screen, and a waiter carrying a tray of drinks.

'What am I, your bloody secretary?' Natalie peered at it, squinting. 'No idea. He has a lot of photos like that, all over the bloody place. It's probably one of his big restoration clients. He was always sucking up to them because they paid the big money.'

Ramsey looked at the photo again.

'Still can't shake the feeling he looks familiar.'

'Maybe he was at the funeral and you saw him there?' Natalie suggested innocently before continuing. 'Oh, wait. You weren't there because you're not the friend you claim to be.'

Ramsey bit off a reply, and walked over to the incinerator, sulking silently. Tinker reached up to the statue, poking at a gun that had been welded into position as part of a wing.

'Please don't do that,' Natalie pleaded. 'I've only tacked that on, so the welds aren't strong.'

'Why only tacking?' Tinker asked.

'Because I'm not sure if I like it there yet,' Natalie replied, as if it was the most obvious answer in the world. 'Once it's properly welded, there's no way it's coming off.'

Tinker noted out of the corner of her eye that Ramsey was poking around the base of the incinerator with his cane. As Natalie looked up at the statue, Tinker saw Ramsey drop to one knee and pocket a piece of charred paper before returning to his lounging position, before Natalie looked back at him.

'What was Seb working on when he died?' Ramsey asked, his mock innocence a little too layered on.

Natalie stared at him suspiciously for a moment before pointing at the cloth covered canvas near the door to the toilet.

'That,' she said, folding her arms, obviously tiring of this intrusion. Ignoring this, Ramsey walked over to the canvas, pulling off the cloth and staring at the half finished painting underneath.

'You know, I could be wrong, but this looks like half of a perfect replica of Turner's *Crossing The Brook*,' he said admiringly. 'He always loved forging this painting. I think he's sold it half a dozen times too.'

Natalie walked over to the half-finished painting, standing beside Ramsey as she stared at it.

'He'd been playing around with it, trying new paints, and using an old canvas to draw it on, so it wasn't likely to be "sold", if you get what I mean,' she explained softly. 'I always intended to get rid of it, but I couldn't bring myself to do so.'

Ramsey nodded at this, as if understanding what Natalie meant. If LaFleur had been intending to sell this as a forgery, the canvas would have been clean and of the correct age. This looked more like a painting drawn for fun.

'I could help,' he offered. 'Take it off your hands.'

'It's sentimental,' Natalie retorted.

'I might offer fifty pounds to soften the loss?' Ramsey was already pulling out his wallet at this.

Natalie looked up at him, narrowing her eyes.

'It was his last work,' she insisted.

'Sixty,' Ramsey began pulling ten-pound notes out of his wallet as he spoke.

'Make it seventy and you have a deal,' Natalie smiled back at him.

Reluctantly, Ramsey nodded.

'Fine,' he agreed, passing over the notes. 'It's a good rendition. He always nailed this one. And I like the idea of the half-finished aspect of a known classic.'

Natalie moved the canvas aside for Ramsey, and on the floor he saw a finished one, exactly the same, behind it.

'As you said, he always loved this painting,' she said.

Ramsey smiled back at Natalie, aware he'd been played, but still happy about what he had.

'I don't know the original,' Tinker admitted.

Ramsey stared back at her in utter horror.

'It's at Tate Britain,' he intoned. 'You should go there. Maybe get an education.'

'In art forgeries?' Tinker chuckled. 'Why do I need one? I've got you, and you're the best.'

Ramsey bristled at this, but the veiled compliment at the end softened the burn that he was sure that Tinker had just given.

'You're right,' he stated magnanimously. 'I am.'

He pointed at the painting; in particular, the large tree on the left.

'See here?' he asked. 'In the bark? S.L. He's signing the forgery. Right there, in the middle of the thing and there for all to see. And nobody ever does.'

'Except you.'

Ramsey shook his head.

'Even I didn't, until Sebastian himself showed me,' he

admitted. 'The man was a genius. You see, by doing this, it can't be classed as a forgery, as he's changed the image.'

'That's the first thing Seb ever taught me,' Natalie, finally warming up, replied. 'Always keep your secrets out in the open, because nobody ever looks there. They all think they're cleverly hidden.'

'Indeed,' Ramsey looked back at the canvas. 'With your permission?'

'You bought it, so go ahead,' Natalie returned to the sculpture, turning the welding torch back on, having decided that the conversation was over. Ramsey nodded, tucking the canvas under his arm.

'Then I think we're done here,' he said, looking at Tinker before turning back to Natalie. 'Oh, one last thing, did Seb ever deal with anyone here about a Vermeer?'

Natalie considered this.

'Not that I can think of.'

'You never saw Seb forging one?' Ramsey insisted. 'Vermeers are quite distinctive.'

Natalie shook her head.

'Sorry, but no,' she replied, pulling down the welding goggles to signify the ending of this interaction.

Ramsey nodded.

'Not a problem,' he said as he motioned for Tinker to unbolt the door. 'Thank you for your time, and sorry for your loss.'

With Tinker opening the heavy metal door for him, Ramsey took the painting from the studio, walking out of the building without another word. In fact, it wasn't until they reached Tinker's Land Rover, parked on the street outside the creative space, that he finally looked back at Tinker.

'Go on then,' she said. 'What is it? I mean, you don't have

a sentimental bone in your body, and you hate giving money away.'

Ramsey placed the painting down beside the Land Rover, rummaging in his pocket.

'Remember the burning smell?' he asked. 'I thought it was welding, but you were sure it wasn't, as you knew burning paper, you sick arsonist?'

He pulled a scrap of charred canvas from his pocket.

'Looks like you were right.'

'What is it?' Tinker leaned in close. The scrap had some kind of painted image on it, but was too small to make out.

'I found this beside the incinerator,' Ramsey explained. 'Likely wafted out on hot air and landed on the concrete. Burned in the last day or so, I'd say.'

'And?' Tinker straightened up as she stared at Ramsey, who slowly smiled.

'And this is a piece of Vermeer's *The Concert*,' he replied. 'The same painting stolen from Danny Flynn.'

'So, LaFleur forged it before he died?' Tinker frowned. 'That's a little coincidental, isn't it?'

'Incredibly so, as he was more a Turner man,' Ramsey nodded. 'One thing's for sure. If Natalie back there *was* the one who burned this, then she lied when she said that she never *saw* it.'

'And the half-finished painting was bought because...'

'Because she said it was painted around the same time, and I need a comparison for the scrap I picked up.'

There was a beep, and Ramsey pulled out his phone, looking down at it.

'Would you do me a kindness,' he said. 'Can you take this back to our resident forensics expert? I'll owe you.'

'You need to be somewhere?' Tinker smiled. Ramsey, in turn, nodded.

'Problem with mother,' he replied. 'I'll catch up with you in the diner.'

'I can drive you to the home if you want,' Tinker offered, already placing the half-finished forgery into the car, but Ramsey was already walking away, down the street.

'Quicker by tube,' he said hurriedly, as he turned a corner, disappearing from view.

Tinker frowned. It was known that Ramsey's mother suffered from dementia and had recently been placed into a care home for her own good, but there was something off with Ramsey, something furtive about his nature just then.

Probably because he's a scorpion, she thought to herself before climbing into her Land Rover and driving off.

7

OPEN-AIR MEETINGS

It took Ramsey another thirty minutes to travel to his destination by public transport, but the time spent on crowded buses and tube carriages was still preferable to the questions he would have to answer if Tinker had been in the car with him.

His final destination was a car park on the South Bank; five storeys high and built in the sixties, this was a brutalist monstrosity, a throwback to a time when concrete was king, and style took second place to functionality. On arriving, Ramsey had ensured that he wasn't being followed, before taking the lift to the top floor, walking up the ramp and emerging onto the open air rooftop parking area.

He'd hated lying to Tinker; he'd hated lying to everyone, to be brutally frank. He didn't owe Ellie Reckless much, and he felt she took him for granted now and then—this current case being a prime example of that—but at the same time, he felt dirty when he went behind her back, speaking to people about her.

Or, rather, speaking to *one particular* person against her.

At the other end of the rooftop car park was a white Tesla Model S, a suited man standing at the side, watching him. There were chargers at the wall beside the car, and Ramsey assumed the car was utilising these while waiting for him, as the other alternative was that they'd deliberately parked as far away as possible, forcing him to walk the entire distance. Which, knowing the nature of who he was meeting with, was also eminently possible.

The man, seeing Ramsey appear at the entrance to the car park rapped lightly on the window, nodding in Ramsey's direction and, as the elderly thief crossed the tarmac towards the Tesla, Ramsey saw the back passenger door open, and a *new* man get out.

He was muscled and lean, wearing branded jogging bottoms and a sweatshirt, his wild, sun-lightened hair roughly pulled back into a small ponytail, as strands tried to escape, in the process clearing his shaven, tanned, smiling face from any obstruction. Patiently, he waited for Ramsey to approach the car, but was already fidgeting by the time Ramsey stopped in front of him.

Ramsey had expected this. He knew that Nicholas Simpson, known as Nicky to his friends, had an incredibly short attention span, bordering on ADHD.

'Ramsey,' Simpson said, now lounging against the side of the Tesla. 'So good of you to find the time to come and see me.'

Ramsey bristled at this.

'I had little choice, really, did I?' he snapped back, before remembering who he was talking to and adding a hasty 'Mister Simpson.'

'Not really,' Simpson agreed, stretching his arms out,

rotating his neck as he cleared a couple of kinks from his spine. 'Pleasant journey?'

'I came on London Transport,' Ramsey stood still, waiting to see where this was going. 'So no, not the best of journeys.'

Nicky Simpson smiled at this, but didn't continue the conversation. Ramsey knew that somewhere deep inside, Nicky Simpson was happy that he'd caused Ramsey Allen some personal discomfort, because at the end of the day, Nicky Simpson was a *prick*.

'So,' Simpson continued. 'What do you have on our mutual friend?'

Ramsey relaxed at this. *Nicky wasn't there to talk about paintings or debts, he was there to talk about Ellie Reckless.* Which was interesting timing, considering the fact that they'd taken Danny Flynn's case on not more than a couple of hours back.

'Nothing,' he replied, shrugging.

'I don't pay you for nothing,' Simpson snapped, and for the first time in the conversation, Ramsey saw that Simpson's guard was down, and his true colours were emerging.

'You don't pay me full stop,' he replied curtly, with a sniff. 'So—'

'How's your mum?' Simpson interrupted. 'In the home? Does she even know where she is? Must be very hard for you, Ramsey. But at least it's a nice place, with nice people around her.'

He stopped, letting the pause emphasise his next comment.

'It'd be a shame if you had to move her somewhere cheaper, somewhere *worse*, you know?'

Ramsey felt the sliver of ice slide down his spine. He knew

that without Simpson's funding, his mother wouldn't be able to stay in the home for more than a few months. Taking a deep breath, forcing back a reply, he swallowed and nodded.

'Look, we don't know anything,' he started. 'She doesn't tell us what her plan is, okay? She keeps doing small jobs for favours, but none of us are brought into her confidence, at least not yet.'

'Go on.'

'That's it,' Ramsey shrugged. 'Meanwhile our regular investigations proceed as usual – they might not be much, but at least they pay the rent, you understand?'

'Feeling the pinch?' Simpson pulled a wad of notes out of his jogging bottoms, counting a few off with his fingers. Ramsey could see that they were fifty-pound notes as Simpson continued. 'Let me help make it all go away.'

Ramsey shook his head, resisting the urge to step backwards, to back away from the man in front of him.

'No, it's fine, I don't need your money—' he started, but Simpson *shhh*ed him, placing around three hundred quid in fifty-pound notes into his upper jacket pocket.

'You've always needed my money,' Simpson smiled as he patted the notes down. 'Don't back out now, not when it's so much fun.'

He walked back to the Tesla, replying as he faced away, staring out across London.

'After all, it's so much nicer when it's the carrot, and not the stick,' he finished.

Ramsey looked at the tarmac of the car park. If he'd felt dirty and shamed before the meeting, that was nothing compared to how he felt now.

'What's the game right now?' Nicky Simpson looked back

at the elderly thief. 'I heard you met in the diner. That usually means fun times.'

'Danny Flynn.'

'What's he done this time?' Simpson asked.

Ramsey looked surprised at this, and Simpson smiled.

'Oh, you're not talking about that bloody painting are you?' he shook his head. 'I thought you were better than that.'

'I take the jobs that I'm given,' Ramsey looked to the floor, as if giving deference, but in actuality, he was trying to work out how much Simpson knew.

Had he been the one to steal the painting?

'You wouldn't know where the burglars came from, would you?' he asked, still ensuring that he didn't make eye contact. He heard a laugh.

'No, but I know where they are now,' Simpson said. 'Tell your boss to have a gander around Battersea. Try Cringle Street. She'll bump into them alright.'

Before Ramsey could ask what he meant by this, the young gangster walked over to him, lifting Ramsey's head up by the chin until Ramsey was looking directly into Nicky Simpson's eyes.

'Tick tock, Mister Allen,' he whispered. 'I'll only wait for so long. Find out what game little Miss Reckless is playing and then come back to me, yeah?'

Silently, Ramsey nodded and, at this Simpson grinned widely, nodding back as he walked back to his Tesla, once more into the guise of the YouTube fitness guru that his public persona had become.

'And say hi to your mother for me,' he said as he climbed into the driver's seat. 'I hear she's doing wonders in the home.'

Ramsey stood alone in the car park as Nicky Simpson, the

bodyguard now sitting in the passenger seat, drove the Tesla at speed away from him, rocketing down the ramp to the lower levels in the strange, enforced silence that electric cars had. In fact, it was so quiet that Ramsey gave himself an extra ten seconds before releasing the breath he held, in case they had parked up just beneath him, and were waiting to see what the elderly thief would do.

Eventually, convinced that he was alone, Ramsey pulled out his phone and dialled a number on it. After a few rings, it went to voicemail, but that was fine for him. It meant he didn't have to speak to her, and right now he didn't even want to speak to himself.

'Ellie, it's Ramsey,' he said. 'Had a hit from a contact, said we might find the burglars of Danny Flynn in Cringle Street, wherever that is. That's all I know. Sorry.'

Disconnecting the call, Ramsey put the phone away, staring out across London. The clouds were greying, and the sun was now hidden behind them, most likely for the next couple of hours. Which was good, because they fitted his mood.

Ramsey hated speaking to Nicky Simpson, because it reminded him he *owed* Nicky Simpson. And he hadn't told Ellie or the others; not because he was ashamed of it, but because he knew that if he did, then he wouldn't be brought back into any jobs where his expertise was needed.

Which meant that his mother would lose her place even quicker.

No, for the moment, Ramsey Allen, Ellie Reckless, and Nicky Simpson's lives were entwined. And the sooner he could help one of them remove the other, the better.

All he had to do, he thought morosely as he pulled the fifty-pound notes out of his jacket pocket, placing them carefully into his leather wallet, *was to decide which of the two he wanted to help, and which of them he wanted to betray.*

And with this thought echoing in his head, he walked away, back down the ramp and to the exit, several storeys below.

———

ELLIE DIDN'T KNOW WHERE RAMSEY GOT HIS INFORMATION from, but he wasn't wrong. As she drove towards Battersea Power Station and the Thames, turning right off Nine Elms, she could already see the blue flashing lights of the police near the end, where the industrial cement factories and yards were situated, deep in the midst of the Thames Tideway Tunnel, otherwise known as the *London Super Sewer.* Due to be finished within a couple of years, and with a promise that *you won't even know we were here,* the area was currently a giant construction site; the sort of spot you could go for some privacy late at night, while in the heart of London.

'That don't look good,' Casey, glancing up from his laptop, and currently sitting in the passenger seat, muttered. Ellie grunted a reply. The kid was right; blue flashing lights meant *blues and twos.*

There was definitely a crime scene ahead.

And unfortunately, that meant police.

Ahead were the recognisable chimneys of Battersea Power Station, but before that, there was a small turn off with a sandwich truck to the left; the amount of construction here meant a lot of hungry workers, and Ellie was actually surprised there weren't more scattered around. Indicating into it, Ellie pulled her Ford Focus to a stop, pulling out her phone and tapping a quick message.

'Aren't we gonna have a look at what's going on?' Casey asked, confused as to the pit stop.

'We will, but we need to have a moment first,' Ellie replied. 'About ten minutes should do it. Want some lunch?'

'You've already fed me,' Casey was suspicious now. 'What's going on?'

'Me and the police? We don't get on that well,' Ellie reluctantly explained. 'I need to sort a couple of safeguards before we arrive. Like first off, whether anyone I know personally is there.'

'Making sure you've got friends in the area?'

Ellie almost laughed.

'I don't think I have *any* friends on the force anymore, but I like your assumption,' she said. 'Do you want a tea? Can of something?'

'Beer?'

'Something more age-specific?'

Casey shrugged.

'Surprise me,' he said, adding, 'but not anything with sugar in it. And not any diet drinks too, as the sweetener tastes foul. Maybe a zero drink.'

'So basically, you want to be surprised with a Coke Zero,' Ellie shook her head.

'Maybe not,' Casey smiled. 'There's a lot of flavours. I had one in my bag, but you made me leave it with my skateboard.'

'Your skateboard was filthy and I didn't want it in my car.'

Casey glanced into the back of the car, checking out the discarded litter.

'What, you thought it might make an alliance with all this?' he asked.

'You'll get what they have,' Ellie got out of the car, walking to the sandwich truck, ordering a coffee for herself.

As she waited, she stared back at Casey, eyes glued again on his laptop. He'd only pulled it out a few minutes ago; before that, he'd been glued to his iPad. Or whatever touch-screen tablet it was that kids used these days. Eventually she gathered her drinks and walked back to the car, climbing in, passing Casey his, while sipping at her own.

'What's this?' he asked, staring at the bottle in confusion.

'It's water,' Ellie sipped at her coffee. 'They didn't have any zero drinks, so I got you that to be safe.'

She smiled.

'Don't worry though,' she finished. 'I made sure it was sparkling.'

'You're funny,' Casey complained, although he unscrewed the bottle and took a mouthful of sparkling water as he did so. 'Hey, who's Millie?'

Ellie looked at Casey, placing the coffee cup in the middle drink holder's space.

'Where did you hear that?' she asked.

Casey shrugged.

'The pissed off bloke you met, you told him you wanted custody,' he replied. 'Is she a daughter? Is she my age?'

He held up the bottled water.

'Is this why you're shit at parenting?'

'You followed me?' Ellie hissed, her voice lowering. Rather than back away, though, Casey just shrugged.

'Of course I did,' he said. 'I ran off, so you'd forget about me, then doubled back on my skateboard. Didn't need it though, because you walked to the restaurant.'

Before Ellie could say anything else, though, Casey held up his hands.

'I had to,' he explained. 'I can't just hack card readers from my computer at home. It's not comic books or a *Mission*

Impossible movie. I have to be on the same network. And I had to be able to lock the correct card at the exact moment. I told the barman I was meeting my dad and watched you from the other side of the room.'

'How much did you hear?' Ellie was still angry, but she couldn't help but appreciate the level of thoroughness Casey had gone through. And, added to that, she was annoyed at herself for not seeing him.

'Nothing really,' Casey admitted. 'Just that you told him Millie cried and you wanted her. By then I was hacking the system, so I was a little distracted.'

Ellie considered this for a moment.

'Millie's my dog,' she replied. 'Well, was my dog. Cocker Spaniel, five years old. We got her together.'

'The man and you?'

'Nathan. My ex-husband,' Ellie nodded. 'I wanted our break up—his idea—to be easy for him; all the shit that landed on us was because of me, after all, but he took Millie out of spite.'

'He doesn't love her?'

'Oh, I'm sure he loves her,' Ellie shook her head. 'He's just terrible at looking after things. The only person I know who ever had a serial killer goldfish. He also kept the apartment, after I moved out, and I bumped into my old neighbour a week back. She told me Nathan's always at work, and poor bloody Millie's stuck in the place alone for hours.'

She looked out of the window, holding back her anger.

'He doesn't even get her walked during the day,' she whispered. 'She needs to come to me.'

'Will you walk her?' Casey asked, instantly regretting it as Ellie looked quickly back at him.

'I don't need to,' she replied. 'That's why I brought you in.'

Before Casey could say anything else, a grey Mondeo drove past. Seeing this, Ellie started the engine of the car, pulling out of the small car park and onto the road.

'So we're going there now?' Casey was confused at the change of plan, and Ellie smiled.

'In a moment,' she said as they drove along Cringle Street, heading towards the Kirting Street turn off, where a dozen police vehicles were parked outside a small car park, blocking off the road.

Spying a particular car, a white Fiat 500 that was parked against the kerb, around ten feet from the turnoff, Ellie smiled.

'Put your seatbelt on,' she said, her eyes still fixed on the car as she sped up.

'I have already,' Casey looked at her suspiciously. 'Why the car safety lecture?'

Ellie slammed her foot onto the accelerator.

'Because we're about to have an accident,' she explained.

8

INSURANCE DETAILS

THE PROBLEM WITH CRIME SCENES IS THAT THE POLICE FOCUS on the crime occurring at the scene, and don't really expect new ones to appear while they're there.

However, that's what happened as Ellie Reckless spun the car left, jumping the kerb as she hammered into the siding, shunting her car at speed into the back of the white Fiat 500 with an abandon that namesake'd her own surname.

At the moment of the crash, two detectives, a man and a woman, had been standing beside the car, talking to a police Sergeant. The man, tall, slim and in his thirties had quickly pulled the woman, currently wearing a shapeless grey overcoat, to the side as the cars impacted, and she in turn glared at Ellie with the look of a forty-year-old Rottweiler as she realised what had happened, pulling back a strand of her long, blonde hair with impotent fury as she recognised the driver.

Ellie, smiling, emerged from the car, hands raised in a placating gesture.

'My fault!' she exclaimed. 'All my fault! Whose car is it? We need to swap insurance and all that.'

She looked back at the cars, then to the turning.

'Although, I believe the Highway Code states that a car needs to be parked ten metres, or thirty-two feet from the junction,' she quoted with the ease of someone who'd already checked this. 'Mainly to give drivers emerging from, or turning into, the junction a clear view of the road they are joining. It also allows them to see hazards such as pedestrians or cyclists at the junction. Does someone have a long tape measure? Because if it's under that, then I think we might have a little bit of an issue here.'

She stopped, returning her gaze to the group as she continued, her eyes widening in theatrical surprise, suddenly recognising the woman currently being held back by her partner.

'Oh, hello Kate!' Ellie grinned. 'This wasn't *your* car, was it? What a surprising turn of events! Do you have your insurance details handy, or should I call the Unit? I think I remember the number still. Although I think your careless parking will mean you'll end up losing your no claims bonus.'

Around her, Ellie could sense more police officers approaching. They recognised her. They knew who she was.

This could be trickier than she thought.

As a forensic officer made his way past, Detective Sergeant Kate Delgado, she of the long blonde hair, shapeless overcoat and furious expression, finally pulled away from Detective Inspector Mark Whitehouse, storming over to confront Ellie.

'You've got fifteen seconds to get your arse off my crime scene before I forget you were once a copper,' she hissed.

'Come on, Kate,' Ellie kept her hands in the air, continually placating the furious woman. 'I told you it was an accident.'

'Ten seconds.'

'Wait,' Ellie looked at the cars. 'Did you know you parked illegally? Is this why you're trying to pressure me to leave? That's not proper policing, is it?'

She leant in, a smile on her face.

'I wouldn't know, you see. After all, I wasn't *proper police*, was I?'

'Leave it, Kate, she's just trying to get a rise from you,' Whitehouse muttered as he approached. Regaining her composure, and backing off slightly while glancing around, finally noticing the audience, Delgado nodded at this.

'It's working,' she hissed. 'Five seconds.'

'Yeah, technically? It's not *your* scene,' Ellie folded her arms now, refusing to move. 'You're a Detective Sergeant, a DS, and therefore beneath DI Whitehouse over there. And because of that, only he can tell me to piss off, and only then if he's not trumped by a DCI on the scene.'

She looked around.

'*Is there a DCI around?*' she shouted.

After a moment, she grinned, seemly enjoying the moment.

'Nope, looks like Mark is king of this hill, currently,' she finished, her eyes flashing, daring Delgado to do something.

Delgado, wisely, relaxed. She knew she was being played, and she also knew the one thing Ellie Reckless wanted more than anything else was to have Delgado physically attack her.

'Fine, you tell her to piss off,' Delgado muttered as she glared back at Whitehouse. 'She used to be your problem, after all.'

'I used to be his *boss*,' Ellie smiled. 'Not quite the same, but I'll let it pass. You've had a bad day after all, what with your illegal parking and all that.'

'Yes, but you're not his boss anymore,' Delgado spun around, her attention returning to Ellie, and for a moment Ellie braced herself for a punch that never came.

Instead, Delgado stared into the car at Casey, almost like she was looking for something to arrest Ellie on.

'You brought a kid to a crime scene?' she shook her head in disappointment. 'Some things never change. Always the one to push that rule as far as you can, to bend it past breaking. Bringing a kid to a crime scene is just...'

She smiled ruefully, aware of the pun she was about to make, but deciding to do it, anyway.

'Well, it's just *reckless,* Reckless.'

'I could say the same to Mark there about you,' Ellie kept going, as she deliberately kept needling at the woman in front of her. By now, more officers had walked over to see what was going on, and a crowd was really building. 'Does it bother you how you've passed forty and you're still a DS, while I was DI at thirty-five?'

'True, but you'd become *nothing* by thirty-six,' Delgado bit back. 'Out on your arse and damned right to be gone. You're scum, Reckless. *Murdering scum.*'

Ellie had been smiling throughout the entire conversation so far, but at this outburst, her face darkened.

Seeing this, Whitehouse moved in, blocking the two women.

'Don't,' he said to Ellie. 'It's what she wants.'

He looked back at Delgado, now staring at Ellie with an expression of triumph.

'And you can stop looking like that, too,' he snarled.

'You're just as bad as each other. Back off, Detective Sergeant. Go sort the chain of evidence—'

Ellie, ignoring him, pushed past, facing Delgado again.

'You can think what you want of me, Kate,' she said, her tone calmer now. 'Doesn't mean you're right.'

'"*I was framed, guv*". Not that bullshit again!' Delgado laughed at this, standing her ground. 'You're just lucky your solicitor was better than ours. I don't deal with fairytales. And I sure as hell don't do favours for criminals.'

Now it was Delgado's turn to lean closer.

'That's *your* thing,' she snapped.

'So much for *innocent until proven guilty*,' Ellie replied, straightening.

'Dirty cops are always guilty. Always,' Delgado was adamant in her reply, and around them, Ellie could see some officers back away. Although the rumours of DI Reckless' dismissal were well known, they were only that. *Rumours.* And many officers remembered Ellie to be a good detective. It wasn't just black and white, no matter what Delgado, now reddening with impotent rage, said.

Noting this, but still standing her ground, Ellie grinned. Delgado had just given her the argument on a plate, and now she threw out the final killer line to push Delgado past breaking.

'*Dirty cops are always guilty,*' she mocked, pursing her lips as she considered this, allowing the moment to build. 'Well, it takes one to know one.'

Ellie had braced herself as she spoke the line; she knew the punch was coming. She'd *wanted* the punch to come. She wasn't intending to block it; she needed to take it, allow the visibility of the moment. And Delgado hadn't let her down, as finally, past breaking point, she spun around and slapped Ellie hard across the cheek.

The entire crime scene stopped, as the echo of the blow was heard further than Ellie could have expected.

After a moment, allowing the silence to extend into uncomfortableness, watching Delgado's expression whiten as she realised what she'd done, Ellie held her hand up to the stinging redness, fighting the urge to wince, keeping her smile on her face as she spoke.

'A slap? You hit like a girl, Delgado,' she whispered. 'Maybe when you learn how to punch, you might get promoted.'

'I'm done here,' Delgado stormed off, leaving Ellie and DI Whitehouse alone. The other officers, seeing the entertainment had now ended, also walked away.

After giving it another moment, Ellie glanced at Whitehouse to see him staring at her, as if disappointed in what he'd seen.

'What?' she snapped. 'You saw it. She hit me.'

'You hit her first,' Whitehouse pointed at the car.

Ellie shrugged.

'She parked illegally and then ran from the accident,' she replied. 'Sign of guilt, if you ask me. I might want to press charges.'

Sighing, Whitehouse followed Delgado, walking away from Ellie.

'Go home, Ellie,' he finished, without looking back. 'You can't see anything here. You're too well known. They won't allow you near any of it.'

And with that, left alone in the road, Ellie looked down at her car.

She'd angled it to be a head on thump, and the bumper

had taken the brunt of the accident. The back of the Fiat 500 was barely touched. As much as she didn't like Delgado, she only needed to distract and annoy her, not give her an insurance nightmare.

Ellie looked back into the car, and at Casey, staring at her in confusion.

'All going to plan,' she said, giving him a double thumbs up.

Casey, in return, shook his head in disbelief.

'Yeah, I get that,' Ellie smiled, feeling the sudden, shaky come down as the adrenaline left her system. 'I get that a lot.'

THEY'D DRIVEN BACK TO THE BURGER VAN IN SILENCE, AND IT was only once they pulled to a stop that Casey spoke.

'So, do you do that a lot? Crash into people's cars and all that?' he asked.

'Not when I can help it,' Ellie replied with a shrug. 'But needs must, and all that. Want another drink?'

Casey nodded.

'A coke, please,'

'Not a zero?'

'I think after that, I need some sugar,' Casey replied, and for the first time, Ellie realised that there was a tremor in his voice.

'Look,' she said carefully. 'I'm sorry. I should have told you I was going to do that.'

'Damn right you should have,' Casey snapped. 'I've never been in a car accident before. Let alone one done deliberately. I could have whiplash. I could sue.'

Ellie nodded.

'You could,' she said. 'And again, I'm sorry. But if you wanted to sue, I'd suggest the woman who illegally parked her pokey little car near a junction.'

She winked.

'No, really, go for it,' she continued. 'I'd pay to see that.'

Casey shook his head, as the grey Mondeo that had passed them earlier pulled into the small car park in front of them. Seeing this, Ellie straightened, nodding at Casey.

'Come on, we need to have a chat with someone,' she said, opening her door. Reluctantly, Casey followed Ellie out, by now genuinely believing that he'd got himself into a worse mess than he'd been in before.

The Mondeo's door opened, and an Indian man in his sixties, with pince-nez glasses over his eyes, climbed out. He was in the same coveralls as the other forensics officers had been, but now wore his hood down, his black turban visible instead.

'Rajesh,' Ellie smiled, shaking his hand. 'Thanks for this.'

'I thought all coppers hated you?' Casey asked, confused.

Rajesh grinned at this.

'They do,' he replied, turning to Casey. 'But forensics, we see the bigger picture.'

'Casey, meet Rajesh Khanna. Main SOCO, or Scene of Crime officer for Mile End police,' Ellie made the introductions. 'And, therefore, not part of the forensic team involved here.'

Casey considered this.

'He walked past the car,' he said to Ellie, realising. 'When you were kicking off at the woman detective.'

'I needed a distraction,' Rajesh admitted. 'Mainly to get past the tape wardens.'

'Tape wardens?'

'The coppers that stand by the scene of crime tape and tell you to bugger off,' Rajesh continued. 'They'd have wanted to check my ID, and that done, they'd then be calling my boss, DCI Esposito, asking him why he'd sent me. And he didn't send me.'

He nodded at Ellie.

'*She* did.'

'But you're police,' Casey didn't understand. 'She's disgraced. Why are you freelancing for her?'

'First off, forensics aren't technically police, but mainly because I believe her,' Rajesh shrugged. 'I was involved in the team investigating the allegations against her. I saw she was being framed. Didn't sit well. Offered my services whenever.'

'What Raj isn't saying is that his evidence also helped get me kicked out,' Ellie punched Rajesh lightly on the arm. 'So it's more guilt than anything else. Anyway, end of the day, I needed to get him in past the police, so I caused a distraction. Taught to me by a Scottish DCI called Monroe once. Miserable bugger, but good in a scrap. What did you find?'

Casey went to reply, but then realised that Ellie had meant Rajesh.

'Red Peugeot 308, 2010 plate. In it were two bodies, both shot in the head, at close range. But you expected that, I'm guessing,' he began, adjusting his pince-nez glasses as he considered his answer. 'I had a quick squizz around, poked and prodded, all that sort of thing, but there's not much there. Looked pretty in and out, which might be deliberate, if you know what I mean.'

'Anything on the victims?'

Rajesh nodded.

'Looks like neither men reacted to the killer when they

were shot. The way they're still sitting in the car, I'd say there were no defensive movements of any kind.'

Ellie considered this, nodding slowly to herself.

'So they knew them,' she said. 'Didn't expect to die, were relaxed, expectant, maybe. Seeing someone after a job well done, perhaps. Good. Anything else?'

'Not much, as I only had a moment, but from what you told me, and from what I saw and heard from the CSI officers, I think the two dead idiots were bringing the stolen painting to the buyer, and were shot for their sins.'

'You sure?'

'There was a blanket in the back, looked like it'd been over something,' Rajesh nodded. 'The part against the seat had a visible ridge. I think the painting was wrapped in it, and then slid out of the back door. The police aren't looking at that though, as they're hunting jewels.'

As he finished, Rajesh's phone beeped. Opening up the one-piece PPE suit, he pulled the phone out of his inside jacket pocket and read it.

'Day job?' Ellie asked.

The slightest trace of a smile kissed his lips.

'I wish,' he said. 'Nothing's been happening in Mile End since the whole Johnny Lucas thing, so I've been crying out for something to do. That was Ramsey; he's just texted me with a comparison he needs.'

'Ramsey's using you now?' Ellie raised an eyebrow.

'I know,' Rajesh adopted a somber expression. 'Look how far I've fallen.'

He looked at Casey.

'Run,' he said mock-morosely. 'Before you become like me.'

'When will you have anything more?' Ellie asked, bringing Rajesh back to the matter at hand.

'You still use the diner as your office?' he asked.

'Only for the special cases.'

'And this is one of those?'

'Of course,' Ellie shrugged. 'Gotta find my answers, you know.'

Rajesh nodded at this.

'Just stay safe on this one, yeah?' he pleaded. 'This isn't the same as the usuals. There's a body count.'

'There's always a body count,' Ellie felt a shiver down her spine as she spoke. 'It's just that we rarely see them.'

'I'll meet you there at ten tomorrow,' Rajesh was already walking to the car, pulling off his PPE suit. 'I should be able to get some ballistics by then, too.'

'Thanks, Raj,' Ellie said to the back of his head as he clambered into his Mondeo. 'I owe you.'

'Not yet, but it's getting close,' Rajesh replied as he shut the door, the Mondeo revving up and then driving away from the street food van.

'Right then, full-fat coke?' Ellie smiled at Casey. 'Good first day, wouldn't you say?'

Casey said nothing. From bodies to car crashes to free-lancing forensic officers, Casey's day had been *spectacular*.

It took another twenty minutes to return to the offices; Ellie wanted to have a word with Robert before she finished, and Casey had left his skateboard in the boardroom, claiming it was why the room was named as such, so she couldn't drop him off on the way.

As it was, they arrived outside the Finders offices just after four in the afternoon, parking in the small underground car park beside the building.

A black SUV was waiting for them.

'This isn't good,' Ellie muttered as a bald, black-suited driver opened the door and climbed out, his hands clasped together as he watched Ellie and Casey park, and then emerge from the car.

'Ellie,' he said.

'Saleh,' Ellie replied, and Casey noted that she'd spoken the name with a nod, as if giving recognition, and perhaps even a little respect. 'The boy needs his bag and then he's gone. He's nothing to do with this.'

'Mister Simpson would like a private word with you,' Saleh patiently replied, not moving from his spot, except to wave a hand to the rear passenger door.

'Is he in there?' Ellie asked, peering closer, trying to look through the black-tinted windows. 'He could get out, we could speak here.'

'Mister Simpson is not here.'

'Course not,' Ellie mused. 'Vehicle like this probably guzzles petrol. Not good for his *zero-emissions* branding, is it?'

'Mister Simpson does like his Tesla,' Saleh admitted.

'Then get him to get in the damn thing and come here, if he wants to talk to me,' Ellie, bored with this now, snapped back. 'He knows where I am. He's always known.'

'Mister Simpson is waiting,' Saleh replied again, still emotionless, as he opened the door. Ellie went to reply, to once more suggest that Casey be left out of this, but stopped as he ran forwards, examining the SUV as he did so.

'Man, this is sick!' he said as he ran a hand along the side.

'This is the new BMW, right? Can you remote park it? Can I see?'

Before Ellie could stop him, Casey climbed into the back of the SUV.

'Come on!' he insisted. 'I want to see what it can do! I'll wait in the car, I promise!'

Sighing, knowing that this was even more of a risk than a car crash, Ellie nodded to Saleh, following Casey into the car, closing the door behind her and hoping to God that the car park's CCTV had picked this up.

That way, when her body was found, they'd know who did it.

9

MACROBIOTIC SMOOTHIES

Nicky Simpson's flagship health club was based just east of Battersea; once a downtrodden area, it had suffered with the closure of many businesses during the seventies, when industry declined and moved away from the area and the then-local councils sought to address the chronic housing problems they had; problems caused by both the Second World War's relentless bombing during the Blitz and the post-war recession that followed. But recently, with large-scale clearances and the establishment of planned housing, it was now a prime target for urban gentrification.

And, as ever, the gentrification of London brought with it change. Working Men's Clubs became high-class restaurants and bistros. Bakeries became artisan bread shops. And long-term eyesores like Battersea Power Station, a Grade II listed building that simply crumbled into ruin from the moment it was closed in the eighties until around five years ago, when it was turned into hundreds of high-class apartments, surrounded by bars, restaurants, office space, shops and entertainment spaces, and with companies like *Apple* offering to take large areas as base locations, were a moneylender's dream.

If you owned land in Battersea or the surrounding areas, it *guaranteed* you'd make money. If you'd owned it since before the war, you'd already made enough to retire gracefully. And this, according to his Wikipedia page, was what Nicky Simpson had done.

A third-generation South Londoner, he'd taken the three houses his grandparents left him, sold them to developers, and by the age of eighteen was already a property millionaire. He'd taken this money and started an empire; a series of exclusive health clubs around the South London area, all filled with white walls covered with inspiring art, ceiling-high windows and beautiful people working out in the gyms and classes at all times.

There were juice bars that gave macrobiotic smoothies, and the latest bio-hacking devices were in small side rooms; items like infra-red saunas and A.I powered exercise bikes that could give you an hour's worth of workout in ten minutes, saving you more time to work, or enjoy your life.

He even had a club in Battersea Power Station, only a stone's throw from the crime scene Ellie had recently attended.

But this one, the one that Saleh had brought Ellie and Casey to, was closer to The Oval cricket ground, just north of Camberwell; Nicky had grown up around here, spending his childhood years allegedly stealing from market stalls at the Elephant and Castle, an area of London just down the road, and it made sense that his base of operations would be in a more familiar setting.

It was a true rags-to-riches story; the young boy who, finding a way out of the South London slums, built up a health club empire and gave free, daily YouTube videos where he worked out with easy to follow High Intensity Impact Training sessions, aimed primarily at the older population. He was a darling of women over sixty, and he made sure he gained every penny from it. Even his meal prep book hit the *Waterstones Top Ten* last Christmas.

What the book didn't mention, however, or what his interviews, or personal YouTube Vlogs never went into, was that this was a lie, created by PR teams who wanted Nicky Simpson to sound like a man of the masses, because he *didn't* make his money through gumption, eagerness or family fortunes.

He made it by *stamping on the neck of every other criminal organisation in the area.*

His grandfather, Paddy Simpson, had been the first to do this; in the sixties, when the Richardson Brothers, the largest criminal gang in South London were arrested and sentenced around the same time as the Krays were also removed from power, Richardson's accountant Paddy—or at least *one* of their several off-the-book accountants—had seen the void created by this removal, and quickly slid into the spot. He was a known face, and he was well liked, especially as he knew where the money was hidden, and likely helped many of the potential rivals with their own financial issues.

And, as the years went on, he was a quiet and reliable moderator of the smaller street gangs that appeared; the Ghetto Boys, the Peckham Boys, all younger, usually black gangs—because of their association with the *colour* black, rather than ethnicity—who respected his non-confrontational style, agreeing to keep their business in their own areas, and take advice from him when needed, so that when

Paddy retired to Majorca in 2000, his son, *Maxwell* Simpson took over.

Nicky was only a child when this happened, but from that point onward, Nicky Simpson lived and grew up within the world of the gangster, seeing both sides of everything. Max wasn't as clever as his father; he was more a *strike first, think later* kind of man, something that caused bad blood amongst his peers, and more importantly, threw away the years of goodwill that his father had built up. He wanted to be the criminal he thought Paddy didn't have the stones to become, never seeing the larger picture; one that even as a teenager, Nicky could see far too well.

Unlike his father, Nicky Simpson was more like Michael Corleone in the *Godfather III*, or Harold Shand in *The Long Good Friday.* He understood the only way they could survive in the new millennium was to become legitimate, something his father never agreed with. And, when Max was diagnosed with Parkinsons in 2014, it was the then nineteen-year-old Nicky who took over the South London firm, changing its narrative, and packing off his father to *go live with granddad somewhere sunny.*

Simpson covered all bases. He allowed the "gangsta" gangs to work, although for a small percentage. He still kept the drug lines open, and worked with the other parts of his family's business to ensure a smooth day-to-day running of the operation with an iron fist, but although having grown up in the world, he wasn't interested in being a gangster.

He had *bigger* ambitions.

And now, standing in his fifth floor, chrome-and-glass office, amongst pieces of art that were each worth more than she made in a year, Ellie Reckless couldn't help but feel intimidated.

Ellie had spent years observing Simpson; as a police officer, she'd crossed swords several times, and since falling from grace had regularly ensured she wasn't ever in a situation like this. She knew every dark secret about Nicky Simpson, except for the ones that would help her.

And now it looked like there wasn't time to find those, either.

Simpson sat behind the glass-topped desk in the corner of his office, tapping on a top-of-the-range MacBook Pro, a collection of post-it notes pasted around it, as Ellie and Casey stood nervously waiting. To his side, beside the full-length window that gave views of the Vauxhall MI5 building and the Thames, was a waist-high IKEA Kallax bookshelf, as white as the walls in the office, and filled with books, awards and YouTube follower plaques. He had over a million now, and this was shown by the gold 'play button' plaque, shown in pride of place on the top of the waist-high shelves, next to a glass-fronted mini fridge.

His mid-length dirty blond hair tousled, likely deliberately so, and wearing expensive jogging bottoms, *Nike* trainers and a Simpson's Health Clubs branded grey hoodie, he looked like he'd recently finished a session, standing out like an overly healthy beacon in the minimal room.

Ellie would have even found him attractive, hot, even—if she didn't already know what an insufferable, psychotic *wanker* he was.

'Excuse the appearance, I've been running an online session,' he explained, as if he felt he looked unprepared for the moment. Ellie, smiling inwardly at the confirmation of her theory, knew this was all for her benefit; he looked good, and he knew it, and this fake self-depreciation was purely done to relax her, something she'd never do within his reach.

The frog relaxed while the scorpion was on his back, and look at how that story ended.

Casey, however, was super excited, staring around the room in wonder, and bouncing around like a child who'd eaten too much sugar.

'Nicky Simpson!' he gushed. 'I'm a massive fan. Can I get a photo?'

Simpson, glancing at Ellie with a mixture of surprise and amusement, rose from his chair, waving Casey over.

'Sure,' he said as he posed for a selfie with Casey. After a couple, he patted Casey on the shoulder, a subtle *we're done* motion that the teenager simply didn't take notice of.

'Want a juice?' he asked. 'I have my own range of E&C macrobiotic smoothies in the mini fridge.'

He pointed at the fridge beside the Kallax shelf as Ellie rolled her eyes.

Of course he had his own range of macrobiotic smoothies.

'Why did you call them *E&C*?' Casey asked as he walked over, examining the labels.

'Elephant and Castle,' Simpson smiled. 'It's where I came from.'

'Silly name for a place,' Casey said absently as he knelt down, pulling out his phone to take a shot of the bottles, probably to show people on Instagram or something. Ellie didn't know what teenagers did, to be honest. And, to be *more* honest, she didn't rightly care.

'It's actually the name of the coaching inn that originally stood there,' Simpson explained. 'The *Elephant and Castle*. Before that it was owned by a cutler; a knife maker.'

'Cool,' Casey was going through the flavours, and Ellie wasn't sure, but he looked like he was picking by colour rather than flavour.

'*The Worshipful Company of Cutlers* have an elephant with a castle resting on its back as a crest,' Simpson continued his lecture, but his enthusiasm for it was waning as his audience ignored him, pulling out bottles and reading the ingredients excitedly.

Ellie put him out of his misery.

'As boring as the history lesson is, can we get to why we're here?' she muttered, shuffling her feet and interrupting the love-fest. 'I mean, come on, you didn't bring us all the way up here for shakes, stories and selfies. And honestly, you could have picked us up when we were south of the river, rather than waiting for us to get back to the office. All you've done is waste my time and your time.'

'I hear you're working for Danny Flynn,' Simpson said simply, ignoring Ellie's comments. 'He owes me money. I would like it back.'

'And I'm looking for a painting he was selling to pay that debt off,' Ellie replied carefully. 'I suppose you know nothing about the theft?'

Simpson's smile didn't even flicker. *This was a question he'd expected.*

'You mean did I do it? No. And I don't appreciate the insinuation,' he replied icily, walking around the desk, passing Casey, who was now playing on his phone, taking artistic photos of the bottles, now arranged on the desk. 'You might be owed a boatload of favours, Reckless, but I own every one of the people who owes you.'

'That's not what I was saying,' Ellie hated to say it, but she knew she needed to lower the aggression level here, if she wanted to get out of the room alive. Simpson, in return, eyed Ellie up and down, as if evaluating her. 'I'm trying to help you.'

'You want to help me? Then tell Flynn he's got until the day after tomorrow, shall we say six pm, to get me my money,' he said. 'I'd make it tomorrow, but I'm getting an award from Princess Anne for my help with the elderly in the afternoon. Promised I wouldn't miss it.'

'And if he can't?'

Simpson's smile didn't flicker as he brushed a crumb off his shoulder.

'He has things I want.'

'Boston.'

Simpson's eyes widened, surprised at this revelation.

'You're good,' he admitted. 'Yeah, if he can't pay, I'll take his daddy's empire from him.'

'And if he doesn't give you that?'

Simpson's eyes narrowed.

'Then I start to get *messy*,' he warned.

Casey looked up from the fridge at this, rising slowly as Ellie slow clapped.

'There's the Nicky Simpson I've heard of,' she said quietly, but with purpose. 'Not this "gung ho health food guru", but the little shit who wants to be bigger than his daddy—'

She stopped, doubling over with a *whuff* noise as Saleh, caring little that she was a woman, slammed his fist into her gut, sending her to her knees.

'Hey!' Casey cried out, now nervous for the first time since they'd arrived.

Simpson slowly turned to face the teenager.

'What? You think anyone's gonna believe her over me? Believe *you* over me?' he hissed. 'Come on, you're not that stupid. You know how it'll go.'

He took on a mocking tone as he continued.

'She slipped, officer. Fell down the stairs. Probably drunk.

She drinks a lot, I hear. I know, terrible...'

He smiled, continuing.

'What's that, officer? You're *glad* she's dead? She was a real bitch, and you're giving me an award?'

'Do what you want to me, Nicky, but leave the boy out of it,' Ellie rose back up.

'Who is he, anyway?' Simpson asked. 'What is it, bring your bastard child to work day?'

'He's my nephew,' Ellie lied, and at this, Nicky Simpson looked at Saleh, his face emotionless.

'Get rid of them,' he ordered. 'Break some limbs, dump them in some foundations, or something, I don't care—'

He stopped as the lights suddenly flashed red, and a piercing alarm fed through the intercom system. Clutching his head, smothering his ears as the shrieking sound filled the room, he glanced around.

'*What the hell?*' he asked loudly, as if someone in the room could explain the sudden chaos.

'It's the perimeter alarm!' Saleh shouted back, frantically tapping on his phone, likely an app that controlled the building security. 'Someone's hacked in!'

'You said it was unbreakable from outside!' Simpson stared up at the ceiling. '*Shut up!*'

The sound stopped as Casey stepped forward, the screen of his phone facing outward. Ellie could see lines of data streaming down it.

'Shouldn't have let me look at your desk, Nicky,' he said, no longer the fawning fanboy. 'Nice router password you got written on one of those post-it notes. Guess a meat-head like you wouldn't be able to remember complex letters and numbers.'

'Why, you little sh—' Simpson started, but was stopped

by Casey's wagging finger.

'Nuh-uh,' he continued to smile as he spoke. 'Let us go, and I cancel it.'

'Cancel what?' Simpson turned towards Saleh, who glanced back up from his phone, a sickly expression now on his face.

'There's a call made to the police when the alarm goes off,' he breathed. 'It's a failsafe.'

'That's right, the call to the police that was made the moment I tripped the alarm,' Casey nodded. 'They'll be here in minutes, a big name like you in danger.'

Casey pointed to a small white CCTV camera in the room's corner. Ellie squinted up at it; she hadn't even noticed it when she entered.

'They can probably see you right now,' Casey continued. 'Checking in, making sure you're all right, and all that.'

Nicky Simpson, now all smiles, waved to the camera.

'Fine, turn it off,' he said through gritted, smiling teeth. 'And get out.'

'Oh, I already did,' Casey walked over to Ellie now. 'And don't feel too bad for having the password in clear sight. I'd already worked it out from your BMW's onboard entertainment system.'

'How?' Saleh asked. 'You were in the back!'

'Wi-Fi, mate,' Casey grinned. 'Can we get out of here, Ellie? I'm having the whole *never meet your hero when they're actually a prick* thing.'

Nodding, Ellie started backing out of the office, Casey by her side.

'I'm not the enemy here,' she said to Simpson, almost apologetically. 'I'm trying to get you what you want.'

Nicky Simpson started laughing at this, and this confused

Ellie immensely.

'He'll pay!' she insisted. 'You just tell me where he needs to put the money once we find the painting and I'll ensure he does.'

'Oh, Danny can pay me in any of my accounts,' Simpson exclaimed as he gathered his breath once more. 'Not that he can, with all that "Vermeer" bollocks. We both know it isn't worth the canvas it's painted on.'

Ellie stopped, staring at him now.

'Are you saying it's a fake?' she asked.

In return, Nicky Simpson walked back to his desk, staring out of the window now.

'I'm saying I don't want excuses,' he replied calmly. 'Goodnight, Ellie. Brat.'

Saleh went to walk with them, but Ellie held up a hand.

'I know the way out,' she snapped.

Saleh stopped, holding his hands up, the slightest hint of a smirk on his face. Ellie wanted to slap it off, but she knew that to do anything would risk the escape Casey had made for them.

Constantly checking if they were being followed, Ellie led Casey down the emergency staircase. It was probably silly, but she didn't want to risk the elevator right now.

'He hates you,' Casey said as he followed her down, two steps at a time. 'You could see it in his eyes. What did you do?'

'He's just worried about what I have on him,' Ellie tried to fob the question off and move on, but Casey wasn't biting.

'And that is?' he continued.

'Nothing, *yet*,' Ellie admitted as they pushed their way out of the ground floor fire door, walking out into the lobby of the health club. 'Shit. We don't even have a car to take us back.'

'Why did you lie to him?'

"What?' Ellie was confused at this.

'You said I was your nephew. Why didn't you want him to know my name?' Casey continued. 'Was it because of my dad?'

'I didn't think he'd earned the right to know, nothing more.'

'Is this what all the favours are for?' Casey was still trying to get answers.

Now out in front of the club, standing in a pedestrianised area interspersed with small raised plant pots and wooden benches, Ellie turned to face him.

I suppose he did save my life, she thought to herself.

'Eventually I'll get the right one, and the whole damn thing will expose him,' she said.

'Well, then you definitely need me on the team,' Casey grinned. 'Because honestly? Seeing your work? All I've seen is you getting punched a lot.'

'Yeah, I call that "weekdays" around here,' Ellie waved down a cab. 'Come on, I'll drop you home.'

'Actually, could you take me back to the office?' Casey smiled. 'You made me leave my dirty skateboard there remember? I can get home quickly with that. And from what I've heard, I don't think mum would want to meet you.'

Ellie faltered as she held a hand out for a cab.

Did Casey know about the affair, or was this a comment about Bryan dying while connected to her?

But Casey didn't continue, and knowing that five storeys above her a psychotic South London gangster was working out ways to end her, Ellie Reckless hailed down a cab, opened the door for Casey, clambered in behind him and left.

10

HEAVY BAGS

It was almost six by the time Ellie and Casey returned to Finders; during the cab ride back, Ellie had sworn Casey to secrecy about the forced diversion to Nicky Simpson, telling him that if asked, they'd *been* taken there, but he'd waited in the café below while she went to see the man himself.

Casey had been annoyed about this, and rightly pointed out that he'd been the one that saved her, and should therefore get full credit, but Ellie countered by explaining that Robert would likely ban her from ever speaking to Casey again if it came out she'd put him at risk, and this would also include allowing him to work with her on either the Flynn case, or the more personal Noyce one.

She didn't have to swear him to secrecy about the favours; he'd already worked out that for some reason she was keeping this from Tinker and Ramsey. The latter he understood, but he didn't know why Tinker was being kept in the dark. Ellie hadn't explained her reasonings in detail, but gave the general impression to him that Tinker wasn't being told because the moment she was, the favours would be irrelevant, as she'd simply go to Vauxhall and blow Nicky Simpson up while he was still in his club.

Interestingly, Casey hadn't been averse to the idea, and, after retrieving his skateboard, had left for home.

Ellie had wanted to go back home too, but she was too wired after the near-death experience of South London, so instead she stopped off at her apartment, situated slightly west of Shoreditch, changed into some gym wear and then went for a run.

Running was something she'd done for a few months now; she wasn't great at it, and was more of a "I've run" than "I'm enjoying the run" kind of person, but there was something calming about the rhythmic flow of step after step, the running trainers hitting the pavement in a constant beat, allowing her to let her mind drift, that she found pleasant and, more importantly, gave her a chance to think through the events of the day in a more relaxed and impartial state.

She hadn't expected Casey to be part of the case when she arrived at the office; she hadn't even expected to be on the case. The Somerville work she'd pulled everyone away from was expected to take a couple more days, and was primarily a job where they had to wait for Marcus, the oldest son and heir of the Somerville fortune to fence the antique Ming vase he'd stolen from his parents.

The Somervilles didn't want the police involved, but with the vase being mid-six figures in cost, they also didn't want it disappearing into someone's collection while their special boy fuelled a drug habit they should have been getting him help for.

A job was a job, though, and Ellie had left it to the others to deal with. She'd been more worried about Nathan and Millie.

She tripped on a raised pavement slab, stumbling, throwing off the beat for a couple of seconds as she moved eastwards onto the Bethnal Green Road, passing a selection of Korean BBQ and Sushi restaurants, smiling as these turned into locksmiths, tailors and a rather curious café and "cat emporium" that she'd wanted to visit every time she passed, but always forgot a few paces later, as the high street now turned into housing estates and apartment buildings, before the *next* stage of high street shops appeared, the landscape of London shifting and changing constantly within hundred-yard stretches.

Usually by now, Ellie would turn off, head south through the wooded paths of Weaver's Fields, looping back to the apartment; but today she needed more, and so she kept on straight, a new destination in mind.

It was another mile, and about ten minutes running before she turned south down Morpeth Street, heading towards Bullard's Place and the Globe Town Boxing Club. She'd last been here a few weeks earlier; there was a case she'd been connected with, one that brought her back into contact with her old mentor, DCI Alex Monroe and his team of City Police, and it'd started in the boxing club with a brutal murder. But to enter it now, you wouldn't know anything had ever happened there; the boxing ring's canvas was updated within days, and now it was once more a simple community boxing club, where for a fee, anyone could come in, use the weights or heavy bags, spar with a trainer or have a fight.

Ellie Reckless needed a fight.

Walking into the boxing club, taking a moment to gather her breath, she wiped at her forehead as she glanced around. It was early evening, and only a couple of others were in the building; many of the wannabe boxers trained during the day, and at this time of evening, the place was closing up.

A track-suited trainer, talking to a young boy, no older than sixteen, looked up, recognising her. Ellie had been a Mile End copper before transferring to Vauxhall, and was a known face, even more so after helping the owner with a problem or two recently.

'Reckless,' he said by way of greeting. 'You need gloves for the bags?'

'More a sparring session, Pete,' Ellie nodded at the empty ring. 'Anyone around, and do I have time for one before you close?'

Pete the trainer looked at a clock on the wall, that said seven-thirty.

'You've about half an hour before kick out,' he replied. 'But I'm training until then.'

Ellie nodded; she'd been aware the chances of a walk-in were low, and was resigning herself to a session on the heavy bags, still enough to get some of her pent-up anger out, when another voice spoke.

'I'll do it.'

The voice was owned by a man in his sixties, his grey hair blowdried back, giving it volume and contrasting with his blue shirt and black suit trousers. He was slim, smiling and incredibly dangerous; this was Johnny Lucas, the boss of the East End, owner of the boxing club and, until recently, one of the two 'Twins' that ran the area.

Now he was alone. And Ellie wondered how he was faring; it was one reason she'd passed by.

'You sure?' pulling on a pair of gloves, Ellie clambered into the ring. 'I don't want you to scuff your shoes or crease your shirt.'

'I don't mind for you,' Johnny smiled still, but it wasn't quite reaching his eyes. 'You could owe me. Or we could call it quits—'

Ellie stopped, realising what this was. Johnny Lucas had owed her two favours for services rendered, one of which had been used the previous evening on top of a building. Ellie knew the favours were problematic; people didn't want to be in hock to her, but were scared of what would happen if they went against her. After all, a favour given to remove a rival was one given a lot more freely.

But she needed them to be.

'No deal,' she said cheerfully. 'I burned one of yours yesterday, I need to keep the other one.'

'Yes, that burned favour,' Johnny was in the ring now, and even though he was putting on the pads and talking genially, Ellie could see there was a frustration, an irritation within him. 'What was that about, exactly? I don't usually fire people when I'm roused from bed.'

'Walker was about to throw me off a roof,' Ellie explained.

'Why?'

'Well, in a way, it was my suggestion,' Ellie shook her head as she realised the absurdity of what she was saying. 'He wanted to shoot me, I was explaining why throwing me was less likely to come back to him.'

'You know, Reckless, when they made you, they really broke the mould,' Johnny slapped the two pads together. 'Why were you on the roof in the first place?'

'He stole Big Slim's godawful lambo,' Ellie replied, cricking her neck and rotating her shoulders. At this, Johnny laughed.

'And Big Slim wanted it back,' he nodded in realisation.

'So what, you had me fire him so his bodyguard didn't kill you?'

'Pretty much.'

'And there was no other way to get out?'

'Oh, I had two or three other ways,' Ellie admitted. 'But this one seemed the least violent.'

Johnny was going to reply to this, but stopped as he stared at the door.

'Looks like you have a visitor,' he said, pulling the pads off. 'And I'm not in the mood for the police.'

Glancing back to the door, Ellie saw DI Mark Whitehouse standing uncomfortably at the doorway. As he caught her eye, however, he nodded quickly and walked over to the ring.

'We close at eight,' Johnny said as he climbed out of the ring. 'If you ever want to use that other favour I owe, I'm always happy to fire people.'

With Johnny Lucas wisely disappearing, Whitehouse now clambered into the ring.

'We need to talk,' he hissed, blinking as Ellie tossed him the first pad.

'And you scared away my training partner,' she replied, 'so strap those on your hands, and we'll talk while I hit you.'

Nodding, Whitehouse did so with the ease of someone who'd done this many times before.

'Different gloves?' he asked as he noted the ones on Ellie's hands.

'Club's ones,' she explained. 'Mine are back at home. This was a spur of the moment arrival.'

She stopped, watching her onetime partner.

'Yet you found me here,' she continued, narrowing her eyes. 'How long have you been following me, Mark?'

Whitehouse shrugged.

'Caught you on the Roman Road,' he said. 'Was returning from Victoria Park.'

'Outside your remit, unless Vauxhall police have really expanded recently,' Ellie motioned for the pads to be raised, taking a stance. 'And we're a way from Victoria.'

'One of the bodies we found was from around here—one, one, two—as you probably already know,' Whitehouse took the strikes with ease on the pads.

'What bodies?' Ellie asked innocently.

'The ones in Nine Elms you caused a scene at, to make sure Rajesh Khanna got a look,' Whitehouse shook his wrists, holding the pads up again, motioning for Ellie to start again. 'And don't tell me he wasn't there for you; it was out of his area, and he's incredibly recognisable with his turban.'

'Are you saying all Indian officers look the same?' Ellie moved in, striking quickly, left-left-right, before stabbing back.

'I'm saying there's only a couple of forensics guys who wear turbans and have pince-nez glasses,' Whitehouse moved around the ring, holding the pads up as Ellie followed, striking. 'And you need to lay off Delgado a little, yeah?'

'She parked illegally.'

'It was a crime scene—come on, harder—and you bloody know it.'

Ellie relented.

'She deserved it,' she said. 'And you're lucky I don't press charges for her physical assault on me.'

'And you deserved that,' Whitehouse smiled. 'Why did you needle her so, anyway?'

Ellie stopped, gathering her breath, boxing gloves on hips.

'There were maybe seven people total in the force who knew Bryan was my confidential informant,' she whispered, watching Pete the trainer out of the corner of her eye, in case he was listening.

'I know that—' Whitehouse started, but Ellie held a hand up.

'Of those, maybe four knew I was sleeping with him,' she continued, 'and maybe two knew we were in love.'

'Oh, come on, Ellie,' Whitehouse shook his head. 'You know how these things go! You can't be certain that your numbers match up.'

'True, but only two people knew I had Bryan's blood on my sleeve the day he was killed, and knew I'd hit him,' Ellie said, thinking back to the night.

I'm sorry, Ellie. I can't do this. I'll lose my son.

'I was angry,' she muttered. 'We'd been drinking. I slapped him out of frustration, not rage. I didn't know he was a bleeder.'

Whitehouse raised an eyebrow at this.

'You punched him square in the nose,' he replied. 'You told me this.'

'No, it was a slap,' Ellie shook her head, frowning. 'I mean, I'm sure it was. Anyway, that's not important. What is important is I mentioned it to you and Kate in the office that day. And by the end of the day Bryan's dead and I'm being taken in by my own team, the blood on the cuff damning me, as it was an exact match.'

'Ellie, Kate didn't set you up,' Whitehouse shook his head, lowering his pads now. 'Forensics spotted the blood when they took your clothes for DNA. We didn't aim them.'

'Kate told them and I know it,' Ellie snapped.

At this, Whitehouse turned, tossing off the pads and walking to the ropes.

'Believe what you want, Ellie,' he said. 'I get you were set up, and yeah, there were a few who knew Bryan was in with us, and who he was spying on. But Kate—'

'Did well by my loss,' Ellie pulled her own gloves off now, spitting the words out bitterly. 'You both did. My dead man's shoes pushed you both up a notch.'

'That's not how the rank structure works, and you bloody well know it,' Whitehouse snapped. 'I came to offer advice, but I can see you're in no mood to take it. Stay away from the case, Ellie. We'll solve it. Your little stunt today made Kate super determined to beat you to it, if only to steal one of your favours.'

'I knew that already,' Ellie muttered. 'You could have sent a text.'

'That wasn't the advice,' Whitehouse replied. 'I saw the boy, Ellie. I recognised him. It's Bryan's kid, isn't it? What the merry hell are you playing at?'

At this, all the anger in Ellie hissed out, deflating her slightly.

'Not my idea,' she said, eventually. 'And it's not the easiest of things, either.'

'Does he know?'

'That I got his dad killed?'

'No, that you—'

'No,' Ellie vehemently shook her head. 'I'd have seen something by now. He knows I was connected to Bryan, nothing more.'

'Then my advice is to back away,' DI Mark Whitehouse climbed out of the ring, jumping down onto the surrounding mats. 'You've already caused the Noyce family enough heartache.'

'Mark,' Ellie walked to the ropes, looking down at him. 'Do you believe I'm innocent?'

Whitehouse smiled gently.

'I do,' he said, tapping his forehead to her. 'But that and a quid still doesn't buy you a coffee.'

'It's a start,' Ellie smiled as Whitehouse walked off. And, before she forgot, she pulled her phone out of the little elasticated strap on her arm, and texted Tinker.

Because unknowingly or not, Mark Whitehouse had given her a lead into the theft; one body had connections in the area, and if that was the case, their friends might know who ordered the theft.

A bell, ringing, brought her back to the present. Johnny Lucas had rapped on a small boxing round bell with a hammer.

'It's eight o'clock,' he said as Ellie turned to him. 'We're closing. Go home, Reckless. We're not a charity.'

He smiled.

'Unless you'd like me to stay open a little longer? I could do it for you—'

'As a favour?' Ellie laughed. 'Nice try, but no chance.'

As she started towards the main door, Johnny Lucas caught up with her.

'I hear you're helping Danny Flynn,' he said. 'I hope it doesn't affect me in any way.'

'Not so far,' Ellie admitted. 'Currently, the only people in firing lines are in Chipping Norton or south of the Thames.'

Johnny grinned.

'That's exactly what I like to hear,' he said as he went to close the door behind her. 'I liked his dad, but Danny's always been a bloody liability. Even when he got played by Simpson.'

'Played? How so?' Ellie stopped.

'That land deal he got into?' Johnny replied, unlocking the door from the side as he spoke. 'We all saw it was dodgy as hell. It's why we were surprised when Nicky got involved. The same developers built his own clubs; they'd have told him to stay away.'

'You're saying he deliberately took a bath?'

Johnny shrugged.

'I'm just saying that if I put almost three million into something that I knew would fail, I'd want more than just double my money,' he replied. 'It's a loss leader. Lose something to win something bigger, and if you're starting big, that's something pretty massive.'

He nudged Ellie out of the doorway now.

'Stay safe, Ellie. You might be a pain in the arse, but you're useful.'

Now out in the chilly evening air, Ellie let out a sigh. She hadn't meant to run this far, and now it was a two-mile journey back.

Performing a couple of warm-up exercises to loosen her hamstrings, she turned to the west, and, with a resigned stride, started running.

11

BREAKFAST BRIEFINGS

IT WAS AROUND TEN THE FOLLOWING MORNING WHEN THE TEAM rejoined, once again in the back booth of Caesar's Diner.

Casey arrived first, and now sat in the booth's corner, eyes glued to the tablet in his hands; when he pulled it out, Ellie had joked about whether he was watching YouTube or playing games, and his withering look of contempt at this actually made her laugh.

Tinker arrived next, hands in the pockets of her army coat, ordering a black coffee and washing down painkillers with it, complaining of a killer hangover, caused by repeated drinking games with ex-squaddie buddies the previous night, and finally Ramsey appeared, as well-dressed as ever, this time with a cravat rather than a tie, but still in the 'old school' colours of the previous day.

As he sat, Ramsey looked at Tinker.

'Can I assume, dear woman, you've told her already?'

'Told me what?' Ellie asked.

'So the forger's dead,' Tinker replied, glaring back at

Ramsey. 'And no, I didn't tell her. I assumed you would tell her.'

'Well, you're her bestie. I assumed—'

'For God's sake, someone *just tell me!*'

Tinker and Ramsey stopped talking at Ellie's outburst, and then Tinker nodded, giving Ramsey the floor. Clearing his throat, he began.

'Sebastian LaFleur died a few months back,' he said, a slight quaver of emotion in his voice, one that Ellie couldn't work out whether it was real or there for theatrical value. 'Crashed his car on a motorway.'

'Accidental?'

'Well, I don't believe it was deliberate,' Ramsey sniffed. 'I spoke to a friend of mine last night in the AA—'

'Alcoholics Anonymous?' Tinker interjected. Ramsey pierced her with a withering gaze, as good as the one Casey had given Ellie moments easier.

'God no!' he exclaimed. 'How would they be able to help? I meant the *Automobile Association.* You know, the yellow vans that come out to you when your car breaks down. If you're a member, that is. You're probably not, with that *Meccano* toy you drive.'

He shook his head as he muttered.

'Alcoholics Anonymous. Give me strength, oh Lord, to bear with these buffoons.'

'So what did they say?' Ellie asked, realising that Ramsey was going off track.

'Well, she works in the call centre, so could look back into the logs,' Ramsey replied. 'All accidents cause delays on roads, and the AA have this live tracking system that takes all the news and passes it out. I knew the rough time, four months ago, and I knew it was around the Headington roundabout, north of Oxford on the M40. It was quite easy to find.'

'And?'

Ramsey shrugged.

'Accident,' he replied. 'Steering went, probably skidded on some diesel on the road, and poor Sebastian went into the middle barrier at about ninety miles an hour. The car flipped over a couple of times, landed on its roof facing the wrong way. Seb, I am afraid, was dead almost instantaneously.'

'What kind of car was it?' Casey looked up.

'I don't know, a *car* car,' Ramsey snapped. 'Four wheels, went vroom...'

'New or old?'

Ramsey looked at Ellie.

'Do I have to answer the child's questions?' he asked.

'The *child's* asking, because if it's an old car—not as old as you, but over ten years, say—then it could be an accident,' Casey replied calmly. 'If it's a new car, though, it's all computers. Your friend in the AA could have told you that; half their relay drivers can't fix the new cars as they need a laptop to connect to the ECG, the brain of the car.'

'Which means?' Ellie was seeing the answer, mainly because she remembered Casey's comments on the BMW the previous evening, but wanted it spelt out.

'If it's new, there's a chance it could be hacked,' Casey continued. 'The steering craps out at a set speed, or the gears seize up.'

'The modern-day equivalent of cutting the brakes,' Tinker nodded. 'But surely cars have failsafes?'

'Ramsey, see if you can find out more,' Ellie said. 'Good catch, both of you.'

Ramsey, annoyed he was sharing credit glared momentarily at Casey, before waving to Sandra for a menu.

'Okay, so while Ramsey looks into that, what else did you find?' Ellie turned her attention to Tinker now.

'There was something odd about his assistant,' Tinker replied, leaning back in the booth. 'I don't think she stole the painting, but she's involved somehow. She told us that before LaFleur died, he paid eighteen month's rent in one go. In cash.'

'Which meant Natalie kept the studio after the accident,' Ramsey added.

'But I checked with the landlord,' Tinker added, 'and he reckons that although the money for the rent in advance came through around the time of Sebastian LaFleur's death, Natalie paid it.'

'Could have been given to her by LaFleur to do, as he was busy?' Ellie suggested.

'Landlord claimed it was a bank transfer, not a cash payment,' Tinker replied. 'Changes the story somewhat.'

'Eighteen month's rent in one go, at roughly two grand a month? That's big money for an assistant,' Ramsey said as, through the door to Caesar's, Rajesh Khanna entered. He wore a dark suit and tie, a pale pink shirt and his police-appropriate black turban.

'I haven't got long,' he said, placing a cardboard file on the table, motioning for Ramsey to budge up a little. 'I told DCI Esposito I had a dentist appointment.'

'Thanks for coming,' Ellie replied, nodding at the file. 'What do you want to go through first?'

'The painting, as Ramsey promised me twenty quid to do it,' Rajesh smiled widely at Ramsey, his hand out for the note. Muttering to himself, Ramsey passed over the money.

'Don't worry,' Tinker, seeing his expression, said. 'I'm sure you'll be able to pad your expenses out enough to cover it.'

Money now squirrelled away in his pocket, Rajesh revealed the first of his A4 printouts; it was a blown up image of the scrap of painting.

'Do you want to share with class what this is?' Ellie asked. 'As neither of you kept me in the loop?'

'You weren't here,' Tinker replied, tapping the image. 'Natalie, the assistant claimed she'd never seen LaFleur painting a Vermeer, but there'd been a recent fire in the incinerator, and that was picked up by Ramsey.'

'I also bought his last painting,' Ramsey added, 'so the good man here could do his forensics stuff.'

Ellie nodded, expecting Ramsey to subtly point out that this too was money he expected back, but Rajesh started talking before Ramsey could speak.

'This is a blown up image of the burned scrap of Vermeer's *The Concert,* that Mister Allen here found,' Rajesh explained. 'But before you think the original was destroyed, fear not, because this burned painting's definitely a fake.'

Now he showed another image; that of a half-finished canvas.

'I compared it to the other one that Mister Allen recovered, and the paints, the compounds, they all match,' he continued. 'Definitely painted in the same location, with the same product. And the brush strokes betray the same hand.'

'So, Seb *was* painting Vermeers,' Ramsey looked triumphant, as if he'd solved the whole thing already.

'But why would Natalie lie to us about it?' Tinker shook her head. 'She must have known it'd get back.'

'Not if she thought she'd burned it all.'

'Unless she wasn't the one who burned it.'

Ellie rubbed at her temples, trying to work through the data.

'Can you date them?' she asked.

'Already have, I guessed you'd ask that,' Rajesh grinned 'I can't be sure, like to the day or anything like that, but I believe, to my best estimation, that both canvases were painted around six, maybe seven months ago.'

'Right before LaFleur's accident,' Tinker mused. 'That can't be a coincidence.'

'True, but it's still not the original painting we needed to find,' Ellie took a mug of tea from Sandra, now arriving with a round of hot drinks. 'Danny Flynn had the original.'

She stopped, remembering Nicky Simpson's words the previous night.

'Although, I'd like to get a second opinion on that authenticity,' she said. 'I have reason to believe it might be a forgery.'

'Oh yes?' Ramsey raised an eyebrow theatrically. 'And who, pray tell, told you that?'

'Nicky Simpson,' Casey replied, eyes still glued to his tablet.

'*What?*' Ramsey rose from the booth's seat. 'How in God's name is he involved?'

'He's sniffing about, looking for the money,' Ellie waved Ramsey back into his seat, playing down the meeting. 'But he mentioned the painting wasn't worth the canvas it was painted on.'

'Well, we won't know for sure until we find it,' Rajesh was already pulling out more A4 sheets. Making sure Ramsey couldn't continue on about Nicky Simpson, Ellie tapped on the first of these, two scans of driving licence photos, both of young, Caucasian men.

'The thieves?'

'Victor Cornell and Keith Molloy,' Rajesh read from the page. 'Early twenties, clean records. Nobodies. Killed close range by a nine-millimetre gun with silencer attached, both headshots, in a car park beside the Thames Sewer works. No CCTV because, well, who wants to steal from a sewer?'

'Do we know what gun?' Tinker asked.

'I've got a friend who's part of the forensics team working the case. She says the rifling on the casing seems to be consistant with a Glock.'

'Nice gun. British Army issue,' Tinker leant back. 'Thousands out there for the right price.'

'Mark Whitehouse said one of them came from East London,' Ellie said, looking at the scans. 'But the addresses are both in Essex.'

'You're talking to Mark?' Rajesh was surprised for a moment. 'Oh, wait, was this after Delgado punched you?'

'She slapped me,' Ellie saw Tinker and Ramsey lean forward at this salacious news. 'And yes. Of course it was then. When else could it be?'

'Well, he's right,' Rajesh tapped the image of Molloy. 'Keith here came from Mile End, but was part of the Loughton mob. Hung around the green near The Standard pub. But it was more hooliganism, nothing to get nicked for, As I said—'

'Clean records,' Ellie nodded, finishing the sentence. 'Strange that they both progressed from squeaky clean to full-on burglary. If you find out anything at Mile End nick, let us know, yeah?'

'What do we know about the bodies?' Ramsey asked.

'Time of death was between two and four am yesterday,' Rajesh went back to lecturing mode. 'Found when the first shift came in at six. And, no defensive wounds.'

'So they knew their killer.'

'Natalie?' Ramsey suggested, but Tinker shook her head.

'The cast she wore means she would have had to shoot with her offhand,' she replied, miming the action with her own left hand. 'And unless she's lying, there's no way she could have carried the painting off alone once she did it.'

'Could she be lying?'

'I checked her social media,' Tink shook her head. 'Not much on there but a few weeks ago she posted images of her on the slopes, and there's one with her holding up the plaster cast. I think it's legit.'

'I've got something, not sure what,' Casey looked up from his tablet now.

'I thought he was playing Candy Crush,' Ramsey stated in surprise. At this, Casey smiled.

''Fraid not, old man,' he said, placing the tablet down onto the booth's table. 'I'm surfing some deep level forums on the dark web.'

'What sort of forums?' Ellie asked, looking down at the screen.

'Hard to find art ones,' Casey replied, using his finger to scroll down a forum's conversations. 'There're tons of threads on this forum about the painting.'

'Our painting?'

Casey nodded.

'Yeah. I'm posing as an art dealer in Brazil. Spoofed my IP and slid through the back entrance.'

Ignoring the fact she didn't understand half of these words, Ellie looked from Casey back to the screen, trying to read the threads. 'What are they saying?'

Casey swiped with his finger, and the screen swapped to a second one, this time with two images on it; two men, both in their middle years. One was a slim man, bald with a full beard, as if making up for his lack of hair, the other a middle-aged black man with short greying hair and a goatee.

'It's more who's saying,' Casey corrected. 'There's been two big players hunting it for years now, Hugo Speer and Christian Wyatt.'

Ramsey leant in now, tapping the image of the black man.

'Him. Wyatt,' he said, looking up at Tinker. 'There was a photo of him and Seb at the studio.'

'You sure?' Ellie looked at Tinker for confirmation. Tinker, in return, nodded.

'I wasn't as close as Ramsey was, but it's definitely the same guy.'

'I've gone back through the archive file since the conversation started almost eight years back,' Casey returned to the forum page now, scrolling through dozens of posts. 'It looks like they've been dancing round each other since the start, and then six months ago Wyatt says he doesn't need to search anymore, and drops off the radar.'

'He stopped searching?'

Casey nodded.

'Completely,' he replied, switching to another thread in the same browser. 'Then, a couple of weeks back, Hugo gobs off that *he's* found it.'

'Danny Flynn. Trying to sell it to pay his debt,' Ramsey suggested. 'Do these guys have the money?'

Casey tapped on the screen.

'Speer's a tech billionaire,' he said, scanning the text. 'Based in Madrid, owns about a dozen companies, even has his own altcoin.'

'And that is...' Ramsey asked, hoping for Casey to finish the sentence.

'Crypto,' Casey obliged. 'Altcoin is what any crypto that's not Bitcoin is called. A mix of Alternative and Coin—'

'I get why it's called that,' Ramsey interrupted. 'So this is like having your face on a coin? Like the Queen?'

'Not really,' Casey grinned. 'There's tens of thousands of altcoins out there. But, if his coin rises in value a lot, then people make money. Like stocks and shares.'

'And has it?'

'Not really.'

'What about the other one?' Ellie asked.

'Christian Wyatt, oil magnate,' Tinker now spoke, looking down at her phone. 'I might not be as quick as the prodigy here, but I do know Wikipedia. Inherited billions from daddy, years ago. One of the richest black people in America, and a staunch Republican. Has a thing for collecting items nobody else can get.'

'So, missing paintings.'

'And statues, vehicles, anything he can retrieve.'

'So five million for this is nothing heavy for them,' Ellie clicked her mouth as she considered this. 'People that rich sometimes make mistakes. Check into him, find out what he knows. And check with Hugo too, see if he's met Danny any time recently.'

'Look, I need to go,' Rajesh rose now. 'But I have two more things for you.'

Reaching into his inside jacket pocket, he pulled out two folded printouts.

'What, no file for these?' Ramsey mocked.

'I caught them as I was leaving,' Rajesh replied as he unfolded them, passing the sheets across the table. 'I know the murder scene was Vauxhall's catch, and covered by Whitehouse and Delgado, but Chipping Norton police were the ones on scene the night of the burglary, and they've put out a request for other Units to keep an eye out for stolen items.'

'And this is the list?' Ellie took the sheets, scanning them. Apart from the painting, which was omitted for obvious reasons, the only things claimed as stolen were a couple of grand's worth of jewellery.

'Just this?'

'Yup. Only Chantelle Flynn's items were ransacked,' Rajesh replied. 'The police believe they were disturbed before they could take more. Luckily, the only jewellery that held any significance was being worn that night.'

'Lucky,' Tinker said. 'What's the other?'

'Transcript of the call to the police the night of the burglary,' Rajesh tapped the paper. 'Only mentions the red car, and people stealing. No mention of any black car, as per the current statement they have. Apparently that was phoned in the following morning.'

'Do the police have any leads?' Ellie stopped Rajesh as he went to leave.

He smiled.

'Only lead is Flynn himself,' he said. 'There's talk of just arresting him for the hell of it.'

And with that, Rajesh Khanna made his excuses and left.

'What I can't get is why Delgado and Whitehouse were even there in the first place,' Tinker mused. 'They're Vauxhall Met, but this was Nine Elms, further west. That's near the US Embassy, and Wandsworth Met would have been the lead Command Unit on this. At worst, it'd be Lambeth. They would have had to call in favours to get this.'

Ellie looked up from the sheet at this. She'd been so focused on Delgado, she hadn't even considered it.

'I'll check into that,' she said.

'Or Nicky Simpson told them to do it,' Casey was still scrolling through pages as he looked up. 'Come on, I can't be the only one thinking that, right?'

'Simpson wants the money, Simpson gets the painting stolen for him,' Tinker clicked her tongue against the top of her mouth as she thought. 'Or he did it deliberately to force Danny to give something else up. Maybe his business.'

'Chantelle wouldn't allow that,' Ellie replied, thinking back to the meeting she'd had with Danny and Chantelle the previous day. 'She very much seemed to be the one with the trousers on in that relationship.'

'What happens to Chantelle if Danny goes to prison?' Ramsey spoke now. 'Surely it has to be discussed?'

'Well, she won't leave him,' Tinker shook her head. 'Robert mentioned it yesterday. They have a prenup. She leaves Danny, she loses everything.'

Ellie rapped on the table as she worked through the options.

'Ramsey, take Casey, go back to Natalie and confirm Wyatt's in that photo,' she said. 'Tink, you're with me; I think we need to find out why Cornell and Molloy were killed, and more importantly, who hired them—and possibly ended them.'

Casey looked up.

'Can the old man and me go somewhere else first?' he asked. 'I just found the hotel Wyatt's staying in. Maybe we could go look, maybe see if he's the same guy?'

'Wait, he's in London? Right now?' Ellie frowned. 'Am I the only one finding that suspicious?'

'Makes sense, if he's beating Speer to the punch,' Tinker nodded. 'Which hotel?'

Casey looked back at the screen.

'*Sea Containers Hotel* on the South Bank,' Casey replied. 'Apparently, he checks out tomorrow at noon.'

'And you know this how?' Ramsey asked, more curious now than irritated.

'His credit card was used last night in the restaurant, so I checked his diary,' Casey tapped the screen. 'He's a billionaire, and his security is great, but his PA uses Google Calendar, and that's a little easier to get access to. I checked through her social media pages, picked a few obvious names—'

'What do you mean?' Tinker frowned at this.

'You know how sites ask for security words, like mother's maiden name, or name of your dog?' Casey replied, looking up. 'Don't use the name you stick on Facebook, on pictures of the aforementioned dog. Really easy to spoof his PA's details through that. I don't have access, but I'm able to see the source data.'

Ramsey frowned.

'We know that hotel,' he muttered. 'I've been sitting in the lobby for three days, as Marcus Somerville has a room there. We even thought he might have the Ming vase in his room.'

'Ramsey—'

'I'm not saying anything,' Ramsey gave his best smile. 'Just that if we're staking out the hotel for Wyatt, we might find Somerville too. And you said we'd work both cases.'

Ellie sighed.

'Fine,' she muttered. 'Go check that and then go to the studio. We'll speak to the friends of Cornell and Molloy and then go visit Danny and Chantelle.'

'Do we have to?' Tinker groaned.

'It's a courtesy, show them where we are,' Ellie smiled. 'And at the same time, we can have a look around the place.'

'What about the police issue?'

'Leave that to me,' Ellie waved for the bill, rising from her seat, sighing as she continued. 'This was supposed to be a simple theft, not a bloody murder enquiry.'

'They're never simple,' Ramsey smiled mournfully. 'Take it from a thief.'

12

GYM BROS

CASEY HAD BEEN UNIMPRESSED WITH THE BATTERED BROWN Rover 25 that Ramsey drove; it was so old it still had a tape player, not even a CD slot, and there was no bluetooth to connect his own music, so Casey was forced to endure Frank Sinatra and Dean Martin as they drove south across Blackfriars Bridge, Ramsey singing badly along with the crooners.

'The wheels won't come off this, right?' he muttered as they hit a bump in the road, the whole car shuddering. 'This thing's older than I am.'

'I have pens older than you,' Ramsey replied. 'What are you, ten?'

Casey didn't reply, settling back into the seat. Ramsey, glancing to the side, watched him for a moment.

'I met your father once,' he said eventually. 'Seemed like a decent chap. Sorry he died.'

'Yeah, me too,' Casey replied. 'So, how come you work with Reckless?'

'She saved my life, so I'm in her debt,' Ramsey indicated right, turning down Stamford Street.

'How?' Casey asked. 'I mean, did she stop someone from killing you? Did she use a favour?'

'Nothing that exciting,' Ramsey actually chuckled at the thought. 'She arrested me.'

'That doesn't sound like saving a life,' Casey muttered.

'You'd be surprised,' Ramsey turned right again, heading north up Rennie Street as he replied. 'I was a mess. I'd found several... vices... that were leading me down a dark path.'

'Drugs?'

'I'll tell you when you hit your teens.'

'I'm fifteen.'

'So you say.' Ramsey turned left into a one-way street. About a hundred metres down, it was an underpass of sorts; a building built across the street, shadowing it from light. To the right, under the cover, was the entrance to *Sea Containers London*, a stylish, if brutalist designed hotel. Pulling up in a bay marked Disabled, Ramsey turned off the engine.

'You can't park here!' Casey exclaimed.

Rummaging around in the glove compartment, Ramsey pulled out one of the 'blue badge' disabled stickers, plonking it on the dashboard.

'And yet magically, I can,' he said.

'You're disabled,' Casey was incredulous.

'I am,' Ramsey argued back. 'Hip issues.'

'And are you also a *Doctor On Call?*' Casey pulled one of the other signs out of the glove compartment. Snatching it back, placing it into the glove compartment and slamming it shut, Ramsey glared at his teenage companion.

'You're here as a favour,' he said.

'I'm here because I found out more than you did,' Casey smiled. 'So, go on, how did arresting you save your life?'

'They put me away for five years, but I was out within

eighteen months,' Ramsey sighed, unbuckling his seatbelt. 'It helped me get clean. You can get a lot of things smuggled into prison, but if you don't want these things, it's a good way to get over them.'

'And so what, you found God or something?'

'Something,' Ramsey replied. 'My mother's old, quite ill. I realised I had to care for her. And I had put nothing away, as most was spent on the horses, my main vice, I'm afraid. I came out of prison looking for my next score, and instead I found myself working for Ellie Reckless.'

'You don't seem to be happy about it when you're with her,' Casey watched Ramsey.

'I said she saved my life,' Ramsey opened the driver's door. 'Doesn't mean I have to be happy about the situation I'm in. Do you know how many people now ignore me the moment they heard I was working with the police?'

'But Ellie isn't—'

'She's *always* police,' Ramsey halted, half out of the car. 'Don't let this dishonourable discharge, or resignation, or whatever she's calling it this week impede the truth. She only cares about one thing; getting back on the force.'

'She cares about the truth,' Casey's face darkened now. 'Finding out who killed my dad.'

'Yes, Bryan,' Ramsey nodded. 'There's more to that, too.'

'Where are you going?' Casey frantically unbuckled his own belt, climbing out of the Rover. 'We're staking out, remember?'

'Dear boy, this isn't like the movies,' Ramsey explained. 'It's warmer, cosier, and there's coffee in the lobby. And we'll see who's coming in and out quite easily from a sofa. It's all about priorities.'

'And what *is* the priority, Ramsey?' Casey asked, grabbing

his bag, locking the car door and following the thief. 'Christian Wyatt, or Marcus Somerville? I know the second one pays you.'

'It does indeed,' Ramsey grinned. 'You're picking up fast.'

———

GETTING TO LOUGHTON HAD BEEN EASIER THAN ELLIE HAD expected, and they arrived within an hour of leaving London, parking up in a small pay and display bay on Smarts Lane, next to the green Rajesh had mentioned. However, as they approached it, they saw no Loughton mob to speak of, unless you counted two seventy-year-old ladies who were sitting on the bench discussing the previous night's *Coronation Street.*

However, The Standard pub was next to it, so Ellie and Tinker walked up the steps to the door—

And stopped.

Although the pub was still in all external aspects a Charrington's Public House, this was a front for what looked to be a posh restaurant; not where their targets would likely drink at.

'So what now?' Tinker asked. 'There's a dozen restaurants around here, maybe three or four pubs—'

'We go south,' Ellie pointed to the other side of the green; across the road was a fish and chip shop. 'I reckon if they're hanging out in the green, they'd be in there a lot. Enough for us to find them.'

Now walking back from the restaurant, Ellie and Tinker crossed the road and entered the fish and chip shop.

It wasn't as fancy as Caesar's Palace; a corner building, two sides of it were floor-to-ceiling glass, the counter directly in front. And along the right were small plastic tables where people could sit and eat. Currently, there were two men, only lads, and a teenage girl, around seventeen, maybe eighteen years of age, dressed in hoodies and jogging bottoms, sitting in the corner whispering nervously to each other, a large chips and a can of Fanta on the table in front of them.

Tinker nudged Ellie as she clocked them.

'I reckon that's our target,' she said.

The woman behind the counter looked up, smiling.

'What can I get you, love?' she asked.

'Two teas and a large chips, open,' Ellie smiled back, passing over a ten-pound note. 'Keep the change if you answer one thing. The guys in the back. Loughton mob?'

The woman didn't reply, just nodded as she poured an amount of freshly cooked chips onto a styrofoam plate.

'Don't want no trouble,' she said. 'Salt and vinegar?'

'Please, and don't worry,' Ellie replied, taking the chips as Tinker picked up two styrofoam cups of tea. 'We have mutual contacts.'

Now with their makeshift snack, Ellie and Tinker made their way over to the three in the corner, looking up at them suspiciously as Ellie placed her tea and chips on the table, sitting down opposite them.

'Did we say you could join us?' the girl muttered.

'I didn't ask, so no,' Elie smiled. 'Judging by your expressions, I'd reckon you're Loughton mob, right?'

'What d'ya mean, expressions?' The lad on the left glanced uncertainly at his friends. 'What's wrong with my expression?'

'It's the look of someone who learned recently his friends are dead,' Tinker replied. 'Maybe last night, possibly yesterday. Police haven't given the names out, but you know Cornell and Molloy are gone.'

At the names, the two lads turned to face Ellie and Tinker, and Ellie held up a hand before they could respond.

'We're not police,' she said quickly. 'We know they were hired to do a job, and then they wound up dead. We're hunting the person who did it to them.'

'And then what, have them arrested?' the girl sneered.

Tinker leant in, smiling darkly.

'As my friend said, we're not police,' she replied. 'Why the hell would you think we'd want them *arrested?*'

'We know nothing,' the middle lad replied, leaning back on his chair. He was shorter and slightly pudgier than his other male friend, who looked like he worked out, but he still had the look of someone who knew how to fight.

'Let me tell you what we know,' Ellie ate a chip. 'And you might find we know more than you, so it's in your interest to listen. Some days ago, someone came to you with a job offer. Victor—or Vic, whatever you called him—and Keith took it on. Late night job, two nights ago.'

'Off they trot, excited at the money they'll make, and then, after that, they don't reply to texts, calls, anything,' Tinker took over now, also taking a chip as she spoke, using it like a pointer as she carried on. 'And then, at some point, you learn their bodies are the two found in Battersea. Both shot in the head, close range by a nine-millimetre gun.'

'They didn't deserve it,' the girl hissed. 'Vic's got a girl-friend. She's pregnant. He needed the money.'

'Then let us fix this,' Ellie replied. 'Who made the offer?'

The three looked at each other nervously. Ellie sipped at the tea, grimaced, and put it aside, taking another chip instead.

'It was a guy,' the first lad eventually replied. 'Knew the

Loughton crowd of old, said the mob were the only trust-worthy people he could use, and made the offer.'

'Break into a house in Chipping Norton, steal a painting.'

'We didn't know the job,' the middle lad insisted, sitting up now. 'The guy didn't give specifics. Just that he'd make sure the place wasn't alarmed, and that he needed us to get him a particular item. We said no—couple of us are on probation and it's not worth it—but as Mercedes said, Vic needed the money. And Keith would always back him up.'

'Had you seen the guy before?' Tinker asked. 'He ever been around here?'

'Nah, no matter what he said about knowing us, he wasn't Essex,' the girl, now identified as Mercedes, replied. 'He was a gym bro though.'

'How so?'

'He was shredded,' Mercedes smiled, and her eyes glittered. 'He was well fit. Like Crossfit-fit, not the dicks who just lift weights.'

Ellie glanced at Tinker at the description.

'Blond? Brunette?'

'Maybe blond? Had it under a beanie.'

'And did he give a name?'

The three looked at each other, each trying to remember.

'Not really, because we turned him down,' Mercedes continued. 'But Keith mentioned it. Ricky or Mickey, something like that?'

'Nicky?' Ellie asked softly, feeling her stomach flip-flop.

'Yeah, maybe,' Mercedes nodded. 'Something *icky*.'

Ellie leant back at this. Nicky Simpson fitted the look and the name. And, being king of the south, nobody would know him to chat to this far north. Even the beanie could have been to reduce any fans of his page seeing his dirty blond hair.

'Thanks,' she said, pulling out a card, passing it across. 'Think of anything else? Drop me a text.'

'When you find them, what you gonna do?' the middle lad asked, taking it.

'Justice,' Tinker replied, and from her tone and expression, the three across the table paled as they nodded.

'Good,' Mercedes said as Ellie rose. 'Hey, can I finish your chips?'

THE SEA CONTAINERS LONDON HOTEL WAS A DESIGNER'S dream; as Ramsey and Casey walked in, they saw what looked to be a great copper hull crashed into reception, up the stairs and to the left, the plating arching out as it reached the ceiling in a riot of copper and brass, a ship marooned on the South Bank, and with a building built around it.

'That's based on the 19th-century clipper the Cutty Sark,' Ramsey said as he pulled Casey to the side of a giant blue statue, that of two links in an enormous chain. 'I need you to keep an eye out for Wyatt.'

'While you look for Somerville?' Casey smiled.

'Someone has to keep the lights on,' Ramsey replied, watching around. 'Do you know which room he's in?

'Wyatt's in a suite, but he's not going to stay there, according to his calendar,' Casey replied. 'Somerville's on the third floor, room three-oh-four, but his phone's pinging off a tower in the City, so I'd say he's unlikely to be in right now.'

Ramsey nodded, heading for the elevators.

'I won't be long,' he said, disappearing around the bulk of the copper hulled 'ship'.

Sighing to himself, Casey looked around, finding a small

couch by the north wall. Sitting down and opening up his tablet, he looked up at the concierge, a middle-aged man, currently frowning at him.

'Hey,' Casey grinned. 'You got Wi-Fi here?'

———

IT WAS EASY ENOUGH FOR RAMSEY TO GET ONTO THE THIRD floor; as he approached the elevators, he accidentally bumped a businessman in his twenties, palming a passkey from his jacket pocket. It was a credit card-shaped piece of plastic that would be waved against the door lock to gain access, and was useless for Somerville's door, but suitable to place against the same lock in the elevator, allowing Ramsey to pick the correct floor.

Now on the third floor, Ramsey saw that the room he needed was almost beside the elevators; this was also good for him, especially when making an escape; however, he still couldn't open the door yet.

A couple of doors down on the right was a cart; the hotel's housekeeping was making their rounds. Card in hand, Ramsey walked up to the cart, peering through the open door into the hotel room currently being cleaned.

'Excuse me,' he said, just loud enough to be heard from within. 'Hello?'

A woman, short, stocky and in her forties, leant back from the bed she was currently making.

'Can I help you?' she asked, her accent European, although Ramsey didn't want to hazard a guess.

'Yes, which way are you moving?' Ramsey pointed back to Somerville's room. 'That way or the other?'

'That way,' the woman pointed the opposite direction,

and Ramsey knew this meant she'd already done Somerville's room.

'Ah, right,' Ramsey nodded. 'I'm two doors down, and I need an extra towel. Can I grab one from here?'

'I already did that,' the woman, now irritated, started towards him. Smiling, Ramsey grabbed a towel from the pile, making sure as he did so to take the master key from the side of the cart.

'Thanks,' he said, hurrying back to the hotel room door, opening it with the master key and opening the door.

As expected, the room was empty.

Clicking the bar on the door to make sure it didn't shut on him, Ramsey now returned into the corridor; the woman, annoyed at her intrusion, had returned to the bedroom. Running back, Ramsey slipped the card onto the cart, before knocking on the door again.

'Sorry,' he said, gaining the woman's attention again. 'Didn't see the one you left. Leaving this here.'

Placing the towel on the top, Ramsey walked to the now open hotel room, chuckling as he heard the faint expletives muttered by the chambermaid. Now in the room, he moved the latch to its original position and closed the door.

He hadn't wanted the woman to get into trouble; that was why he'd returned the key, but it gave him a slight issue, as he still didn't have a key that worked for the room. And, looking at the side table, he knew he needed one.

There was an antique Ming vase on it; a vase he'd spent three days hunting.

Walking to the phone, he dialled reception.

'Yes, Mister Somerville?' the voice at the end of the line spoke.

'Hello, yes, sorry, I have a bit of an issue,' Ramsey replied. 'When did I say I was checking out?'

'Not until—' the sound of a keyboard was heard down the line, '—Saturday.'

'Good,' Ramsey smiled. This gave him a day or two to work with. 'I need a little help, then. My card isn't working on the door. Can you send up a replacement?'

'Absolutely,' the voice replied. Ramsey was about to disconnect when an idea came to him.

'Actually, do you have a safe?' he added. 'For larger, more expensive things?'

CASEY WAS ABOUT TO CALL RAMSEY WHEN HE SAW CHRISTIAN Wyatt walk to the reception desk, a hard case cabin bag in his hand, arranging a car with the concierge. Rising, putting his tablet back into his messenger bag, Casey looked around nervously. He wasn't sure how to stop Wyatt from—

He paused as a security guard carrying a Ming vase exited one elevator, with Ramsey following. A momentary flash of fear ran down Casey's spine; *had the old fool got himself caught?*

But then the security guard placed the vase on reception, all smiles, as the receptionist nodded at whatever Ramsey was saying, taking the vase away from reception and into a back room.

Shaking the guard's hand, Ramsey walked over to Casey.

'What the hell?' was all the teenager could say.

'It's an expensive vase,' Ramsey replied casually, already watching Wyatt as he finished speaking to the hotel concierge. 'It shouldn't be left in a room. I've asked for it to be placed in a more secure vault, in their back room, and with a number code of my choosing.'

'Because they think you're Marcus Somerville.'

'I opened the door to my room as such,' Ramsey sniffed, already focusing on the next task, now walking towards them. 'Mister Wyatt?'

Christian Wyatt, cabin bag behind him, paused, looking over at the well-dressed old man and the teenage boy beside him.

'Can I help you?' he asked, his accent deep, and possibly Texan.

'We might be able to help each other,' Ramsey smiled. 'I knew Sebastian LaFleur.'

'Don't know the name.'

'Sure,' Ramsey nodded. 'Then maybe I can tempt you with a Vermeer I currently have in my possession? I hear you've been looking for it?'

At this, Christian Wyatt turned fully to face Ramsey.

'*The Concert?*'

'Indeed.'

'Then this Sebastian you speak of must have sold you a fake,' Christian laughed. 'Because it's missing, and likely in a personal collector's vault.'

He thought for a moment.

'Although Hugo Speer might want it, as he ain't getting the original. Good day.'

And, taking his cabin bag once more, Christian Wyatt walked away from the now frowning Ramsey Allen.

'"Likely in a personal collector's vault",' he muttered. 'That's a nice way of saying "I have it and it's secure", wouldn't you say?'

'If he already has it, then maybe he was the one who stole it?' Casey asked.

'Either that, or he's too stupid, or arrogant, to realise he has one of Seb's forgeries,' Ramsey was pulling his phone out, tapping on it, as they started down the steps, returning into the street and the battered Rover. 'And remember, he stopped looking for it six months ago. It's more likely a forgery.'

'What do you reckon's in the bag?' Casey watched Wyatt lift it up, placing it in the back of the cab. 'Doesn't look too heavy.'

'Probably picking up something stupidly rare and expensive later,' Ramsey shrugged. 'Come on, let's go see the assistant again. After I let the City Police know of a stolen vase being held in a vault.'

13

PROFESSIONAL JOB

ELLIE HAD BYPASSED LONDON ALTOGETHER AFTER LEAVING Loughton, taking the Waltham Abbey junction of the M25 around to the M40, and then heading west. It was a long journey, close to two hours with the increased traffic around the M1 junction, but even though the Chipping Norton police had managed the best they could do with the search before Danny had arrived, there was still a chance they may have missed something.

And besides, Danny had been nervous when they met the previous day, and Ellie didn't trust his wife one bit.

As they drove down the M40 motorway through the hills of Aston Rowant, Tinker, sitting in the passenger seat and flicking through her phone, looked over at Ellie.

'So,' she said, 'when do we talk about Nicky Simpson?'

'What about him?' Ellie kept her eyes on the road.

'The fact he kidnapped you last night?'

Ellie chuckled.

'I think you've been reading too many spy stories,' she replied.

'Okay then, explain to me how you knew he reckoned the painting was worthless?' Tinker turned to face Ellie now, shifting in the seat. 'I wrote it down. You said "he's sniffing around, looking for the money". How did you find this out?'

'I have my ways?' Ellie suggested innocently.

'Sure,' Tinker smiled. 'Maybe Saleh told you when he forced you into his car.'

At this, Ellie instinctively gripped the wheel, and the car swerved slightly. It was only half a second, but Tinker saw it.

'Yeah, I watched the CCTV,' she said.

'And why were you watching the CCTV?' Ellie was getting angry now, but more at herself. When Saleh had told her to get into the BMW, she'd hoped someone would see it; now, safe and out the other side, this was a complication she didn't need.

'Do you remember why I joined the team?' Tinker asked, settling back into the seat, watching the road as it passed by. 'You came to me. Said you needed someone with my particular set of skills to keep you alive.'

'I remember.'

'Well, I was using those particular skills last night,' Tinker folded her arms. 'I saw you pull up, then Saleh appeared, I watched the kid run to the car and get in, with you following. Almost an hour and a half later, you reappear by your car, alone.'

'I—'

'*I haven't finished yet,*' Tinker hissed, stopping her. 'I checked the other cameras. Casey came back to pick up a skateboard, worked on one of the computers briefly, probably checking emails, and left. You both arrived by cab, split with him at the front of the building. Now, taking the hour and a half you were missing, it's easy to work out a half hour drive somewhere and back, and about twenty minutes there. A half hour's drive from Finders is Nicky Simpson's empire. And here you are, knowing something he says.'

'I was fine,' Ellie lied.

'I should have been there with you.'

'Yeah, and then what? You'd have killed Saleh? I know you've got history. Nicky wasn't going to do anything.'

Tinker watched Ellie carefully.

'Stop the car at the next service station,' she said.

'If you needed the loo—'

'I don't need the toilet,' Tinker stared out of the window sullenly. 'I'm leaving. I can't work for you if you're going to keep me from things, or lie to me. It's bad enough you're lying to the kid. Drop me off, and I'll hitch a ride back to London.'

'Tink—'

'I'm serious, Ellie,' Tinker looked back, and for the first time, Ellie saw utter fear in her expression. 'I'm not stupid. I've realised the whole point of your favours is to find how Nicky, if it even was him, framed you. And now you're visiting him? Tell me you weren't in danger at any point. Just tell me that. I'll know if you're lying. If you're not? I'll give it a rest.'

Ellie stared at the road ahead, sighing.

'He wanted me dead,' she muttered. 'I got gobby at him, got a smack for it. I deserved it, and it was more for show. But Nicky hit his limit. Told Saleh to get rid of me, he didn't care how.'

'So what happened?'

'The kid,' Ellie chuckled. 'Hacked Nicky's entire system, set the alarms off. Nicky knew the police would check in, so he had to smile and let us go. He'll not make that mistake again.'

'And this is why you need me.'

'It wasn't my decision to go there,' Ellie glanced over at Tinker. 'If I were ever deliberately going there, I would have you with me. Always.'

Tinker sat in silence for a long moment.

'How much does the kid know?' she asked.

'Not enough,' Ellie admitted. 'By design.'

'You should come clean with him,' Tinker shuffled in her seat. 'He's clever. He'll work it out, find something on his bloody dark web browser. Better he hears it first.'

'Let's talk about it later,' Ellie indicated left, taking the Ford Focus off the A34 Oxford turnoff.

'Sure,' Tinker replied with the tone of a woman who never expected to hear about it again.

IT WAS ANOTHER HALF AN HOUR BEFORE THE FORD FOCUS reached Danny Flynn's house; by now it was mid-afternoon, the two women having paused to fill the car up and buy a service station sandwich for a late lunch, their earlier chips being left with teenagers in Loughton.

The house was a wide, seven-bedroomed one, built out of red brick with a white and black mock-Tudor frontage over the first-floor windows. To the left as they approached was a double garage, and next to that was a red-brick extension "coach house", as fake as the main building in design, and likely where the driver stayed. The entire estate was surrounded by a three-foot-high brick wall, with another four feet of wrought-iron railings above. There was a double wrought-iron gate at the front, and beside it an intercom.

Ellie pulled up beside it, pressing the only button on it.

'Hello?' a man's voice, the accent Mediterranean, spoke through the grille.

'Ellie Reckless, here to see Danny.'

There was a pause.

'You are not on a list,' the voice replied cautiously.

'No,' Ellie replied. 'But he'll want to see us.'

'You are not on a list,' the male voice repeated.

'Fine,' Ellie sighed. 'Tell Danny we drove two hours to talk to him, but if he's screening calls, he can come to us for updates on who stole his painting.'

There was a long moment of awkward silence, possibly long enough for the security guard to speak to Danny, and then the wrought-iron gates slowly opened inwards.

'Yeah, this is going to be jolly,' Tinker muttered as Ellie started into the driveway.

As they pulled to a stop, the front door of the house opened and Danny Flynn emerged; his hair hadn't been combed, he wore the same clothes he'd worn the previous day, and Ellie wondered whether he'd even been to bed.

'Have you found it?' he asked nervously, looking past Ellie, almost expecting a painting to be withdrawn from the back seat.

'Not yet,' Ellie locked the car door, turning to face him. 'But we've found the people who did it.'

'And?' Danny's head was swivelling from Ellie to Tinker and then back. 'Do they know who has it?'

'They're dead,' Tinker replied, mimicking a gun with her finger. 'Two to the head.'

Danny paled at this.

'It wasn't me,' he whispered.

'We assumed that, but eventually the police will learn of their connection, and they'll place you at the top of the list, so

I'd make sure your story is straight,' Ellie suggested. 'We already know forensics are linking the gravel in their tyres to this drive, so expect them at some point. So, we're here to have a look around, work out how they got in and out.'

Danny nodded as, through the doorway, Chantelle appeared.

'What are they doing here?' she muttered to Danny.

'What you're paying us to do,' Ellie replied, still finding herself not warming to the woman.

At this, Chantelle sniffed dismissively.

'I ain't paying you to do anything,' she leant against the doorframe, glaring at Ellie, her Essex accent appearing through her clipped tone. 'He's the bloody fool doing that.'

'Not now, Chantelle,' Danny muttered. 'Just give them what they need, yeah?'

'We'll need to have a chat in a moment, but we'd like a look around first,' Ellie forced a smile, returning to Danny. 'The police report is minimal—'

'That's because I didn't talk to them,' Danny interrupted. 'Just gave them a list of things the bastards nicked.'

'The jewels,' Tinker added.

Danny nodded.

'I had a ton of good shit they could have taken, but they didn't bother,' he replied, almost annoyed at this. 'Guess some people have no taste.'

'So, how did they get in?' Ellie asked, looking around. 'I don't recall you mentioning any signs of a break in.'

'They opened the gate from the inside,' Danny nodded at the double wrought-iron gates. 'Someone in a black car climbed over the wall, got in and then opened them up so they could bring the car in, fill up and leave. Police told us this morning they'd had a witness.'

'And why do you think they took nothing else?' Tinker added.

'Because they were sent by Simpson to get one thing,' Danny snapped.

'You sure it was Simpson?'

'Who else could it be?' Danny spat to the side of the drive. 'He wanted me owing him. Taking the picture doubled his income. He can sell the painting and still demand what I owe, and in the process, get into America.'

'How?'

'He's hinted, shall we say, that if I can't pay, he'll take a percentage of my business,' Danny muttered. 'And once he's in, he'll see how it works. He'll have access to my contacts. I'll be choke-slammed out of my firm and with that gone, I'll have nothing.'

He waved around the mansion.

'Even this is owned by my company,' he shook his head in resignation. 'I did it as a tax break, but once Nicky takes me out, I'll lose it to him. And of course he'll want to live here; all his influencer mates go to Soho Farmhouse down the road. He gets all this if I can't pay by tomorrow night.'

'Why did you borrow money from him in the first place?' Tinker was examining the side of the garage door as she spoke. 'Surely you had to know he was going to screw you over?'

'Not many options for millions of pounds business loans in my field of business,' Danny shrugged. 'Nicky's dad knew mine, and I thought he was solid when he offered me a life jacket a couple of years ago.'

Ellie nodded.

'Yeah, we've heard that before,' she stepped back, looking up at the house. 'How did they get into the house itself?'

'Side door, down there,' Danny showed the end of the garage block. 'Picked the lock, got in through the garage, entered the kitchen, took out the burglar alarm.'

'They knew the code?'

Danny snorted.

'Those things aren't worth shit,' he shook his head. 'We only have one for the house insurance. They can fritz it a dozen different ways.'

'And how did they do it for you?'

Danny stopped at this, frowning.

'Actually, I don't know,' he replied. 'And the little pricks didn't help.'

'Help?'

'Yeah, do one for me, you know?'

Tinker, seeing Ellie's confusion, leant in.

'This was a professional job,' she said. 'In and out, targeted item. There's no sign of a break in, the alarms were turned off with no explanation, the car brought in later, purely to pick up stock. The problem though—'

'No sign of forced entry,' Ellie finally got it. 'The insurance won't pay out.'

'Oh, they will, but they'll be knobs about it,' Danny whined. 'When my lads did something like this, they'd take out a window pane, or smack a doorframe with a hammer to break the seal, anything like that, something after the event that, should the victim need to avail himself of the insurance firm recompense, he'd be able to point at, and say "that's where they did it." Nothing this time. Pricks.'

Ellie clicked her tongue at this.

'So if the neighbour hadn't called the police, you'd have arrived home with no idea anything had gone.'

'Pretty much,' Danny glared across the street. 'The

coppers said it was an anonymous tip, but I reckon it was the curtain twitcher there. She's always watching me.'

'Well, if it was, you should be grateful,' Ellie patted Danny on the shoulder. 'She made sure the police could create a crime number for you—or, at least, for Chantelle's jewels. Do you have a number yet?'

'Crime number, or amount stolen?' Danny clicked his tongue against the top of his mouth. 'Probably about ten grand's worth. I've already given a list to the insurance company. I'm guessing the police found nothing when they found—they found the bodies?'

Ellie watched Danny. For a gangster, he was rather squeamish about violence, it seemed. *Definitely not someone who could shoot two people in the head at close range.*

Looking across the road, Ellie saw movement through one of the upstairs windows.

'Stay here,' she said to Danny, nodding at Tinker to follow her. 'I want to have a chat with the curtain twitcher.'

'Why?'

'Because you've got nothing more you can tell me about the theft, and they might have witnessed something you missed,' Ellie walked to the gate now. 'Open it up for us, will you? And put the kettle on. I'm gasping.'

As the gates opened enough for the two women to emerge into the street, Tinker looked at Ellie.

'No way Cornell and Molloy did this,' she breathed. 'They were muscle, nothing more. Neither of them had the record for break-ins of this quality.'

'Clean records could just mean they hadn't been caught,' Ellie countered.

'Come on!' Tinker stopped, incredulous. 'You saw their

friends! Smash and grab, sure! But locks? Beating alarm systems?'

Ellie smiled.

'I agree,' she said, rummaging in her jacket. 'I just like seeing you get angry.'

Pulling out a black leather wallet, she walked through the gate, along the driveway and up to the door of the house facing Danny Flynn. Unlike his small fortress, many of the houses on this side didn't have brick and iron walls and remote controlled gates, but that didn't detract from the worth of the houses.

'You're doing *that?*' Tinker looked around, nervous. 'You're asking for trouble.'

'If you want, stay here,' Ellie used the door knocker to rap on the door. Tinker, looking around, shifting her stance as she did so, sighed.

'Just don't make me one of your bloody fictional detectives,' she muttered. 'Last time, you said I was DS Morse, and I spent half an hour being talked to about sodding John Thaw—'

She stopped as the door opened, and an old lady, slim, well dressed and in her seventies observed them. She was wearing a long cardigan, with a tartan skirt and a grey blouse under it. On her right wrist, the only one visible, was a silver bracelet with a diamond-encrusted bird on it.

With a smile, Ellie flipped open the warrant card.

'DI Reckless,' she said, showing it for a moment before placing it away. 'My companion here is DS Walsh. We'd like to talk to you about your phone call to the police.'

'I don't know what you mean,' the woman replied uncertainly.

'Please, Ma'am, we know you phoned in the call,' Ellie lied.

'It's supposed to be anonymous,' the woman muttered. 'I didn't want to be involved in any police business.'

'That's fine,' Ellie smiled. 'In that case, I'm Ellie, this is Tinker. Let's talk about it as women, over a cup of tea instead?'

Sighing, the elderly woman walked off, leaving the door open in an unspoken invitation.

Tinker glanced at Ellie.

'DS Walsh?' she raised an eyebrow. 'He won't be happy you demoted him.'

'He'll never know,' Ellie grinned, pushing the door open and entering.

14

CURTAIN TWITCHER

'I'M NOT MAKING YOU A TEA, I DON'T WANT YOU IN HERE longer than I have to,' the woman said as she entered the dining room of her house. 'The people across the road are criminals. I don't want them coming back at me.'

'I get that,' Ellie replied, noting a couple of photo frames on the mantelpiece. One was a man and woman, in their forties, and the second was a woman, only a teenager, her hair pulled back and in dungarees.

'They're nice,' Ellie nodded at it. 'Daughter?'

'In law,' the woman looked over at it. 'As well as my son and my granddaughter.'

Ellie looked back at the photos.

'I don't see a group shot,' she mused. 'Don't see them much?'

'Haven't spoken for over five years,' the woman replied. 'Although what that has to do with this...'

'No husband?'

'Never needed one,' the woman watched Ellie, as if daring her to respond. 'My son was born out of wedlock.'

'Must have been hard,' Tinker said from the window.

The woman shrugged.

'You might have guessed from the house that I come from money,' she replied. 'He didn't. My parents weren't happy with me seeing him, and when I became pregnant, they made sure we never worked.'

She stroked at the bracelet on her wrist absently.

'We wouldn't have worked, anyway,' she replied. 'Different worlds. He never knew about Sylvester, our son, and Sylv never knew about his father. Well, until I told him, five years ago. And, as I said...'

'You should try to build bridges again,' Tinker replied suddenly. 'I had issues with my family, and I regret not doing that before... before it was too late.'

'I spoke to my granddaughter recently,' the woman stated sadly, still rubbing at the bracelet on her wrist absently. 'It didn't end how I'd hoped.'

'Sorry,' Ellie said, regretting the conversation now; it obviously weighed on the woman's mind, and from the sounds of things, the moment the son realised the truth of his parental status, he cut his mother off.

She was probably better off without him, if that was the case.

'Look, can I confirm your name?' she eventually asked.

The woman stopped, turning around in confusion.

'Surely you know that?' she replied. 'You came to me, remember?'

'*I* know your name,' Ellie lied smoothly, 'but I need to know *you* do. Make sure you're the same person. For all I know, you could be an imposter, pretending to live here. If I was to say your name aloud first, you'll know it.'

'Ah,' the woman looked unconvinced at this. 'June Hudson.'

'Well, June,' Ellie smiled. 'Tell us what happened that night.'

'Well, they left in their bloody ugly car, and about an hour later another car came back,' June replied as she walked into the conservatory. She was out of sight for a moment before returning to view. 'It was a black one. It drove in—'

'The gates opened?'

'I didn't see them open, but when I saw the car, they *were* open,' June corrected. 'I assumed they knew the code, as the car drove in.'

'And then?'

Then, about two minutes later, a red car turns up,' June carried on, and Ellie noted that at the moment she'd been out of sight, she'd removed the bracelet. She almost chuckled at this; that the old lady still didn't trust them to mug her, even after the warrant card was shown, was a tribute to good, old-fashioned British distrust. 'They don't go in, but park on the corner. Lad got out, walked around the house. A couple of minutes later he waves and the car drives in, as the other one drives out and leaves.'

'And you called the police why?' Tinker asked now, staring out of the front window. 'They could have been friends who had the code.'

'They didn't enter a code,' June replied. 'They waited until the door opened, and there's only Flynn, his wife and their chauffeur-come-whatever who live there. And they were all out.'

Ellie nodded at this, understanding.

'And then?'

'And then they left,' June sniffed, walking to the window and pointing past Tinker. 'I can see the door, and they walked out of it, something under a blanket. I knew they were thieving scum and so I called the police.'

'Mighty civic minded of you,' Ellie patted June on the shoulder in what was supposed to be a reassuring manner, but was surprised to see the woman flinch at this. 'We saw the report, the transcript of the call. You didn't mention the black car. How come?'

'I didn't think it was relevant.'

'But the red one was?'

'That was the one they put the stolen goods in,' June crossed her arms, as if daring Ellie to argue anymore. 'I called back the following morning, and pointed the black car out as well, though.'

'Of course,' Ellie smiled, relenting. 'We'll leave you alone now.'

Walking to the door, she suddenly stopped, spinning back around.

'One more thing,' said, doing her best Columbo impression. 'You're a member of the Neighbourhood Watch, right?'

'I am,' June looked surprised at the revelation. 'How did you know?'

Ellie didn't want to reply with the truth, that many busybodies and 'curtain twitchers' were often members of organisations and resident committees, and shrugged.

'As I said, Mrs Hudson—'

'*Ms* Hudson.'

'As I said, *Ms* Hudson, we checked up on you in the office,' Ellie continued. 'I wondered, while keeping a wary eye out on the street, did you ever see any other suspicious characters come and go from across the road?'

'He's a gangster and a criminal,' June replied with an

expression of disgust. 'Him and his wife, they're always argu-ing. It's no wonder she looks elsewhere—'

She stopped, as she realised what she was insinuating.

'Of course, that's only gossip,' she finished. 'I'm above that.'

'I'm sure you are,' Ellie shook June's hand and nodded to Tinker to open the door. 'Thank you for your time.'

'What exactly are you doing over there?' June asked as they walked back out onto the driveway. 'I saw you talk to him before you came over.'

'Trying to solve the case, Ma'am,' Tinker smiled. 'Just trying to solve the case.'

Walking back across the road, Ellie looked at Tinker.

'Did you see the bracelet?' she chuckled. 'She took one look at you and hid it. You're obviously a wrong'un.'

'And proud of it,' Tinker replied as they entered through the gates once more, nodding at the open garage door. 'Inter-esting about the black car. The one Danny has in the garage over there is more of a beige.'

'I think it's called champagne.'

'Still looks beige. And a curtain twitcher wouldn't miss a detail like that.'

Danny Flynn was waiting by the door as they returned.

'Well?' he asked. 'Was it her? Nosy bitch.'

'No,' Ellie lied, walking past him and into the house. 'Come on, get those brews going. We need to have a chat.'

The last time Ramsey had been to Sebastian LaFleur's studio in Hoxton, he hadn't known what to expect. He certainly hadn't expected to find a man he'd worked well with in the past to be dead and buried, and he *hadn't* expected to feel so bad about it.

Sure, he could claim it was because he hadn't been invited to the funeral, but what exactly was the etiquette there? It wasn't the same as being uninvited to a wedding. It wasn't exactly a glorious occasion, even if some wakes he'd been to over the years had been insane, raucous affairs.

But it still galled him to admit he hadn't been liked enough to even be informed of Sebastian's death.

As he walked down the path from the road to the complex where the creator studios resided, Tinker's words came back to him.

'You screw everyone over. You're like a well-dressed scorpion.'

Ramsey shook his head to shake away the bad thoughts, and this slight movement alerted Casey, looking up at him.

'You okay?' he asked cautiously.

'Why wouldn't I be?'

'I dunno, I don't know you,' Casey admitted, pausing at a window and nodding in approval at a painting. 'Look at this. Now that's art.'

'What is it?' Ramsey frowned. It was an oil portrait, but of what, he had no idea.

'It's C3PO from *Star Wars,* but with a Wheaton Terrier's head,' Casey explained knowledgeably. 'My aunt used to have one.'

'A painting of C3PO, with a Wheaton Terrier's head?'

'A Wheaton Terrier,' Casey started walking again. 'I asked if you were okay, because you just broke into a hotel room, stole a priceless Ming vase and locked it in a hotel safe.'

'I *retrieved* a stolen vase,' Ramsey corrected. 'Different situation completely.'

'So what happens now?'

'I told the police where it was, so they can't claim I stole it,' Ramsey explained. 'And then I texted Robert. It's his job to sort these legal things out, so he'll make his way to the hotel, explain the situation and use the police to his advantage.'

'How?'

Ramsey smiled.

'Well, I would imagine by the time he gets there, he'll find a rather irritated Marcus Somerville wanting his items back. A police audience might stop that.'

'Have you told Ellie?'

'Why should I?' Ramsey stopped, turning to face Casey. 'I work for Finders, not her. I might be on her team, but I work for whomever provides me with the most money.'

'Yeah, I got that the day I met you,' Casey stared up at Ramsey, his eyes cold. 'Only giving a damn about money. But then I also heard your mum's in a home, and that has to cost, so I get why you'd be like that.'

'Thank you, I think,' Ramsey frowned. 'Look, I decided to pass it on to Robert, because I knew he wouldn't have his head torn off if he told *her*. If she knew I'd gone off book, and stepped away from her Quixotic crusade for one moment, then she'd be angry.'

'What is this crusade, anyway?' Casey asked. 'I mean, I get you mean *Don Quixote*, we did it at school, but from what I can work out, she wants to find dad's killer, and I know she was set up, but she seems to risk a lot of things for effectively a clean sheet at a job that doesn't want her back. Why?'

Ramsey went to reply, but then stopped himself.

'You really don't know,' he said, more as an observation than a question. 'I think you need to ask her that. Maybe when all this is over.'

'So there's definitely something?'

'There's definitely something,' Ramsey walked up to Sebastian LaFleur's door. 'You just might not like it.'

And, with that ominous prophecy given, Ramsey went to knock on the door—but stopped.

'Listen,' he said. 'What do you hear?'

Casey strained his ears for a moment.

'Nothing.'

'Exactly,' Ramsey still held his hand up, paused mid-knock. 'She was playing rather progressive rock music the last time we were here.'

'So?' Casey frowned. 'Maybe she got sick of it.'

'She was also working,' Ramsey lowered his hand. 'You could hear generators. Underlying noise. There's nothing coming from within.'

'Maybe she's out?'

Ramsey knocked on the door.

After a moment, he knocked again.

'You might be right,' he said, pulling a leather pouch out of his pocket.

'Is that what I think it is?' Casey looked around the corridor nervously.

'I don't know,' Ramsey knelt in front of the lock, placing the tension rod of his lock picking kit into it. 'You're ten or something, so you might think it's some kind of... actually, I have no idea what a ten-year-old would think.'

Opening the door with a click, he rose, placing away his pouch.

'I thought we were only asking questions?' Casey asked as they entered the studio.

'Well, she lied to us last time, so she'll probably lie to us again,' Ramsey clicked on the light switch, even though the windows gave in an adequate amount of light. 'If we have a look around first, we might find something that can help us.'

The studio was exactly as it was the last time Ramsey visited, although this time quieter and without Natalie welding on her statue. Also, there were more papers scattered around, and several of the drawers were opened haphazardly, as if someone was searching for things before leaving quickly.

'Someone was desperate to find something,' Ramsey commented, checking a drawer. 'I wonder what they were looking for?'

'You think someone burgled this place?' Casey turned to the side; the statue was also still there, and still unfinished. Casey looked up at it in wonder.

'Possibly,' Ramsey shrugged. 'I mean, technically, we've done the same.'

'Not unless we steal something,' Casey replied. 'Currently it's just breaking and entering.'

Ramsey grinned.

'Who said we're *not* stealing anything?' he asked. 'Anyway, when we were here last time, there wasn't anything here worth stealing. I reckon Natalie sold everything she could the moment Seb died.'

Casey picked up a phone from the side; it was a cheap, pay as you go style; nothing more than phone calls and texts, and was as analogue as you could get in a mobile device.

'Doesn't even have a password,' he said as he flicked through the calls. 'What's 01608 the code for? She had a number call her from there, at—' he checked his own phone, '—just before seven am yesterday.'

'Write it down, we'll check later,' Ramsey suggested.

Casey tapped the number into his phone's notes app and then looked back up at the statue.

'Are they—'

'Guns, yes,' Ramsey was already rifling through unopened mail. 'Replicas, apparently. It's a protest against the industry of war.'

Casey was impressed.

'And you can tell that by looking at it?'

'Of course,' Ramsey examined his nails as he spoke. 'Tinkerbelle got very excited about it, but then that's all guns for her.'

'Should you be calling her Tinkerbelle?' Casey smiled. 'Especially with her love of weapons?'

Ramsey looked up, mock horror on his face as he scanned the room. Then, this done, he relaxed.

'Nope, she's not here,' he said. 'I can say what I want. Tinkerbelle. Tinkerbelle. Tink—'

He stopped as his phone buzzed.

'Say her name and she shall appear,' he half-whispered, looking down at the message with a slight expression of horror. 'Nope, she's miles away. They've arrived at Flynn's house.'

'You should tell them about the vase.'

'Who are you, my confessor?'

Casey ignored the jibe, walking over to a photo on a workbench.

'That's Wyatt,' he said as he picked it up. 'And it's not that old, because he looked the same when we saw him today.'

'Tinker was right,' Ramsey walked over now, examining the image. 'It's a party. Has to be six months to a year at least, purely because Seb died six months ago.'

'Six months matches when he stopped searching for the

painting,' Casey placed it back on the shelf. 'Maybe they met here?'

Ramsey was still staring at the image, in particular the woman in the back.

'We need to see if we can find that woman,' he said. 'She might be able to tell us how recent this was. Can you scan it, maybe—'

'Run some facial recognition?' Casey smiled. 'That's very much a movie thing, I'm afraid. And even if I could, she's only partially facing the screen. Maybe Natalie could—'

'No, Tinker asked her,' Ramsey picked up another photo, one of an elderly lady, a much younger Natalie, standing on the other side. It was outside, maybe on a farm, or some kind of countryside restaurant, and at least five, maybe ten years old. 'Looks like this isn't just Seb's shelf.'

As Ramsey looked around the studio, Casey pulled out his phone, taking photos of the two frames, placing them back in their original positions.

'Look,' Ramsey had walked to a pile of canvas frames resting against the wall in the corner, and was now flipping through them. 'These are all half-finished forgeries. He must have died before he finished them all.'

He stopped, however, as he picked up a piece of paper left on a table beside them.

'Oh, bother,' he muttered, already looking around the studio.

'What?' Casey asked. Ramsey stared back at the sheet.

'It's a handwritten suicide note,' he said. '*I'm sorry for everything, Nat.*'

There was a door at the back of the studio, and now, with impending urgency, Ramsey walked over to it.

'Touch nothing,' he hissed. 'Grab a cloth, wipe down anything you've handled.'

He opened the door, staring down at the floor.

'Well, that's bloody inconvenient.'

Casey angled so he could see into the room and wished he hadn't.

On the floor of a small kitchenette was Natalie; obviously dead, a small, open plastic tub of pills scattered around her on the floor. Her face was pale, almost blueish, her eyes rolled up into her head, her mouth open, with what looked to be bile down the side of her cheek.

'Is she dead?'

Ramsey looked back at him angrily.

'I said *wipe your prints!*' he snapped. 'We were never here!'

'Is she dead!'

Ramsey rose, stepping away from the body as he nodded.

'Lack of breathing's a bit of a giveaway,' he muttered, looking around the studio, almost in a daze. 'She's been dead for a while. But there's something very wrong here.'

'Like what?'

'Like how did she write the note?' Ramsey pointed at the wrist. 'She told us it was hard to use. And the penmanship doesn't show any issues.'

'He observed the scene, clicking his tongue in irritation.

'And why scatter the pills like this?' he eventually questioned. 'If you commit suicide like this, you take them *all*, to make sure you get the blasted job done. This looks like someone had a very theatrical view of how a pill overdose should look, and dressed the place as such.'

Casey walked backwards, shaking his head.

'We need to get out of here,' he whispered. 'Before the police turn up.'

Ramsey was wiping down anything he'd touched, nodding as he did so.

'Clean up, then move out—' he started, but stopped as, in the distance, he could hear police cars, their sirens blaring, getting louder.

'Too late, time to go,' he said, grabbing Casey and pulling him out of the door to the studio, quickly kneeling and locking it behind him. 'We can't be found here.'

'And how do we get out?' Casey pointed at the entrance, where through the frosted glass the faint flashing blue lights of the police could be seen. 'They're already here. We could tell them we just arrived?'

'No, they wouldn't believe us. One of the other residents here must have seen me pick the lock and called them in,' Ramsey said as he looked around. 'It's *incredibly* bothersome. This suit's vintage, and I don't really want to be climbing walls in it.'

'But we didn't do anything!'

'They won't care, kid,' with a growing urgency, Ramsey started up a staircase, aiming for an upper level, motioning for Casey to follow him, as, at the frosted window, they could see figures approaching. 'And our prints will be in there. If not from today, they'll be there from the last time we turned up.'

Nodding, Casey followed as, with Ramsey ahead, he ran from the scene of a potential murder before the police arrived to arrest them.

15

CRASH TEST DUMMIES

Chantelle was sitting in the living room when Danny entered with Ellie and Tinker, walking them over to a coffee machine in the kitchen area against the south wall of the room, just past the giant television screen.

'Glad you have time for a drink,' she snarled at them. 'I'd hate to think you were working non-stop for us or something.'

'We needed to see the burglary scene, and speak to witnesses,' Ellie replied, taking a cup of coffee from Danny, and walking into the room. At this, Chantelle seemed to lose a little of her bluster.

'What witnesses?'

'Don't worry,' Ellie gave a slight smile. 'We'll keep you in the loop.'

She looked around the room; it was pretty much as the police report stated; white leather sofas against two of the walls, a black IKEA unit with a massive, sixty-five inch 4K HD television, connected to a surround sound system that had speakers around them.

'Here's my question,' Ellie said, walking over to the TV. 'Why didn't they take this?'

'Too big, wasn't it?' Chantelle replied.

'Yeah, but they took the painting, which was similar in size, and they had a car out the front,' Ellie turned to face Chantelle now. 'And they checked the house, because they stole your jewels.'

'I'm guessing you didn't find those yet?'

'Not yet,' Ellie shook her head. 'But we do have a list of what was stolen.'

'How?' Chantelle looked at Danny. 'We haven't given a list to the police yet.'

'Yeah, but I had to give a rough list to the insurance company, so they probably have that,' Danny replied, almost apologetically, scratching the back of his neck as he looked in any direction except for Chantelle's.

Who, at this moment, was furious.

'I haven't worked out what was taken,' she hissed.

'You'd written an itinerary in the box, so I ticked off what was missing,' Danny mumbled.

'I thought they took all of it?' Tinker asked now, sipping at her own coffee. 'Ooh, that's nice. You'll have to tell me the blend before we leave.'

'Bugger the blend!' Chantelle snapped. 'You have no right to pry into things—'

'Things that were stolen?' Ellie leant closer. She was starting to really dislike Chantelle. 'Would you rather we just found the painting? Leave your jewels out of it?'

'I have my own people hunting the jewels,' Chantelle replied huffily. 'I spoke to them today about it.'

'She did, they're in Bristol,' Danny replied. 'She and our driver were out all morning.'

'Is there anyone else who works here, apart from the driver?' Ellie asked.

Danny shook his head.

'We have a cleaner who comes in, but she's only a few hours a week. I used to have a cook, but Chantelle didn't like her food.'

'She didn't understand my dietary needs,' Chantelle muttered. As she said this, the door opened and the chauffeur, in black trousers and white-collared shirt, leant in.

'Do you need me any more?' he asked, and Ellie realised this was the accent she'd heard through the intercom. She also realised that, although speaking to Danny, he was looking directly at Chantelle.

'Not until this evening,' Danny replied, looking back at Ellie as he explained. 'We're off to Clarkson's gaff. Bit of a party going on.'

Ricardo, nodding, disappeared back through the door.

'What about him?' Ellie pointed her thumb at the door. 'Could he have done it?'

'Ricardo? Definitely not,' Chantelle said, a little too quickly.

'He could have driven back here,' Ellie added, deciding not to mention the fact that June Hudson had said the car hadn't returned.

'He's been with us for ages,' Chantelle snapped, angry now. 'He's family.'

'He ain't my family,' Danny muttered. 'He's always pandering to your needs when I'm the one who pays him.'

'Not my fault I have needs,' Chantelle replied with a smile. 'I'm a needy kind of girl.'

Ellie bit her tongue, forcing back a reply to this as she remembered June Hudson's gossip.

'You get a lot of parties around here?' she asked, changing the subject.

'A fair few,' Chantelle said from the sofa, pulling out her phone, tapping on the screen.

'For God's sake, can you stay off Instagram for five minutes?' Danny, exasperated, asked. In reply, Chantelle placed the phone beside her on the sofa.

'You ever *host* any parties?' Tinker asked now. 'Maybe someone saw how your security worked when they came in?'

'Nah, we never hosted,' Danny shook his head. 'Didn't like people around here.'

'What about Ms Hudson?' Tinker added.

At this, Chantelle rose from the sofa, irritated now.

'What about her?' she snapped angrily. 'What's your fixation with her?'

'You don't get along?' Ellie enquired innocently.

'Oh, they get along fine,' Danny held his hands up, walking between the two women. 'Chantelle gets along with everyone. Ain't that right, love?'

Ellie somehow doubted this.

'So, the people that did this,' Chantelle changed tack. 'What do you know about them?'

'They weren't local, but they knew the house,' Ellie replied, deciding to tell the truth, to see if it threw anything out into the open. 'They were in and out before anyone even realised.'

'And they were shot?'

'Yes, both in the head,' Tinker added now. 'The weirdest thing? No defensive wounds. Like they knew their killer.'

'Maybe they did,' Chantelle sniffed. 'Nicky Simpson probably hired them after all.'

'Maybe, but they weren't South London boys,' Ellie

watched Chantelle now. 'They were from Loughton. Essex lads.'

At this, Danny whitened.

'This was done by people from my own manor?'

'Looks like it,' Ellie walked over to the wall, staring up at the painting-shaped, faded rectangle on it. 'Looks like all loyalties died when you moved to the Cotswolds.'

'So whoever killed them took the painting, and it's likely gone forever.'

Chantelle spoke it as a fact rather than a question, and Ellie shrugged in response.

'That's a possibility,' she replied calmly, deciding to throw another grenade into the conversation. 'It definitely wasn't on them.'

She glanced at Tinker as she continued, tapping the space on the wall.

'But it's looking like more than a simple theft,' she said. 'I believe your painting, the one right here, that was taken a couple of nights back, was a forgery.'

Danny spluttered at this, and Chantelle picked up her phone again; Ellie wondered if she was about to take a photo of him, but instead she started tapping on the screen, obviously bored with this.

'Bullshit,' Danny eventually managed to get out. 'My dad gave it to me, swore it was the real thing.'

'That doesn't mean he was right,' Tinker replied. 'Although I'm sure, over the years, you've had the painting, and thinking it was the real deal, you had it authenticated?'

Danny's eyes widened in horror as he slowly shook his head.

'It was stolen goods,' he mumbled. 'If I'd done that, someone would have learnt of it.'

'I think they learnt of it when you started selling it on the dark web,' Ellie stated. 'Surely you discussed this with Christian Wyatt?'

Danny frowned.

'Who?'

'Sorry, I mean Hugo Speer,' Ellie smiled.

At this name, Danny nodded.

'He was going to get his people to do it,' he said, looking at the space on the wall. 'I had to tell him it was gone. He wasn't happy.'

'I'll bet,' Ellie said. 'And the delay isn't helping you with the debt.'

'And what do you know about that?' Chantelle asked irritably.

Ellie returned her attention to Chantelle, now shifting uncomfortably on the sofa under the sudden intense gaze.

'I had a chat with Nicky Simpson last night,' she replied. 'It was a little tense, but incredibly enlightening.'

'Oh yeah?'

'Yeah,' Ellie hadn't taken her eyes off the woman. 'Let's just say that he's impatient for his money.'

She frowned, pacing now.

'The issue I have is this,' she continued. 'Danny owes Nicky. Danny goes to sell his painting to pay the debt. This would mean the debt is sorted, Nicky would have his money back, all good. In fact, he'd make double his investment, a good two million in profit. But if Nicky takes the painting, then Danny can't pay him.'

She looked back at Danny.

'And as we know, if you can't pay him, he takes everything.'

'My Danny won't allow that,' Chantelle replied. 'My Danny—'

'Is broke,' Tinker interrupted.

'It was a good land deal,' Danny muttered, staring at the floor. 'Until it wasn't.'

The room was silent as Chantelle stared at her husband.

'I'm not waiting around for him to make good on his threats,' Danny looked at his watch. 'It's four pm now. If you can't fix this by tomorrow evening, we're off.'

'You'd run?'

'What other options do I have?' Danny hissed. 'He'll gut me. I can't give him Boston. I've got more chance staying out of reach until I can sort something to clear the debt.'

'And where would you go?' Tinker shook her head. 'He'll find you. He'll be watching airports, train stations...'

'Got a yacht waiting,' Danny said, glancing at Chantelle. 'It's a friend of Chantelle's. We can use it.'

Ellie's phone rang; pulling it out, she saw the name and nodded to Danny.

'Sorry,' she said. 'I need to take this.'

Leaving Tinker with the other two, Ellie walked out of the living room and into the hall.

'What do you have?' she asked.

'A rather unfortunate amount of trouble,' Ramsey's voice echoed through the speaker. 'Natalie's dead. Looks like an overdose. Maybe suicide, as there was a note, but there was also a provincial theatre's level of artistic detail in the death scene, so I'm not sure.'

'Where are you?' Ellie could hear running, and Ramsey was out of breath as he spoke.

'Escaping from the police before they decide we did it,' Ramsey replied. There was a strange scrabbling noise down the phone, and a muttering of something being *vintage*; Ellie assumed this was the sound of Ramsey climbing a wall or something.

'Casey's sending you the photo of LaFleur and Wyatt,' he said. 'Don't know if it'll help. Wyatt didn't blink when we confronted him, either.'

'You confronted him?' Ellie exclaimed. 'I don't recall telling you to do that.'

'Not now, Elisa,' Ramsey snapped, and Ellie realised that the pair of them were likely running for their lives. *The last thing he needed was an argument.*

'Text me when you're safe,' she said, disconnecting the call.

There was a beep, and a WhatsApp message came through, appearing on the phone's screen. It was a picture taken of a picture, so the image wasn't as well-defined as she could hope for, but it was what she needed; Sebastian LaFleur and Christian Wyatt were at a party together. Now she just had to—

She stopped, zooming in on the photo.

And, looking up, she smiled as she re-entered the living room.

Tinker, now by the window, watched her warily.

'You okay?' Tinker asked.

Ellie nodded.

'Quick question,' she said, walking over and showing Tinker the photo. 'Is this the photo you saw in the studio?'

'Yeah, that's the one,' Tinker replied, before her eyes widened. 'And—'

Ellie held a finger up, pausing Tinker as she looked back to Danny.

'So there's this forger. Guy named Sebastian LaFleur,' she

said, glancing from husband to wife. 'Either of you know him?'

Danny shook his head, while Chantelle shifted uneasily in her seat.

'Should we?' she asked irritably.

Walking over, Ellie showed Chantelle the photo on her screen before showing it to Danny. On it, they could see the two men, in black tie, smiling to the camera.

And, in the background, talking to someone off camera, was Chantelle Flynn.

'You seem to move in the same circles,' Ellie said.

Chantelle rolled her eyes theatrically as she sighed.

'I go to a lot of parties,' she replied.

'Would have been about seven months back.'

'I'll check my diary,' Chantelle replied with the tone of someone who definitely wouldn't be doing that. Danny, however, took the phone back, looking at the photo again.

'Who are they?'

'This one's a world class forger,' Ellie said as she tapped the image of Sebastian LaFleur. 'The other's a billionaire who's wanted your painting for years.'

At this, Chantelle rose.

'You're fishing,' she stated icily. 'And we need you to find a painting before some psycho kills us, not blame us for your shortcomings. I think it's time for you to leave.'

Looking over to Tinker and nodding, Ellie shrugged.

'Sure,' she said. 'Whatever you think is best, Mrs Flynn.'

'What I think best is you never coming here again,' Chantelle snapped. 'Look at my husband! He's a mess! And you're not helping here at all!'

Ellie walked to the door, but stopped as she got to it.

'One more thing,' she said as she looked back at

Chantelle. 'We saw the list of items stolen. You had some large cost items taken, but I was just wondering whether there was a reason you had on that specific necklace that night?'

Chantelle smiled; a cold, humourless one that chilled Ellie to the bone.

'Just lucky, I suppose,' she replied. 'It was my grandmother's. She was looking out for me.'

At this, Ellie considered the answer, looked back at Danny, and then carried on through the door, Tinker following.

'Yeah,' she said as she left the house. 'Real lucky.'

IT WAS ABOUT AN HOUR DOWN THE M40, AN HOUR SPENT mainly discussing Danny Flynn's interior decorating taste, before the conversation finally turned to the case.

'So, what did you make of Chantelle?' Ellie asked as she pulled out into the middle lane.

'Apart from the fact that she's screwing the driver? Not much,' Tinker smiled.

'You think they're sleeping together?'

'I don't think *sleeping's* ever been involved,' Tinker grinned. 'But did you see him when he came in? Asking his boss if everything was okay, but staring at her?'

She settled back into the passenger seat.

'Probably been going on for months.'

'Maybe he thinks Chantelle's his boss?'

'Oh, I think we can both agree that Chantelle's the boss of everyone there,' Tinker replied, looking at Ellie. 'Danny is the most beta Essex man I've ever met. How did they meet?'

'Chantelle was in TOWIE,' Ellie explained, sighing when she saw no recognition in Tinker's eyes. '*The Only Way Is Essex*. Was a massive TV show a few years back.'

'I was in black ops a few years back.'

'And one day, you'll tell me all about that,' Ellie smiled. 'Anyway, she's from Chingford, but *TOWIE* was filmed around Brentwood, where Danny came from. They met in a club, moved on from there.'

'How close are Chingford and Brentwood to Loughton?' Tinker asked.

'Brentwood's miles away, but Chingford's definitely closer,' Ellie considered. 'Three, maybe four miles?'

'So she may have known the Loughton mob then. It's worth considering,' Tinker suggested. 'If the Nicky Simpson angle doesn't work out.'

'Maybe they're working together?' Ellie overtook a transit van, pulling back into the lane. 'She looked like she does a lot of working out.'

'Typical trophy wife,' Tinker shrugged in the seat. 'And the tits are totally fake.'

They drove for a moment in silence.

'What are we missing here?' Ellie asked. 'Why would Natalie be removed from the board? The two thieves, sure, but what was Natalie's role?'

Tinker pulled out her phone, typing.

'Ought to see if Ramsey got arrested,' she said, pressing send.

'He's too good to be caught.'

'He had Casey with him, and you can't hack your way out of a custody cell,' Tinker replied.

Ellie snorted.

'If I had to put money on anyone doing it, I'd place it on Casey Noyce.'

'You have to tell him, you know.'

Ellie sighed.

'I know.'

Tinker placed the phone away, looking out of the passenger window.

'Simpson's laughing his arse off,' she said. 'If he's behind it.'

'Well, he's still out a few million, so probably not that hard,' Ellie was coming up behind a lorry; accelerating, she went past it. 'Although this whole US scheme is worth way more.'

As she said this, passing seventy-seven miles an hour on the dial, the radio, currently playing nineties songs at a very low volume, spluttered and crackled.

'What the hell?' Ellie said, looking at her dials.

'It's probably just the aerial—'

'I'm not talking about the radio!' Ellie replied, her voice rising in fear. 'The car's not responding! It's speeding up and the brake's not responding!'

Slamming her foot onto the brake pedal to emphasise this, Ellie tried to turn the steering wheel as she sped past another car.

'It's sluggish to steer,' she continued. 'It started when the radio fritzed.'

'Hold on,' Tinker said as she pulled up the handbrake.

Nothing happened.

'The brake's been cut!' Tinker exclaimed.

The car was veering wildly now, crossing lanes almost with abandon as Ellie struggled to control it, forcing it to avoid the other cars, smacking the horn repeatedly.

'It's not the brakes!' she replied. 'The car's speeding up, stopping me from controlling it. Someone's doing this—'

Ellie stopped speaking as they slammed into the back of a caravan; the caravan wobbled, but as they'd both been moving, all the thump did was loosen the bumper, and slow the Ford Focus down a little, before the acceleration kicked in again.

'If we go over, we'll take out more than just us!' Ellie cried out as, unable to be stopped, the car swerved across to the middle barrier of the motorway.

'Hold on!' she cried out as the car crashed into the barrier railings, sparks flying up where the side of the chassis struck metal. It slowed the car, but not enough, and as Ellie pulled at the wheel to get away from it, the cars behind already slowing down to avoid them, the Ford Focus veered sharply to the left, skidding, the back of the car pushing past the front as it spun—and then rolled, the car smashing onto its roof as it overturned, still scraping along the motorway, smoke billowing as it slammed into the hard shoulder of the motorway, stopping on its side as it hit the grassy verge.

Cars were pulling up now, drivers climbing out and running over to the vehicle, calling out to each other to *phone the police, call an ambulance,* anything that could help.

But for Ellie and Tinker, lying unconscious in the car, covered in blood, and with torn airbags and wreckage now scattered around them, their journey home was over.

16

BEDSIDE VIGIL

I<small>T WAS SEVEN IN THE EVENING WHEN</small> R<small>AMSEY ARRIVED AT</small> Wycombe hospital. Guided to the second floor by a lady on reception (after an uncomfortable and extensive conversation where she thought he was Ellie's father) and running into one of the upstairs waiting rooms, he slowed to a walk at a fearsome glare from another of the nurses, making his way quickly to Robert, sitting on a plastic chair, who rose from it as he saw Ramsey appear.

'Any news?' Ramsey asked.

Robert raised an eyebrow.

'I would have texted you,' he replied, now sitting back down, Ramsey taking the chair beside him. 'You didn't have to come all the way here.'

'Felt like the right thing to do,' Ramsey shrugged, looking around the waiting room. 'And I'm terrible at waiting.'

'You've never known what the right thing is,' Robert stated icily. 'Come on, out with it. Why are you really here?'

Ramsey, in response, simply stared at Robert.

'You really think that little of me?' he whispered, as if finally realising.

'No, actually, I think a lot of you,' Robert sighed, leaning his head against the wall behind him. 'When I was a criminal solicitor, I watched your trial, the one that finally put you away with a little envy.'

'Because you wanted to be the one that put me away?' Ramsey gave a wry smile.

'No, because I knew I could have got you off,' Robert said, looking back at him. 'I knew how to angle the case, I saw the reasons you did what you did, and I realised very early on how your solicitor dropped the ball on the whole *addict* angle.'

'You could have told him before I was sentenced,' Ramsey mused.

'Wasn't my case to defend,' Robert shrugged. 'And besides, I also saw the other side of it, and knew how, as prosecution, I could make sure you did at least ten to fifteen.'

Ramsey didn't reply to this.

'Anyway, when Ellie said she wanted to bring your skills on board, Finders had to agree to it,' Robert continued. 'I was the one that signed off on you.'

'Well, I hope I didn't disappoint.'

'Not until now,' Robert replied calmly, before changing the subject. 'So you know, Tinker's still in A and E; she's not too bad, but she's a little battered. Small head wound, and a possible broken rib, but she was telling everyone about half an hour back she was checking herself out the moment she could.'

'And Ellie?'

Robert's face darkened.

'Still waiting,' he replied. 'She was driving, took the brunt of the roll. She's unconscious, and she's also got some scrapes and bruises, although there's nothing broken.'

He tapped his head.

'Well, apart from up here,' he finished. 'We have to wait until she wakes to see how bad it is.'

He stopped, looking around, as if realising for the first time there was something wrong with the picture.

'Where's Casey Noyce?' he asked. 'I thought you were with him?'

'I dropped him at home,' Ramsey said. 'He wanted to come as soon as we heard, but I knew it'd likely be an overnight deal, and I can't see his mother allowing that.'

'No,' Robert muttered. 'Almost as much as her allowing him to be taken to a murder scene, or involving him in a car accident.'

Ramsey held up his hands at this.

'In fairness, we didn't know Natalie was dead when we went there,' he replied quickly. 'And I wasn't the one who rammed my car into the back of a police vehicle. And, if I can be brutally honest, Robert, *I* wasn't the one who *placed a teenage boy with a group of criminals*.'

'Criminals? Is that what you think you are?'

'Have you seen what she's had us doing recently?'

Robert shook his head.

'I should have stuck with the legitimate work for her,' he scratched at his arm irritably. 'I shouldn't have let her talk me into this.'

'Talk you into what?' Ramsey snapped. 'What are these favours for, anyway? Nobody tells us a bloody thing!'

Robert didn't reply, and Ramsey rose from his chair, angrily pacing.

'I didn't ask to do these blasted favours,' he hissed. 'I do the paid work. And while she was fiddling about, looking for stolen paintings, I was the one finding the vase we'd been hunting.'

'Yes, I was meaning to speak to you about that,' Robert replied, staring up at Ramsey. 'I wanted to congratulate you for being a *prize bloody idiot* and costing us that fee.'

'What do you mean?' Ramsey frowned, stopping his pacing as he looked down at his boss. 'I found it! I made sure Marcus Somerville couldn't sell it!'

'What you did was alert him to our presence by performing a criminal act!' Robert hissed, now rising back up to face the confused Ramsey. 'You broke into his hotel room! You took the vase!'

'Nobody can prove I took it from his room—'

'You called a bloody security guard up to take you to reception with it! You told them you were Marcus Somerville, and you had them lock it away for you!'

'And then I called the police,' Ramsey replied, straightening. 'I was trying to stop Marcus from selling it.'

'And a right awful job of that you did!' Robert was reddening with anger now. 'Can't you even see what you did? Imagine the scene. Marcus Somerville turns up shortly after you leave and finds his vase gone. He calls security, stating he was robbed. He shows security his identification, and is recognised as Marcus Somerville from CCTV when he checked in. Security realise the man they gave a pass to, who took a vase to the safe earlier, was an imposter. When told what happened, Marcus, realising he's been rumbled, explains "it was all a funny prank by an old friend, and can he have his vase back?" Of course, the hotel agrees. They're mortified they were taken in by this in the first place. He takes the vase and goes back to his room.'

'This isn't sounding that fictional,' Ramsey mused.

'It isn't, because it's exactly what bloody well happened, about twenty minutes after you buggered off,' Robert hissed.

'But the police—'

'And, when the police arrive,' Robert held up a hand to cut Ramsey off. 'In our imagined scenario, when they turn up, the hotel explains it was all a misunderstanding. The police go to speak to Somerville, and guess what?'

'He's gone,' Ramsey mumbled, looking at the floor of the waiting room.

'Of course he's sodding well gone,' Robert, exasperated, snapped. 'The moment he got back into his room, he threw everything into his duffel and ran out through the car park.'

'We'll find him again,' Ramsey insisted, silently cursing his stupidly. 'I thought I—'

'You thought you could cut corners,' Robert replied. 'You thought you could get this sorted quickly, as you didn't know how long you'd be involved on the Flynn case, you were pissed at Ellie for even putting you on it, and you needed a payday.'

Ramsey nodded.

'Yes,' he stated. 'My mother—'

'Is being looked after very well by Nicholas Simpson,' Robert leant in, nodding at Ramsey's stunned expression. 'Yeah, I know about that. I know also how he's leaning on you, wanting inside information on what Ellie's doing.'

Ramsey opened and shut his mouth a few times, before slumping onto the chair.

'Does she know?'

'Nobody knows,' Robert sat back down. 'Christ, Ramsey, do you think Tinker would even talk to you if she knew? She'd break your arms off and feed them to you.'

'How—'

'It's my job to know things like this,' Robert replied. 'Just like it's my job to monitor anyone who's acting against Ellie, and in part, us.'

'You think I'm acting against her?'

'I think you don't know who you're acting for,' Robert shook his head.

At this, Ramsey nodded, sadly.

'I needed money,' he said. 'It was before Ellie brought me on. I was supposed to get a payout for keeping quiet in prison, but my partner, Mickey Two-Suits, who kept the money and stayed out of jail, rather annoyingly died while I was in, and didn't leave a forwarding address to the funds I'd been promised.'

'Harsh.'

'My mother wasn't well, she was displaying signs of early onset dementia, and I didn't know what to do. The council offered to help her while I was in prison, but when I got out I saw what they offered, and I could see she needed more. Special needs, expensive care, all that,' Ramsey explained. 'I'd let her down all my life, Robert. I wasn't going to do it now.'

He stared at the wall for a moment, breathing heavily, forcing back tears.

'I wasn't going to be that man again,' he whispered.

'Ramsey—' Robert started, but Ramsey held up a hand, regaining control.

'Anyway,' he continued, his voice calm again. 'A friend suggested I speak to a friend of *theirs*, and so on and on, and it went on like that until someone gave me the money to get her into a place that could look after her.'

'Simpson.'

'I didn't know, I swear,' Ramsey pleaded. 'He did it through a known face, and I found out a couple of months after I started working for you. Simpson pulled me into his car one day while I was returning from Caesar's and explained he could have mother kicked out, force me to pay back the money in one lump. Or, I could give him the scoop on what was going on, have an easier life.'

He slumped in the chair.

'She was making progress in the new place. She was playing her violin again. She was happy, and she seemed proud of me. And I'm ashamed to say I took the easy way out.'

'Of course you did,' Robert sighed. 'You bloody stupid bastard.'

Ramsey sat in silence for a moment, mulling over his words.

'I'll fix this,' he said.

'Damn right you will,' Robert looked up to the entrance of the waiting room now, where through the doors walked DI Whitehouse and DS Delgado. 'If you're not arrested first. I'm hoping you didn't touch anything when you were in the studio? Let the boy touch anything?'

Ramsey looked over at the approaching detectives and groaned.

'We tidied as best we could,' he breathed. 'And we got out across the roofs, came back onto the street about a block down.'

Nodding at this, Robert rose, smiling warmly at Delgado while shaking Whitehouse's offered hand. 'Detectives. It's been a while.'

'Since your previous firm convinced a court to allow a

murderer to walk free, yes, it has,' Delgado muttered sullenly, ignoring Robert's outstretched hand.

Without missing a beat, he removed it.

'Have you come to check on Ellie?'

'We came to make sure she was dead—' Delgado started, but stopped as Whitehouse spun on her.

'*Enough*,' he hissed. 'If you can't act professional, then piss off back to the car. She was one of us, no matter what you think, she was my bloody partner for years, and she *almost died*. Might *still* die. So shut up or bugger off.'

Delgado blinked, realising what she'd said, paling a little.

'Sorry,' she mumbled softly. 'I didn't mean to say that aloud.'

'That you *thought* it isn't better,' Robert looked back at Whitehouse. 'We're waiting for the doctor to give an update. She was driving, is unconscious, although there are no major physical wounds, and there's pressure on the brain, so they're taking it slow.'

Whitehouse nodded.

'You have my number?'

'I can find it.'

'Keep me updated, yeah?'

'Of course,' Robert folded his arms. 'And now, with that out of the way, you can tell us why you're *really* here.'

'Did anyone breathalyse her?' Delgado asked innocently, backing off when Whitehouse glared at her. 'I just wondered. We know she likes a drink. Or three.'

'We wanted to check—that is, *I* wanted to check she was okay,' Whitehouse moved in front of Delgado, effectively barring her from the conversation. 'But we also needed to chat to Mister Allen here.'

'And you knew he was here how?'

'ANPR cameras.'

'Should I be speaking to your superiors about why his car was being stalked?' Robert asked, but Whitehouse chose not to respond.

'Do I need my solicitor present?' Ramsey asked now, concerned.

'Your solicitor *is* present,' Robert said, suddenly all business, still staring coldly at Whitehouse. 'What's the nature of the conversation?'

'Dead artist in Hoxton,' Whitehouse replied. 'Apparently it was suicide, but considering they were talking to you about Danny Flynn—'

'Hold on, how do you know that?' Ramsey asked.

'Because we spoke to her a couple of hours after you did,' Delgado leant in, moving around Whitehouse to do so. 'You're not the only one with connections.'

'You mean you followed us,' Ramsey snapped. 'Hoxton's out of your remit. Why were you there?'

'We had reason to believe it was connected to our case,' Whitehouse replied.

'Oh? How?' Robert raised an eyebrow, pulling out his phone and pressing *record* on the voice recorder. 'This being the case that Wandsworth police should have taken on?'

'That doesn't matter,' Delgado was tiring of the conversation, becoming antsy as she spoke. 'What matters is we found Mister Allen's fingerprints in the studio.'

'Seb was my friend,' Ramsey replied. 'I was paying my respects.'

'To a man who died six months ago.'

'I've been busy,' Ramsey sniffed. 'Been a tough year.'

'Mister LaFleur was a suspect in a case we were examining,' Robert interceded. 'Mister Allen was unaware of his passing.'

'Listen to you,' Delgado mocked. 'Talking about suspects and cases like you're real police.'

'Listen to *you*,' Robert snapped back. 'Talking about *real* police.'

Delgado went to reply, but another glance from White-house stopped her.

'By the way, you still haven't explained why you were there,' Robert continued, his voice quite amiable. 'If I was a suspicious type, I'd think you'd gone off books, fixating on an ex-colleague, and pushing yourselves into cases you had no right to be involved in, just for ego's sake.'

He looked back at Ramsey, nodded, and then sat back down on the plastic chair, crossing his legs.

'Either way, though, my client's fingerprints were there from a previous time.'

'Your client touched a lot of things,' Delgado, unper-turbed, continued. 'Photo frames, canvases—'

She stopped.

'But you know what was really interesting?' she changed tack now. 'In this place where a dead body was found? The *lack* of prints.'

'My lack of fingerprints was interesting?' Ramsey frowned.

'No,' Delgado smiled darkly. 'The lack of *any*. All items gather prints over time, and our forensics always has a nightmare with that. But sometimes they find items here and there with no prints. None whatsoever. And you know how that happens?'

'A good cleaner?' Ramsey suggested.

Delgado ignored the mocking comment.

'In a way, you're correct. But more specifically, singular areas being wiped down, is usually someone making sure that items they touched don't have their prints on. And in the studio, we found several singular areas wiped down.'

'So, let me get this right,' Robert frowned. 'The *lack* of my client's fingerprints brought you here?'

'We came to check on Ellie,' Whitehouse repeated. 'But we wanted you to know, as a professional courtesy, that whatever your *employees* are doing, whatever favour they're working for? Leave it alone and walk away. There are three bodies in this so far, and eventually your *employees* will be arrested and brought in.'

'And when they are, I'll be there with them,' Robert leant in. 'I'll pass on your wishes to Ellie when she wakes up. But, unless there's anything else? Piss off, yeah?'

Now it was Whitehouse who stepped back as if slapped.

'Now—'

'No,' Robert interrupted. 'I was there, remember? I saw how you turned your backs on her. I saw how you pushed to have her removed. So don't come here and act all concerned. You're sniffing around a case you only know half the information on.'

'So give me the other half.'

Robert chuckled.

'Quit and come work for me, and I'll consider it,' he smiled.

Delgado snorted and walked off before saying anything else, and sighing, Whitehouse watched after her.

'Keep me updated,' he said, following his partner.

And, as Whitehouse and Delgado left the waiting room, Robert sighed.

'Bloody marvellous,' he muttered to himself. 'What could go wrong now?'

He should have kept his mouth shut, because the moment the two detectives left, a new, familiar face entered the ward, its expression that of a man who really didn't want to be there.

'Christ,' Robert muttered as he rose once more, nodding to the newcomer. 'Hello, Nathan.'

———

17

WAKE UP

'Personally, I'm not sure what you expected out of all this,' Bryan said as he stared out over the sea, munching on his ice cream. 'You had to know something like this would happen.'

'Come on,' Ellie waved her own half-eaten ice cream at him. 'You know this wasn't like that.'

'How would I?' Bryan grinned as he turned to look at her, and for a second, Ellie's heart caught in her mouth. He was everything to her; shaggy black hair and Prada glasses, a pale checked shirt rolled up at the sleeves, and a pair of Levis on, he could have been anyone, done anything...

But he stayed with her. He wanted to be with her.

Please don't say anything more my darling

'Come on, how would I?' Bryan finished. 'I wasn't there. I'm *dead.*'

Ellie staggered back, clutching at her chest as a lightning bolt struck her through the heart, dropping the ice cream onto the promenade floor as she looked up at Bryan, now leaning back on the railings, staring out across Brighton beach.

'You are, aren't you?' she whispered. 'This isn't real.'

'It was, once,' Bryan didn't look at her as he spoke, still eating his ice cream. 'Remember the day? It was awesome. We had a great time. For an entire weekend, nobody knew who we were. Nobody needed us. I was Bryan, you were Elisa, and we were newlyweds.'

'And then Rebecca called on the Saturday night, telling you Casey was sick,' Ellie nodded. 'You had to go. I didn't understand why. We both knew she was lying, using him as a pawn. He was perfectly fine, but you wouldn't admit it. We fought. I stayed.'

She looked out at the sea.

'I always seem to stay when you go,' she whispered.

'How's he doing?' Bryan's voice cut through her thoughts as he turned to face her.

'Why do you care?' Ellie snapped, feeling the loss building up, a pain that threatened to swallow her whole, tear her apart. 'You're not real. You're just in my head.'

'You sure about that?' Bryan tossed the remains of his ice cream cone to the floor, watching as a seagull swooped down and picked it up, flying off in one smooth motion. 'Maybe I'm here to take you through the veil, walk you to the other side.'

'No,' Ellie hugged herself, pulling back from him. 'It's not my time.'

'Nobody knows their time,' Bryan smiled, but now it wasn't friendly, or welcoming, and Ellie felt cold, looking up as the clouds moved in above them. 'I didn't know it was my time until about a millisecond after I died.'

'Well, I do,' Ellie hissed back, feeling the anger build, allowing it to do so, if only to feel something, to prove to herself she was still there. 'And it won't be my time until you're avenged.'

'And how do you intend to do that?' a voice spoke behind her, and Ellie spun to see Kate Delgado, sitting on a small fire engine, the type that you would place a child on, insert a coin and watch it rock back and forth as the child rode it.

The fire engine wasn't moving; Delgado had placed no money in.

Ellie frowned, about to ask how Delgado had got there, and even turned back to Bryan to ask if he'd invited her—

But Bryan was gone.

Even the ice cream, taken by a seagull, was no more.

It was as if he'd never been there.

No God not again don't let me lose him again

'See? Even the dead don't have faith in you,' Delgado mocked. 'Hey, you got a quid? This isn't moving.'

'Get out of my head, Kate,' Ellie snapped, walking away from the Detective. 'This is my dream and I don't want you in it.'

'You think you're asleep?' Kate climbed off the ride, following Ellie. 'You'd wake up if this was a dream. Go on, try to wake up. Oh wait, you *have* tried, haven't you?'

Ellie kept walking.

'This is something far worse than a dream,' Delgado mocked. 'Do you even remember how you got here?'

'I said *get away from me!*'

'I killed Bryan,' Delgado stated suddenly, and Ellie stopped, spinning around as she continued. 'I knew you were shagging, and I was jealous. I told Nicky Simpson about it for ten grand. And, when you were found with his blood on you, I saw a way to remove you from Mark's side, so I could have him as well.'

Ellie couldn't speak, as Delgado walked towards her.

'I've always hated you,' Delgado continued. 'I've wanted you dead for so many years. That's what you want to hear from me, right? All that, wrapped up in a bow for you, closing the case?'

'Are you saying it's not true?'

'How the hell do I know?' Delgado laughed. 'I'm a figment of your imagination! Of course I'm going to agree with your opinion of me, maybe even play to the beliefs, in the way the real Kate Delgado wouldn't. Would you like to know how I helped kill him, perhaps? Your subconscious has some very interesting theories.'

Ellie ran now, trying to get away from Delgado, now returning to the fire engine ride and shouting after her.

'Don't forget to try the fish and chips!' she yelled. 'You really liked them the last time you were here!'

Turning the corner, Ellie leaned against the wall and started sobbing.

'Come on, you dozy bitch, wake up,' she muttered as she wiped her eyes, searching her memory for clues to her current situation.

How had she got here?

She remembered a car, some problems steering, Tinker yelling as the car—

There was an accident.

Tinker was in it.

'Christ,' Ellie muttered as she looked up at the skies. 'If you can hear me, body, I'd really like to open my eyes right now.'

'You will when you're ready, lassie,' a soft, Scottish lilt spoke behind her, and Ellie turned to face her old mentor, DCI Alexander Monroe. He looked like he did the last time they met; his hair was whiter, and he now sported a goatee, but she'd recognise him anywhere.

'Bloody hell, if you're in here, I must be in trouble,' she quipped. 'You the ghost of Christmas past or something?'

'You tell me, it's your bloody head.'

'There was an accident,' Ellie nodded.

'Are you sure about that, lassie?' Monroe asked, raising an eyebrow. 'Because it looked to me like you had someone screw with your vehicle.'

Ellie couldn't recall what exactly happened, but something Monroe said rang a bell.

'I need to get out of here,' she said.

'You need to make sure you're doing the right thing,' Monroe replied. 'You're following breadcrumbs, and you dinnae know who laid them.'

'Nicky Simpson.'

'Are you sure about that?' As Monroe looked back at the pier, Ellie followed the gaze and saw a distant figure running along the esplanade, effortlessly jogging over to them.

Nicky Simpson.

He was in shorts and a vest, and, once arrived, started doing star jumps as he spoke.

'I might not like you,' he explained, 'but two and a half million quid is two and a half million quid. I'm not going to throw that away for shits and giggles. I'm not some nineties pop band or anything, burning millions for a press stunt.'

Ellie considered this, shaking her head. Danny had no way to provide him with the money he needed, and his businesses couldn't make the funds up. But the contacts Simpson would gain could make the money, on a longer basis. She already knew this had to be his plan; Nicky Simpson would have an entrance to the US.

'Short term pain for long-term gain,' she whispered. 'Isn't that what you say in your YouTube videos?'

In response, Simpson got down onto the promenade floor and began doing pushups.

'Like and subscribe,' he said to her with a wink.

Ellie looked over to Monroe, who was now running on the spot, puffing as he did so.

'Oh, for God's sake,' she muttered, walking away from the scene. 'I'd really like to wake—'

———

'HEY,' THE VOICE SAID; IT WAS MALE, SOFTLY SPOKEN AND concerned. Ellie recognised it, but was confused why it would even be there.

Her eyes wouldn't open yet; it was like she'd woken to a sleep paralysis.

A hand held hers and gave a squeeze.

'I think she's awake.'

Slowly, and with great effort, Ellie opened her eyes.

'What the hell are you doing here?' she croaked at Nathan, as he slowly went from blurry outline to defined image.

'You never changed me on your NHS details as your next of kin,' he said, letting go of her hand and sitting back in the chair. 'They called me last night. I've been here for hours now. But you're welcome and all that.'

'Well done,' Ellie sighed, closing her eyes again, feeling a tightness around her head as a headache was beginning. 'Less than ten seconds and you've already made it about you.'

She opened her eyes again, suddenly feeling the icy trickle of terror down her spine.

'I can't feel my left leg,' she whispered. 'Did I—did they—
'

'Ah, no, sorry,' Nathan reddened. 'I was sitting on it when you woke up, I think I numbed it.'

'Idiot.'

'Yeah, I'll take that. Millie says hi, by the way. Actually, Millie says *I love daddy more than you and I'm living with him now, so deal with it.*'

'Now?' Ellie growled. 'This is the time you want to make these jokes?'

Nathan's face darkened.

'Who said they're jokes?'

'What happened?' Ellie closed her eyes for a moment.

'You were in a crash on the M40,' Nathan explained. 'Your friend, Tinkerbelle?'

'She doesn't enjoy being called that.'

'Really? I couldn't give a shit. Well, she was in the car too, but did better out of it than you. She was kept in overnight, but she woke up hours ago. Nothing more than a few scratches and bruised ribs.'

'And me?' Ellie half rose, blearily looking down at her body. She didn't seem to be in plaster, and although her left wrist was bandaged, and her head had some kind of wrap around it, she seemed strangely okay.

'Sprained wrist, but it's your left one, so you can still punch people and knock back a few,' Nathan forced a smile. 'Gash on the leg, so don't expect to be doing any marathons soon and you have a wicked black eye, and a nasty cut on the temple. Oh, and probable concussion, so expect to have a really shit time when you try to stand.'

'Your doctor's manner needs to improve,' Ellie tried to sit

up, and felt a spinning sensation, unpleasantly like being drunk, but without the fun parts.

'Good job I'm not a doctor then,' Nathan replied. 'Your lawyer bloke's outside. And some creepy old queen dressed like Kenneth Williams. They've been here all night. Doctors would only let me in, though.'

'And I bet you lorded that over them,' Ellie muttered.

'I've been harsh on you,' Nathan nodded. 'And we both know it's not undeserved. But the people you work with? Seem a good crowd. Didn't go home when they knew you were okay. Even Tinkerbe—even your friend, and the influencer guy.'

He rose from the chair.

'I'm glad you found people, so maybe pick one of them as your next of kin, yeah?'

'I want Millie,' Ellie responded.

'I'll send you her dog collar,' Nathan replied. 'I'm getting her a new one. To go with her new name.'

'You wouldn't dare.'

Nathan smiled, flipped Ellie the finger, and then walked out. Ellie leaned back on the pillows, sighing. It sounded like Robert, Tinker and Ramsey had been outside while she was unconscious, and that meant the world to her. But there was something nagging at her, something just said, that she hadn't commented on, hadn't—

'And the influencer guy.'

Looking at a clock on the wall, Ellie saw it wasn't even five in the morning yet; the window, although closed, had only the faint glow of streetlights behind it, and the one side lamp kept half the ward room in darkness.

The door opened, and a shadowed figure walked in.

'Ellie Reckless,' Nicky Simpson said as he sat down

beside her. 'I hear you had a spill. Did you find my money before it happened?'

'I'm still trying,' Ellie muttered, her head throbbing. *How did Nicky Simpson know she was here? Why hadn't Robert stopped him from entering?*

'How did you get in?'

'Nurses love me,' Simpson grinned. 'I do a lot for the NHS. Wonderful people.'

'Look,' Ellie tried to sit up. 'You said the painting was a forgery. What do you know about it, that we don't?'

'I know you're looking at the wrong suspect,' Simpson smiled. 'I know that because you're looking at me, and I know I didn't do it.'

'You've done a lot of other things,' Ellie hissed, and Simpson leant closer.

'Is that what this is?' he asked. 'All these favours, are they to do with me?'

'Don't flatter yourself,' Ellie pulled back, pushing herself into the pillows. At this, Simpson leant over, pulling one out from behind her, plumping it up.

'Here, let me help you,' he said, holding it now with both hands, and for a second Ellie thought he was about to smother her with it. But after a drawn out moment, he pulled her shoulder forward, placing the pillow behind her.

'I'm not an enemy you want,' he said, standing now. 'I could be a very good friend.'

'I have all the friends I need,' Ellie forced a smile, knowing it was more a grimace. 'But I'll put you on the standby list.'

'You do that,' Simpson walked to the door. 'Because I'm reckoning you'll have a few vacancies in that area opening up soon.'

And with that cryptic statement made, Nicky Simpson slipped out of the door once more, leaving Ellie alone in the ward.

She wanted to scream. She wanted to call for help. She wanted to bring her friends in.

But the fact of the matter was she was exhausted and in pain, and ten seconds after Simpson left, Ellie was unconscious again.

———

18

VISITING HOURS

It was almost ten in the morning by the time Ellie awoke once more. Her head wasn't aching as much as it had before, and, when sitting up, she noticed with a small smile of satisfaction that the dizziness seemed to have gone as well.

Looking around, she couldn't see her personal effects anywhere, and was about to hunt for a buzzer to call a nurse when one walked into the room.

'I thought I heard movement,' the nurse smiled, walking over. 'Sit back, let's take some readings.'

After having her pulse and temperature checked, Ellie sat up.

'Where's my stuff?' she croaked irritably. 'I need my phone. I have people I need to call.'

'The people are probably the ones outside,' the nurse smiled. 'I'll let them know you're awake, if you're up for visitors?'

Ellie nodded and, a moment after the nurse left, Robert, Ramsey, and Tinker entered through the door. Robert and Ramsey were both in suits, although Robert had removed his tie, and Tinker was still in the same clothes she had worn the previous day, although there was a little more blood spatter on her coat than usual, and she had a wicked-looking plaster on her temple.

'You look like shit,' Ellie smiled, her voice soft and hoarse.

'Not as much as you,' Tinker grinned. 'Glad you're up.'

'I was up earlier, but I don't know if it was a dream or not,' Ellie admitted. 'Was Nathan here?'

'Long enough to sign forms,' Robert nodded. 'He went to see you, was around maybe ten minutes?'

'And Nicky Simpson?'

Robert looked at Ramsey, who shook his head.

'I didn't see him,' he replied.

'That might have been a dream,' Robert suggested. 'We didn't see him.'

Ellie nodded at this, but there was some part of her that knew this had been as real as Nathan's visit.

'Well, we don't need to worry about that now,' Robert continued. 'Just know we'll keep looking for the painting—'

'Hold on, when did you become part of the "we" here?' Ellie asked.

'When *you* stopped being part of it,' Robert replied. 'Come on, Ellie. There's no way you can continue today, and six pm is Simpson's deadline for the debt.'

'We have to have something here, if only to save Danny from a beating, or worse,' Ramsey added.

'Since when did you care about Danny Flynn?' Ellie frowned.

'Since the body count started to rise,' Ramsey looked away, and Ellie knew something was wrong here.

'What's happened?' she asked.

Ramsey sighed.

'I screwed up,' he said. 'I thought I could kill two birds with one stone, and when we went to look for Wyatt, I—well, let's just say I might have alerted Marcus Somerville to our surveillance.'

'He's in the wind,' Robert added.

Ellie leant back against the pillows, closing her eyes. The only way she convinced Finders to allow her the leeway she had was by closing the paid cases.

'It's okay,' she said.

'It's not—' Ramsey began apologising, but before he could continue, Ellie waved a hand to stop him.

'We'll find him,' she replied. 'We just need to find the person he was selling to and follow them.'

'It could be anyone—' Tinker started, but then stopped. 'No, wait.'

Ellie nodded.

'Wyatt,' she said simply.

'He's here to buy the painting,' Ramsey frowned. 'Not a vase.'

'Maybe both,' Ellie reached for the table and from it grabbed a cup, drinking water before continuing. 'Maybe we're looking at this the wrong way.'

'You don't think it was Simpson?'

'I'm wondering,' Ellie forced herself upright. 'As much as I'm starting to think Nicky Simpson may have been right about the painting being fake. We know Christian Wyatt was looking to buy the painting before Hugo Speer did. We also know that six months ago, he stopped searching.'

'Six months ago, Sebastian LaFleur died,' Ramsey added.

'And his rent was paid for eighteen months,' Tinker nodded. 'You think he bought it then?'

'Or put a down payment on it, maybe said he'd take it

when needed,' Ellie shrugged. 'Either way, Danny has always believed the painting is real. That wasn't changed six months ago, and he believed it enough recently to try to sell it again. Until someone stole it.'

'He can't claim insurance, as it's stolen goods, and never announced,' Robert sat on the chair beside the bed. 'He wasn't playing a scam here. Danny's legitimately scared.'

'And then Wyatt turns up, in the same hotel as Marcus Somerville?' Ellie clicked her tongue against the top of her mouth, wincing as she touched a cut there. 'I don't think so. I genuinely think Wyatt's here for the vase. We need to see if the two of them have been in contact. If they have, then maybe Marcus might still try to sell to Wyatt.'

'I'll go check,' Robert said before Ramsey could reply. 'I'll take Ramsey with me.'

'So what, I'm demoted even lower?' Ramsey muttered.

'Well, as I'm technically your boss's boss, and I go to meetings with her, surely you coming along is a kind of promotion?' Robert said sarcastically, but Ramsey smiled at this, taking it as a compliment.

'Well, in that case, I'm fine with that.'

'Does someone know where my clothes are?' Ellie asked, swinging her legs over the edge of the bed. 'As much as I like you all, even Ramsey, this gown leaves nothing to the imagination behind me, and I'm not comfortable going around town in it.'

'I'll find them,' Ramsey said, backing out of the room, and Ellie couldn't work out whether it was the act of helping, or the fear of seeing Ellie's naked arse cheeks that made him run. The thought made her chuckle.

'How bad is the car?' she asked.

'Totalled,' Tinker replied. 'Police took it, and I think it's being examined by Wycombe forensics, but as far as they were concerned, this was driver error, as nothing seemed to be broken.'

Ellie sighed.

'And that's the easier answer for a quieter life,' she replied. 'What do you think?'

'I think someone hacked your car,' Tinker replied. 'It's new, has computers in it, and this is why people should drive rust buckets like mine.'

'Right then,' Ellie nodded, wincing again as her head felt like it was rolling off her shoulders. 'We should have someone check it.'

There was a pause as Ellie went to speak, but then stopped.

'You okay?' Robert asked, glancing at Tinker. 'She's not having a moment, is she?'

'I am, but not one you'd think,' Ellie looked back at him. 'There was a list of stolen jewellery. Rajesh got it from Chipping Norton nick. Do you have it?'

'On my phone somewhere,' Robert started scanning through his emails. 'Why?'

Nodding to himself, he passed it over.

'Here,' he said. 'Only five or six items. A couple of bracelets, a necklace—'

'That's what I wanted,' Ellie looked up at Tinker as she read. 'Silver and diamond swan bracelet.'

'June Hudson was wearing something similar when we knocked,' Tinker replied, realising where Ellie was going.

'I don't get the significance?' Robert was confused.

'Chantelle Flynn loses items in the theft, but there's a chance at least one item is now in June Hudson's possession,' Ellie passed the phone back. 'She was wearing it when we arrived but immediately removed it, as if worried we'd recognise the bracelet.'

'It was when she thought we were police,' Tinker nodded.

At this, Robert scowled.

'Is there a reason she'd think you were police?' he asked innocently, but Ellie could taste the salt in the question.

'She's old, confused,' she smiled, smiling wider as Ramsey returned with a pile of clothes. 'Excellent. Thank you.'

Ramsey, however, wasn't smiling.

'Have you seen the news?' he asked. 'I had a text from our resident surly teen.'

'I thought *you* were the resident surly teen?' Tinker asked, checking her phone. 'Nope, nothing for me.'

'He may have texted Ramsey because he assumed the rest of you were with me,' Ellie waved with her hand for Ramsey's phone.

'And he *didn't* think I'd be here?' Ramsey seemed both surprised and hurt by this revelation.

'Don't take this the wrong way,' Ellie was opening up the phone now. 'But you're standing in front of me, and even I don't believe you're here.'

She checked the link Casey had sent; it was a piece on the *Metro* newspaper's site, talking about the apparent suicide of prominent London artist, Natalie Myles.

'Poor cow,' Ellie muttered. 'Luckily, they're saying it was apparently suicide, so it looks like Ramsey and Casey got out—'

She stopped as she reached an old photo of Natalie on the page.

'Is this her?' she asked, turning the phone around to show Ramsey.

'Yeah, that's her,' Ramsey replied. 'Why?'

'When we were in June's house, I looked at her family photos,' Ellie looked at Tinker. 'I think you were talking with her at this point. But there was a family photo I commented on.'

'Yeah, I remember,' Tinker nodded. 'I was looking out of the window at the time, wondering if she could have seen the car from the ground floor.'

'The photo had a teenage girl in it, who June claimed was her granddaughter,' Ellie tapped the image. 'It was Natalie. A few years younger, but definitely her.'

'Good God,' Ramsey muttered, taking back his phone. 'Grandma and granddaughter were in this together?'

'It's definitely suspicious that she was wearing stolen items, and her granddaughter was burning forged paintings,' Ellie was pulling on her jeans now, ignoring the averted gazes of everyone. 'We can't speak to the daughter, but we can still talk to grandma.'

'She claimed Flynn's beige car didn't come back,' Tinker pondered this now. 'But if she's an unreliable narrator, maybe it did?'

'Champagne car.'

'Whatever.'

'I'll contact the golf club, see if we can contact any of the other drivers there,' Ellie was pulling on a bloodied jumper now, her back to the others. 'If we can confirm their driver did indeed leave the club, then we might have something.'

'If he did, and she lied? Then they're in it together,' Robert was writing this down on a small reporter's notepad. 'It still doesn't explain where the painting is though.'

'One step at a time,' Ellie smiled, but then let out a string of expletives.

'Are you okay?' Robert asked, genuine concern in his eyes. 'Are you in pain?'

'I'm a bloody fool,' Ellie snapped, leaning against the bed. 'A bloody, bloody fool.'

'Well, we all knew that,' Tinker quipped. 'But why exactly this time?'

'I've been so obsessed with chasing Nicky Simpson, I wasn't thinking of the other side of it,' Ellie shook her head. 'Monroe was right.'

'DCI Alex Monroe?'

'Well, the dream one. Last night. He told me I was following breadcrumbs, and didn't know who laid them.'

'That's not Monroe, that's your subconscious,' Tinker replied.

'Yeah, I know,' Ellie forced a wry smile. 'He said that too.'

'So come on then, what was your make believe dream mentor right about?' Robert asked.

'We were told a muscled man in a beanie, name Ricky or Nicky, hired Cornell and Molloy,' Ellie explained. 'I instantly went to Nicky Simpson, but we saw the chauffeur yesterday.'

'Muscled, pale hair, named Ricardo,' Tinker smiled. 'Yeah, it could be him. Ricky for Ricardo, rather than Nicky for Nicholas.'

'But what now? We can't arrest him,' Robert replied. 'You're not the police anymore. And to be blunt, I'm not sure passing this on actively helps you.'

'Not yet,' Ellie nodded, pulling on her bloodstained *Converse* trainers. 'We need proof first. We need confirmation that Ricardo was the guy who hired the burglars. And maybe killed them too.'

'Taking the painting and passing it to Wyatt, perhaps,'

Ramsey mused. 'Still doesn't explain the burnt forgery, or Seb dying in his freak crash—'

'Exactly,' Ellie wobbled as she turned, forcing herself not to grab at her head, allowing the pain to fade. 'Sebastian LaFleur had a freak car accident, just like ours. We need to work out if the two cars had the same error.'

'I could speak to the child, see if he could find out?'

'Get him onto those dark web pages again,' Ellie ordered, now walking gingerly to the door of the wardroom. 'See if he can find Wyatt and Somerville talking. It'll keep him out of trouble for the moment.'

She leaned against the door, forcing her head to stop spinning, covering it by looking back at the group.

'Why did he try to kill us?' she whispered.

'Because you're annoying?' Ramsey suggested lightly.

'No, I'm serious,' Ellie placed her head against the frame of the door as she considered this. 'We were working for Danny, trying to get the painting. Something happened that made us dangerous, turned us into targets. We must have picked up something. But what?'

'It was when we went to June Hudson's house,' Tinker thought about this. 'We were fine before that. And then, after we did that, someone fixed the car.'

'We spoke to Chantelle about the photo, and Wyatt,' Ellie added. 'Maybe—'

'No, she wouldn't have had the time,' Tinker shook her head. 'Danny told her to stop going on Instagram while we were there, and she picked up the phone again when you talked about the painting being a forgery.'

'She knew,' Ellie's face darkened. 'And she didn't want us learning anything more.'

'We should have another chat with Mrs Flynn,' Robert

muttered, glaring at Ellie. 'She's not allowed to try to kill my employees. Only I'm allowed to try to kill my employees.'

Straightening from the door frame, Ellie nodded.

'Robert, Ramsey, go back to the hotel and see if there's anything on Wyatt and Somerville,' she said. 'Link up with Casey, too. Go in Robert's car.'

'Why Robert's car?' Ramsey shook his head as he realised. 'No, Ellie. No.'

'I don't have a car and I need one,' she held out her hands for the keys. 'And it's old, so we won't need to worry about it being hacked.'

'It's also my pride and joy, and you've crashed twice in as many days.'

Tinker placed her hand on Ellie's arm, lowering it.

'Ellie, he's right. You're in no state to drive,' she said, looking back at Ramsey. '*I'll* drive instead.'

'Well, that's okay,' Ramsey pulled his keys out, passing them over. 'I know you love antiques, and you'll look after her.'

'Dude, it's just a Rover—' Tinker started, but stopped at Ramsey's glare. 'Yes, absolutely. Where are we going, anyway?'

'Back to have a word with June Hudson, and then the golf club,' Ellie had pulled out her phone, tapping a number on it. 'After we find wherever the remains of the Focus are.'

She held the phone to her ear.

'Big Slim,' she said as it answered. 'Ellie Reckless. 'You know you owe me that favour? I'm calling it in. You're an expert in cars, right? All that *Fast and Furious* stuff, pretty shit hot, right? Who's your best guy, in particular on the computer side of cars?'

She listened for a moment.

'Awesome,' she replied. 'I need him to check two wrecks and see if they were tampered with. That done? Then we're done.'

Disconnecting the call, Ellie looked at Robert.

'Burn a favour to gain a prize,' she smiled. 'We have around eight hours before all hell breaks loose.'

———————

19

FAST AND SPURIOUS

BIG SLIM WAS TRUE TO HIS WORD, AND BY THE TIME ELLIE FOUND her battered and buckled Ford Focus in a custody yard near Wycombe command unit, Big Slim and his expert, a small Indian man named Jeet, who had some kind of nervous tic in his neck that meant he was constantly twitching, had arrived on site.

Big Slim was also true to his name; almost seven feet tall and stick thin, he looked like a man that'd been stretched on a rack for way too long, or Mike TeeVee from *Charlie and the Chocolate Factory*, but after he was placed in the "stretching room". He was well dressed, wearing a collection of *Prada, Tom Ford* and *Gucci*, and his hair was short and brown, matching the groomed stubble on his face.

Big Slim was a record producer who'd come up through the West London gang system. Now in his late thirties, he was an old man compared to his peers, but he was still a name in the rap world, and his collection of gold and platinum discs, visible to anyone who visited his studio, showed that he was good at what he did. Good enough to buy a Lamborghini that

Weasel had stupidly stolen, which had then brought Ellie into the situation.

'Reckless,' Big Slim smiled as he nodded at Ellie and Tinker. 'Psycho.'

Tinker grinned back, taking the nickname as a compliment.

'Thanks for coming,' Ellie said, walking over to the remains of the Ford Focus and staring down at it. 'Christ, how the hell did we survive this?'

'From the looks of things, you didn't,' Big Slim pointed at Ellie's clothing, and she looked down at herself; unable to change since the previous day, her jacket was torn, her jumper spattered with blood from her still-bandaged head wound, and her jeans and trainers stained with blood, having seeped through the denim from the gash on her thighs. She looked more like an extra in a horror movie than an investigator. And Tinker, with her plasters, bruises and bloodied army coat, looked just as brutal.

'Yeah, you could say that,' Ellie shuddered.

'Anyway, you said to come, and that's how the debt thing works, innit?' Big Slim sauntered over to the back of the car, whistling as he took a photo. 'For the boys. They'll get a kick outta seeing what almost killed ya.'

Putting away the phone now, he straightened, and his full height shadowed over Ellie.

'To be honest, I thought you'd hit me up for Coachella tickets, or VIP passes for Glasto,' he admitted. 'Didn't expect this.'

'Wait, could we have had those?' Tinker looked over at Ellie. 'Is it too late to change the deal?'

Ellie smiled at this.

'Needs must, and all that,' she said. 'Someone tried to kill us, I'm sure of it.'

'Or you could be a shit driver,' Jeet muttered, his neck flinching as he spoke.

'Possibly, but this wasn't normal,' Ellie ignored the jibe. 'The problem is, I don't know how they did it.'

Jeet tried the door to the car; it was locked.

'Key?'

Ellie rummaged in her pockets, pulling out the remote for the car. Taking it, Jeet examined the remote for a couple of seconds before clicking the open button. Even though the car was written off, the driver's door could still be opened, the twisted metal creaking as he did so.

'It's a button starter, right?' he asked. 'You keep the remote on you and it senses it?'

'Yeah, I think,' Ellie replied. 'I mean, it's a car, I don't know much more than that.'

'You drove around in this every day and that's all you know?' Jeet looked horrified.

'He's very precious about cars,' Big Slim smiled.

Jeet was now rummaging around the space above the pedals, pulling off a small plastic cover, and exposing some of the car's guts.

'This hides the OBD2 port,' he explained as he pulled a satchel onto the seat, pulling out a laptop and a cable. 'Stands for *On-board diagnostics*. A trained operator, using something like *FORscan* to connect to it, can look up fault diagnostics and all that, but sometimes, it can even change your car's controls through coding.'

He plugged the cable into a socket under the dashboard, opening up a program on the laptop. Then, this done, he looked at the dashboard display, tutting.

'Don't help it's mashed,' he muttered, half to himself.

'Sorry,' Ellie replied sarcastically, glancing at Big Slim, who once more shrugged. 'I'll do better next time.'

'Your cruise control's been altered,' Jeet was running through lines of code now. 'There's a lot of custom shit here. I'm guessing you didn't do that?'

'What do you mean, custom shit?' Ellie moved closer now, staring down at the screen, and wishing she understood what the hell she was looking at.

'Someone's put in some fail-safes, and turned off others,' Jeet was scrolling through pages of code. 'It's good shit, but it's *known* shit. You can get this for sale on the black market. It wasn't recent, either, as it's an out-of-date version that did it. You can see by the coding protocols.'

Ellie looked over at Tinker to see if she understood this at all.

'Basically, someone OBD'd your car and mushed it up,' Big Slim explained. 'You use cruise control on a motorway, right? You press a button, set the speed to a number and take your foot off the pedal. Car senses when vehicles are approaching, slows you down. They leave? You speed up. New ones like this also sense the lines on the lanes, so it even steers for you. Within reason, yeah?'

'I don't use cruise control,' Ellie frowned.

'Yeah, that don't matter,' Jeet disconnected his laptop, looking up. 'It's set that the moment you hit seventy-seven miles per hour, it clicks on. And then it's fireworks.'

'How so?'

Jeet shrugged.

'The brakes are suddenly told everything's fine and you've stopped, so they don't need to work no more. And the steering wheel's told everything's clear and follows a curved road, even if there ain't one coming. And the accelerator's told you're twenty miles slower.'

'And so it speeds up,' Ellie nodded at this, understanding. 'So it's like Doc Brown's Delorean in *Back To The Future*, except when it hits eighty-eight miles per hour, or rather seventy-seven, instead of going back in time, it tries to kill me?'

'Apart from the speed, yeah,' Jeet clicked his tongue as he looked down. 'You'd have found the brake not working, the steering would have been a bitch to hold, and you would have sped up. Honestly, you're lucky you're alive.'

Ellie felt a shiver down her back at this. And, as she was about to reply, her phone buzzed; Pulling it out and glancing at the now-cracked screen, she saw a text from Casey.

Understand you need LaFleur car. DVLA registered Mazda 3 Sport Lux 2.0 Skyactiv year 2019. C

'Do you know when the code was created?' she asked, looking back up. 'Or if you can see when it was last used?'

'Only on this car,' Jeet replied. 'But if it helps, the software that made it was updated around March, so about five months back.'

Ellie nodded silently at this. *This could have been how Sebastian LaFleur died.*

'How did it get in there?' Tinker asked. 'Is it like Wi-Fi?'

'No, man, it needs to be cabled in, like I've just done,' Jeet shook his head. 'You'd only need a minute at best, but you'd need to crawl in and connect. Car don't need to be on, either. All you need to do is get through the door security. And that could be done by cloning a key through a relay attack, or even just using a locksmith's tool. Anyone used to stealing cars could do this.'

'Danny's got a history of car theft,' Tinker said to Ellie.

'Yeah, but he needs us,' Ellie replied. 'When could this have been done?'

'Any time,' Jeet was putting his items away, looking over at Big Slim before continuing. 'It clicks when you hit the speed. You drive around London? You're unlikely to go that fast.'

'I drove that fast to Danny with no problems,' Ellie surmised. 'So it can't have been Simpson. It has to be when I was there.'

Remembering the text, she looked back at Jeet.

'Hey, would this also work on a Mazda 3 Sport Lux 2.0 Skyactiv?' she asked. '2019 model?'

Jeet considered this before nodding.

'Yeah, it'd do the same, I reckon. You need me to look at it?'

Ellie shook her head.

'I know all I need to know,' she replied.

'Good, then we're done,' Big Slim motioned with his head for Jeet to leave the car park. 'We're clear, right?'

'Until you need another repo job,' Ellie nodded, offering her hand. Big Slim took it, shaking it.

'You're all right for a Fed,' he replied, walking off. 'And don't be fooled; you are one, badge or not.'

Ellie and Tinker stared down at the remains of the Ford Focus.

'It had to be Ricardo,' she growled. 'Danny and Chantelle were in the room.'

'It could have been any of them,' Tinker replied. 'We walked across the road after we arrived, remember? Danny was literally beside the car. What if Nicky Simpson said to him he'd waive the debt, or give him longer to pay it off, if he killed us?'

'That's not something I want to consider,' Ellie took one last, dejected look at the Ford Focus and started walking back to the entrance to the compound. 'Also, how did they get to LaFleur's car?'

'We know he was at parties Chantelle was at,' Tinker mused. 'Maybe it was done around then.'

'Maybe,' Ellie sighed. 'Come on, we have a long drive ahead of us.'

'Why a long one?'

Ellie smiled.

'Because I'm never going over seventy miles an hour again,' she said.

ELLIE AND TINKER ARRIVED BACK IN CHIPPING NORTON IN Ramsey's Rover shortly after noon.

Getting out, Tinker thumbed at the house opposite June Hudson's, the gates closed and unwelcoming, the driveway empty.

'Want to go say hi?' she asked, a half-smile on her face. 'Might scare them a little, especially the way we look right now.'

Ellie was almost tempted to go across the road, but shook her head.

Let's get this done first,' she said as she opened the gate that led from the street into June Hudson's front garden and started down the drive to the front door. 'We know she has a habit of watching through curtains. I'd rather she didn't run before we got to her.'

Walking up to the door, she rang the bell, looking back across the street. Only a few of the houses on it had walls and gates; the south was far more welcoming, it seemed. June's driveway was just as long as Danny's, but for some reason, it felt a little more—

There was a crash from somewhere in the house, and Ellie turned back to the door.

'Hello?' she shouted, banging on it. 'June? It's Ellie Reckless. We spoke yesterday.'

'*Side!*' Tinker shouted, running off down the left side of the house, pushing through some bushes that partially blocked the way, and slamming open a wrought-iron gate that led into the back garden. Following her, Ellie saw what had excited Tinker so; a black-clad figure had run out of the side door on the other side of the gate, and was now sprinting across the expansive garden. Starting after her friend, Ellie pulled up short after only a couple of steps; an incredible pain ran through her hamstrings as the gash in her leg screamed in protest. Leaning against the side door for a moment, forcing back the urge to throw up, Ellie regained her composure and entered the house, finding herself in the kitchen.

'June?' she called out again, limping through the room, grabbing a kitchen knife from a magnetic holder against the wall. She'd seen one intruder run from the scene; there could be others, as far as she knew.

Better to be prepared.

'June, call out if you can hear me,' Ellie continued as she walked into the hallway, looking around. 'We're here to help—'

She'd walked into the living room by now, heading

towards the conservatory at the back, when she saw the figure on the floor.

'June!' she cried out, running to it; June Hudson was on her back and sprawled out on the carpet, her eyes closed and a worrying dark red stain spreading out behind her head.

Kneeling, Ellie checked June's neck for a pulse; it was weak, but it was there.

'Come on, June, wake up,' Ellie said, now leaning down and searching for the source of the bleeding. A head wound, behind the right ear and viciously given, seemed to be the culprit. Looking around, Ellie spied what looked to be a pewter statue, only a foot in height, of the Irish hero Cú Chulainn tied to a stone. It was an iconic image of a hero at the time of his death, and now was even more grotesque because of the splotches of fresh blood and hair on the edges. It'd been brought down with a lot of force, and Ellie worried about how bad the injury truly was.

'Nat...' June mumbled, and Ellie returned her attention, leaning close.

'Yes, it's Natalie,' she said, hoping this would bring the older woman back. 'Open your eyes. Don't go to sleep.'

'I lost the bugger at the back of the garden,' Tinker, now clutching her ribs, walked into the conservatory. 'If I'd been at full fighting power, I'd—oh damn.'

'Call an ambulance,' Ellie said, waving her hand as Tinker pulled out her phone. 'Use the land line, don't give a name.'

Tinker, nodding, hastened across the room, picking up the phone and dialling 999. Ellie knew she was being paranoid, but with her team already linked to one location where a dead body was found, the last thing she wanted to do was give Kate Delgado more ammo.

June was mumbling incoherently now and reaching for her bare left wrist; Ellie saw it was red, scratched, as if something had been forcibly removed from it. The last time June had spoken to them, she'd been wearing a swan bracelet similar to one claimed stolen from the Flynn house.

What was stolen once can obviously be stolen again, she thought to herself. In fact, Ellie wondered if this was the attacker's plan—but if so, why?

'Ambulance is here in fifteen minutes,' Tinker said, replacing the handset. Ellie finished making June comfortable, placing a cloth under the head to stem the blood, and then rose.

'Then we have less than ten minutes to search the house and find what we need,' she said.

'And currently, we have no idea what that is.'

'Let's get searching,' Tinker said, walking back out into the conservatory. Wincing at the dual pain of leg and head, Ellie sighed, deciding to take the stairs to the upper floor. June looked stable and was breathing regularly now, even if her face was pale and she moaned softly every few seconds, but Ellie felt a little better about leaving her. Taking a woollen throw from the sofa, she wrapped it around June like a blanket and, with a determined eye, left the room.

They had less than six hours to solve the case, and their principal witness wasn't talking any time soon.

20

HOUSE CALLS

WITH ONLY A SHORT TIME TO SEARCH THE HOUSE FOR ANYTHING that could help them, and with the only person who could tell them where to look unconscious on the floor, Ellie and Tinker split the house into floors, with each of them scanning the rooms as quickly as they could.

While Tinker was examining the living room, doing her best not to knock anything, her latex gloves flicking through paperwork, photos, and trinkets in her side cabinet drawers, Ellie was examining the bedroom; a large double bed with two side tables, the most exciting thing Ellie found was a letter opener in the shape of Excalibur; but why it was there and not in the living room was beyond her.

Maybe June just liked swords.

There were a couple of saved cards from 'Nat', mainly birthdays, always signed to "Granny" rather than "June", and all older than five years in age, but nothing gave Ellie any more clues on where the painting could have gone, or even if June had been part of this.

She'd been given jewels taken from Chantelle's jewellery

box; that much Ellie was sure of. The bracelet was on the stolen item list, and June had been cautious of wearing it when believing Ellie was still police, taking the bracelet off mid-interview. Which was logical, if it was an item likely to be on any list, such as a stolen item one.

To have it stolen again, though, seemed unlikely. Unless Chantelle had learnt of the theft, and had demanded it back, perhaps? Could the black-clad figure have *been* Chantelle? Maybe Danny, learning of it, and looking for anything that could gain him some last-minute funds, more likely to escape than to pay off Nicky Simpson?

She'd been staring absently at the painting at the end of the bed for about thirty seconds before she realised what it was.

Turner's *Crossing The Brook.*

'*Tink!*' she yelled, walking over to it, staring closely. It was an incredible forgery, and, beside the seated woman on the distant bank of the titular brook, Ellie could make out a faint *S.L* drawn in the sand.

Running, wincing at the pain in her ribs, Tinker stumbled into the bedroom, a golf club in her hand.

'What are you doing?' Ellie asked as Tinker, realising there was no immediate danger, tossed the club to the floor.

'You called out!' Tinker replied angrily. 'You didn't say *come look at this* or *I've found something,* it was one word! In a house where a woman was attacked! Of course I'm gonna grab a weapon!'

Calming, she looked over at the painting.

'Ramsey said this was one of LaFleur's favourites,' she said as she examined the frame. 'He also said LaFleur forged this a lot. Do you think Natalie gave it to her grandmother?'

'No,' Ellie ran her latex glove along the top of the frame,

showing Tinker the gathered dust. 'They haven't talked for years, and this has been hanging here a while.'

Taking the sides of the painting's frame in her hands, she slid it sideways, showing the faded wallpaper behind.

'See—' she started, but this turned into a '*Whoa!*' as the painting came off the wall; the nail the wire had been hanging off slipping out of the hole, sending the heavy frame to the ground with a solid thump, and, now out of Ellie's grasp, falling onto its front on the bedroom carpet.

Ellie and Tinker stared down at it silently for a moment.

'What the hell is that?' Tinker eventually said.

Attached to the back was a photo, the corners secured by old masking tape. It was an old, faded one, the colours paling, the contrast almost gone, easily fifty years old. It was of a young couple, laughing at what looked like a funfair. The woman ate candy floss, wearing a brown leather jacket, while the man wore a blazer and white polo neck.

'She looks like Natalie,' Ellie said, pulling the picture carefully away from the frame. 'You can definitely see the family resemblance.'

'And that's a young Sebastian,' Tinker showed the photo that Casey had sent the previous day, of an older LaFleur, arm around Christian Wyatt. The face was older, the hair whiter and thinner, but it was unmistakably the same man.

'Bloody hell,' Ellie looked up. 'Natalie was his grand-daughter. Do you think she even knew?'

'I don't think so,' Tinker shook her head. 'And June said yesterday he kept away.'

'Not too far, it seems,' Ellie turned the photo over, finding a handwritten note. 'Look. "*My darling June, although our time has passed, I will always love you. And I will remember you every time I paint this. S.*" And then a kiss.'

'This was why he always painted it,' Tinker crouched down, pulling a small flat card from the inside of the frame. 'Hey. It's a camera SD card.'

Ellie took the SD card from Tinker, examining it.

'Not even hidden,' she muttered. 'Anyone could have found it.'

'Nobody would have looked that close at the back of a fake painting,' Tinker smiled. 'Always keep your secrets out in the open, because nobody ever looks there.'

In the distance, they could hear the faint sound of an ambulance.

'Time to get out of here,' Ellie said, pocketing the photo before placing the frame upright against the wall. 'We'll go around the block and then return, knock on the door across the street.'

'I wouldn't bother,' Tinker was watching out of the window. 'I can see from here the garage is empty, and the car is gone. They're not there. They've probably run.'

She picked up something from the windowsill; turning it around to show Ellie, she frowned.

'An SLR camera,' she said, already turning it upside down and checking the battery case. 'And no SD card. I reckon Ms Hudson was filming things she shouldn't.'

'We need to go now,' Ellie took the camera, placing it back on the sill as she half-pulled Tinker out of the door. 'We'll look at the card when we're somewhere safe.'

And, with an old forgery left alone in a bedroom, Ellie and Tinker ran down the stairs, checked quickly on the unconscious June before exiting out of the conservatory, following the route the black-clad thief had taken, albeit at a far more gentle, and painful pace.

CASEY WAS WAITING OUTSIDE THE SEA CONTAINERS HOTEL, skateboard in his hand and bag on his shoulder, when Robert and Ramsey arrived.

'I've got news,' he said with a smile. 'But it can wait, as I want to see this.'

'I'm not apologising,' Ramsey muttered.

'You'll do whatever I tell you to do,' Robert replied as he passed Casey, walking through the doors to the hotel. Now walking up to the reception, he gave his most fierce expression.

'Who's the manager here?' he asked.

The receptionist, seeing Ramsey walking up behind Robert, stepped back, calling to the side door.

'He's back,' she said, 'Security—'

'Isn't needed,' Robert replied, placing a business card on the reception desk. 'Mister Allen here was part of a sting operation, working on behalf of the Finders Corporation and your parent company. And to be honest, you came up short.'

'I'm sorry, but what is this?' an older man, obviously higher up the food chain, now arrived, picking up the card and reading it. 'I'm the duty manager here. We weren't told about anything like this happening.'

'Of course not,' Ramsey, realising what was being pulled here, leant in. 'What's the point of doing this if you're *aware?*'

'The only people in the know were Mister Allen here, Mister Somerville, myself and your CEO,' Robert added, pulling out his phone. 'If you want to call him right now, we can wait. I have his number here somewhere.'

The duty manager paused at this, and Ramsey knew what was going through his head. Marcus Somerville had claimed it had been a friend playing a prank and had then disappeared. This wasn't a normal situation, and this suit-wearing, officious man might be telling the truth.

'No, that's fine for the moment,' the duty manager replied carefully. 'Could you just explain what happened for us?'

'Absolutely,' Robert smiled. 'We were asked to check your hotel security.'

'By who?'

'Above your pay grade, I'm afraid,' Robert continued, ignoring the interruption. 'My men took two roles; one of hunter, and one of hunted. The latter, Marcus Somerville, took a room here for four days, in the process leaving a large, fake Ming vase on display. This was to test the honesty of your cleaning staff. You'll be happy to know they passed this.'

'Oh, good,' the duty manager said, his expression revealing he still wasn't sure where this was going.

'And, while he did this, Mister Allen here took up residence in your lobby, spending three whole days over...' Robert looked inquisitively at Ramsey, who pointed at a comfy-looking chair by the far wall.

'In that chair, reading the *Racing Post*,' he replied, turning back to the duty manager, poking him with his finger. 'And not once during those days did any security guard, or even any staff, come over to me and ask about my business! I could have been a serial killing stalker for all you knew!'

'I—that isn't usually our policy,' the duty manager stuttered. 'Are you sure it was three days?'

'Check your security cameras,' Robert suggested. 'Anyway, on day four, we decided we needed to take this a little further. Your owners provided us with a room card to gain access to the elevators—'

'Well, of course,' the duty manager, seeing a potential win

here, puffed his chest out. 'We're incredibly cautious of who we give our keys to.'

'Oh, yes,' Ramsey replied, pulling out several room keys and placing them onto the reception counter. 'Here's a few others I forgot to give back.'

The duty manager stared down at the keys in horror.

'How—'

'Oh, you know, left here and there,' Ramsey replied, forgetting to mention how one had been stolen from a leaving guest to gain entry to the elevators, another was picked up from Marcus Somerville's room and the last two were the ones the security guards gave him. 'You have them lying around all over the place.'

'Not good,' Robert added. 'My man here went to Mister Somerville's room, gained entry—'

'How?' the duty manager, now embarrassed, snapped.

'It'll be in the report,' Robert waved a hand. 'He gained access, called reception, asked for replacement keys to be sent up, giving him an actual entrance to a room not his—'

'He said he was Mister Somerville, and he was in the room,' the duty manager was seeing his position crumbling.

'Mister Somerville is a man in his late twenties,' Robert replied coldly. 'He's been quite visible over the week. Mister Ramsey is a man in his seventies—'

'Sixties.'

'—who has been sitting in your lobby, in clear view for days before making his move.'

Quietly, the duty manager nodded.

'Anyway, we took the vase and placed it in your safe, to show how we could have removed it from your premises,' Robert finished. 'The "police" who arrived were actors, and after Marcus picked the vase back up, he left.

And at no point did you challenge his story of a simple prank.'

'So, what now?' the receptionist, noting the now silent duty manager, asked.

'Now, I pay the outstanding room charges for Mister Somerville, you give us a key card for the room and we pack his items,' Robert pulled out a platinum credit card with FINDERS CORPORATION on it. 'He's already on another job, at the Hilton in Kensington.'

The receptionist took the card, glancing at the duty manager, who nodded. Swiping it, she looked back.

'Are you paying for the extras too?'

'No,' Robert replied. 'Just the room rates. The extras will be taken from his expenses.'

'We have a dinner outstanding,' she replied. 'Two nights ago. A meal for two, running at over a hundred—'

'Ah, no, that's on the wrong room,' Ramsey interrupted, playing a hunch. 'That should have been put on Christian Wyatt's tab. It was *that* dinner, right?'

The receptionist checked the records and nodded.

'Yes, the reservation was in Mister Wyatt's name, but Mister Somerville charged the bill to his room.'

'Has Christian left yet?' Robert asked.

'I don't think so,' the receptionist clicked again. 'No. He checks out tomorrow, but I saw him leave this morning for the day.'

'Hold the charge then, and we'll pay the bill tomorrow,' Robert took the platinum card back. 'We'll check with Mister Wyatt as to whether or not he should pay that. We'll obviously add the extra day to the amount owing.'

'Do you still need to go to the room?' the duty manager, now all smiles, asked.

'No, I think we can take our time with that,' Robert replied, still keeping his cold exterior. 'I'll send someone later, after I've sent your superiors the report.'

'Are you sure we can't discuss this?' The duty manager was sweating now. 'I get how mistakes have been made, but people could lose their jobs on this.'

'I'll do what I can,' Robert promised, placing his wallet back in his jacket. 'Until tomorrow.'

Turning and leaving the desk, Robert was striding through the lobby as Casey and Ramsey struggled to keep up with him.

'That was amazing,' Casey said, genuinely impressed. 'I didn't know you were a con artist too!'

'What I am is about to be violently sick,' Robert pushed his way through the main doors now, breathing in the outside air. 'That was terrifying. How do you do that all the time?'

'Practice and innate talent,' Ramsey said as he finally emerged. 'So now what?'

'We know Marcus Somerville met with Christian Wyatt, likely to sell him the vase,' Robert considered. 'If Marcus is hiding, and we can't find him, we'll need to get hold of Wyatt instead, and come at this from the other side.'

He looked at his watch.

'But, with five hours to go before all hell breaks loose, let's turn our attentions back to that, yes? Because I need to get to the office, and hunt some kind of new lead up.'

'Oh, about that,' Casey smiled. 'Remember I said I had news?'

'I remember you saying it wasn't important,' Ramsey replied.

'I said it could wait. Different context,' Casey smiled. 'And it has waited. Now it's time to tell you.'

'Tell us what?' Robert opened the door to his car, and as Ramsey slid into the passenger seat, Casey clambered into the back.

'So, did Ellie explain how we got out of Simpson's?' he asked.

'You hacked something,' Ramsey looked back at the kid. 'Infuriated the fellow immensely, apparently.'

'Yeah, but it's the hacking that's important,' Casey explained. 'When I hacked the system, I dropped a worm.'

'That sounds disgusting,' Ramsey shuddered.

'A virtual worm, a section of coding,' Casey grinned. 'I knew they'd change the password the moment we left, and I'd be locked out, so I placed a backdoor in, so I could get back through.'

He looked apologetically at Robert.

'I had to open a corporate account with the health club,' he admitted. 'I did it when we got back.'

'You hacked our system too?' Robert was incredulous.

'Yeah, but to be honest, you left me in a room with an ethernet connection for two hours earlier the same day,' Casey shrugged. 'I was bored.'

'Go on,' Robert sighed. 'Before I regret bringing you on board even more.'

'Don't worry, it's a seven-day trial,' Casey grinned. 'You can cancel it for free. But once Finders had a corporate membership, you gained access to the membership portal, and that's where I'd thrown the worm.'

'And what did you find?' Robert started the car now, as Ramsey, his phone vibrating, checked his messages.

'Two things, but I'm still searching,' Casey pulled out a tablet now, tapping on it. 'First off, Chantelle Flynn used to be a member of the club a couple of years back.'

'Makes sense,' Ramsey replied. 'It's an influencer club. She was a reality TV star.'

'True, but she had a personal trainer there,' Casey tapped the screen again. 'Richard Vieceli.'

Ramsey looked down at the image.

'Attractive, muscled, so what?'

'So, I popped out for some air while Danny and Chantelle were chatting in the boardroom,' Casey explained. 'He was by their car. Because, for the last year, Richard, known as "Ricardo", has been the Flynn's chauffeur and mechanic.'

'Ricardo worked for Nicky Simpson as a trainer?'

'No, and that's the other thing,' Casey was tapping through the system. 'He was Chantelle's personal trainer, but he wasn't on the books. He was a member in his own right, but his own profile says he used to work in a garage in Battersea. I sent an email to them, claiming to be a new garage asking for a reference for him, and learnt he used to focus on diagnostics and custom firmware for cars while there. I then messaged an old friend of his on social media, asking if Ricardo was still working *off* the books, altering firmware for stolen cars, as I had a job for him. It was a hunch, but it panned out, as the friend came back saying Ricardo hadn't done that since he had a caution when he was sixteen, nine years ago, and his mum had gone ballistic on him.'

'Who did he do it for back then?' Ramsey closed his eyes, sighing softly to himself. He already knew the answer.

'Max Simpson,' Casey replied. 'You see, Richard's father, Andrew Vieceli, was Max Simpson's driver, until Max retired. And ol' Ricky was the childhood chum of Nicky Simpson.'

Ramsey whistled through his teeth.

'Remind me to *never* annoy you,' he said.

'We need to have a chat with Ricardo then,' Robert replied, but Ramsey shook his head, looking at his phone.

'I've had a message from Elisa and Tinkerbelle,' he interrupted. 'Apparently June Hudson was attacked and left for dead, and Ricardo, Danny, and Chantelle are in the wind.'

'Tell me you have more,' Robert's voice was tight with anger.

'In a few hours, I might have some bank accounts?' Casey suggested.

'We don't have a few hours,' Robert took a left, pulling onto Battersea Bridge, and the City of London. 'I'll take whatever you can get right now.'

21

ACCOUNT DEPOSITS

IT TOOK ANOTHER TWO HOURS BEFORE ELLIE AND TINKER arrived at Caesar's Palace; It was now just past four in the afternoon, and in the booth waiting for them were Casey and Ramsey, the former looking smug, the latter looking concerned.

'Is she okay?' Ramsey asked.

'June?' Tinker frowned. 'We're not sure. We bailed before the ambulance got there, wandered around for a bit and then, after the ambulance left, we walked back to the car and drove off—'

'Not the woman, my car!' Ramsey exclaimed. 'She's a classic!'

'Well, I'm not too sure "classic" is the term we should be using here,' Ellie motioned for Casey to scoot over as she slid into the booth, waving to Sandra for a menu. 'But she's fine. Parked in the basement, not a scratch on her.'

Sandra walked over, menus in hand, but stopped as she saw Tinker, with her bruises and plasters, and Ellie, bandage still around her head, and bloodstained jacket.

'Long night,' Ellie explained as she took the menus from the stunned waitress who, after a moment longer, shook her head and walked away.

'You could have gone home to change,' Ramsey muttered.

'I'll do that when we pass six this evening,' Ellie shrugged, examining the menu. 'After that, it doesn't matter anymore.'

'It does if Danny runs,' Tinker added. 'Because then he'll be hunted, he'll be in danger.'

'I have a feeling Danny's already up to his neck in danger,' Ellie waved for Sandra once more. 'I'm starving. I don't think I've eaten today.'

'And technically last night, either,' Tinker nodded in agreement. 'Your body's probably screaming out for sustenance.'

'Well, it's getting a cheeseburger and dealing with it,' Ellie tapped at an image on the menu, as Sandra wrote it down. 'And a Fanta, please. Quick as you can.'

'No tea?' Ramsey looked horrified at this obvious faux pas. 'You really did suffer a head injury.'

With Tinker ordering an all-day breakfast, and with the other two in the booth already eaten, Ellie looked back at the group.

'Robert texted me what you found,' she said to Casey. 'That's bloody good work.'

'Kid's found more,' Ramsey replied, sipping his tea. 'But we can get to that. What's this about a photo and a frame?'

'Yes,' Ellie reached into her bloodied jacket, pulling out the old photo and the SD card, passing the latter to Casey. 'Can you see what's on that?'

As Casey pulled out a dongle for his tablet, clicking it in and inserting the card, Ramsey stared in wonder at the image in his hand.

'All these years I knew him, he never once mentioned it,' he whispered. 'I actually thought he was gay, you know.'

'In fairness, we've thought the same about you,' Tinker replied. 'Nothing against that, by the way. "You be you", as they say.'

'I might be gay,' Ramsey gave an impish smile. 'Or maybe I'm just choosy. You'll never know.'

'It's a video,' Casey said. 'Well, it's like half a dozen photos and then two videos. They're of flowers in a garden, a bird in a tree; I think she didn't format the drive first.'

'Can you read them?'

'Of course,' Casey smiled. 'Here.'

He turned the tablet around to show the group. On it, a video was playing; a camera placed at the window of June Hudson's house. In the image, they could see the streetlamp-lit road, the walls of the opposite house imposing, the night quiet. However, on the bottom right, a red car could be seen parked up.

'It's been there for half an hour,' June's voice was heard. 'I think they're looking to break in. Either that or they're looking at breaking in here. I really should get some cameras.'

'God, she really was a curtain twitcher,' Tinker muttered as, on the screen, a champagne coloured Bentley pulled up beside the gates.

'Oh, looks like they're home early,' June said through the speakers. 'That'll piss the thieves off.'

'She lied,' Tinker noted. 'There's no way she mistook that for a black car.'

'They lied,' Ellie added. 'When they said Ricardo hadn't left the golf club.'

On the screen the gates opened, and the champagne

Bentley drove into the driveway. However, rather than closing behind, the gates stayed open as the red car now followed, driving in behind it.

There was a little back and forth, as the first car repositioned itself to leave, and Ricardo could be seen to leave the driver's side, walk to the edge of the garage for a moment, and then return, getting into the car, waiting inside it without a word to the red one facing him.

'So Ricardo was involved,' Ellie said as, on the screen, two men exited the red car and walked around the side of the house. Nothing happened for a long moment before June's voice spoke again.

'They might be workers,' she muttered. 'They were let in, but they're sketchy as hell. If they're not out in ten minutes, I'm calling the police.'

The group watched the video some more, and were rewarded by the front door to Danny's house opening, and the two men walking out, holding something large and flat, like a television, or more likely a valuable painting.

'Their driver is stealing their stuff!' June exclaimed on the audio. 'When the police find out—damn!'

There was a knock of the camera here, and it fell to the floor, angled now at the bedroom as June crouched down.

'I think they saw me,' she whispered. 'I think I'll keep this video safe, in case I have to show it to someone.'

She turned the camera to the window now - both the champagne Bentley and the red car were leaving, before the video stopped.

'So now we know,' Ellie leant back. 'June Hudson saw the crime and lied to the police later on.'

'A lie that might have been organised by Chantelle, judging by the bracelet June had,' Tinker added. Casey opened the second video; it was the same scene, a good view of the house, from June's window. This time, there was no commentary to go along with it.

'The video's six hours long,' Casey said, checking the file size. 'It pretty much ate up the rest of the card space.'

'She must have left it filming. Scroll through it, see if you find anything,' Ellie suggested. At this, Casey started scrolling through the video.

'Police are quick to turn up, they're out the front—' he stopped. '—damn. It's corrupted.'

'How come?'

'Probably because it ran out of data,' Casey replied. 'I can fix it, but it'll take some time. Six hours is a long video to check for corrupted data.'

'Do what you can,' Ellie nodded.

'It sounds to me like Ricardo and Chantelle are working together here,' Tinker spoke now.

'Yeah, she knew,' Ellie nodded her head, wincing a little. 'She wore her most personal, precious items the night of the burglary. She knew her jewels were being taken, and she wanted to make sure that she didn't lose the relevant pieces.'

'This is getting way too complicated,' Ramsey replied. 'We have Danny's wife and driver stealing a painting that's claimed to be a forgery, six months after the man who would have painted it died, to stop a man owed a debt from receiving payment, even though losing everything Danny has would actively hurt her.'

'How did they kill the thieves?' Tinker asked. 'It's a two-hour drive to London from Chipping Norton. That's four hours, round trip.'

'Danny took a pill,' Ellie mused. 'Chantelle said he was

out all night, while she only got a couple of hours. Maybe he was asleep while she did it.'

'Still a long bloody journey,' Ramsey scratched at his moustache.

'We're still missing something,' Ellie rested her head against the back of the booth, trying to will the approaching headache away. 'Why kill Natalie? How was she involved?'

'Blue sky thinking,' Tinker said now, smiling as Sandra brought over two plates of food. 'Danny owes money. Decides to sell the painting. Maybe Chantelle doesn't realise it's worth so much. She wants to run away with Ricardo, decides to forge it, sell the real one to Christian Wyatt. She brings in LaFleur, but he says no. Wanting to make sure he doesn't tell anyone, Ricardo fixes his car to kill him.'

'Still doesn't explain the Nicky connection,' Ellie nodded. 'Ricardo worked for him, was aimed at Chantelle and then "leaves" him, and works for her.'

'Nicky wants Danny's contacts,' Ramsey pondered the scene. 'He knows Danny can't pay the debt, so calls it in. Danny reveals he has this painting; Vermeer's *The Concert*. He wants to sell it for a bargain five million.'

'Five million's a bargain?' Tinker asked.

'In 2015, it was valued at a quarter of a billion dollars,' Ramsey reminded her. 'That's two hundred and fifty million—'

'I know what a quarter of a billion is,' Tinker snapped back. 'So why not ask for more?'

'Because it's stolen,' Ellie paused from eating her cheese-burger, her mouth still half-full. 'He could go to a black market auction, maybe gain a bit more for it, but Nicky wants the money now. It's a fire sale.'

'But Nicky doesn't want the money,' Ramsey continued.

'He'll make more millions once he gets into the US through Boston. He needs to make sure the painting isn't sold. So, he gets Richard, or Ricardo as he's known, to honey trap Chantelle. Probably wanted her to steal the money and run with it, so Danny loses everything. Once done, Ricardo would screw over Chantelle, and Nicky would get that as well.'

'But it all depends on Christian Wyatt buying the painting,' Ellie continued now. 'He's in town, the painting is stolen —that can't be a coincidence.'

'And Marcus Somerville?'

'We don't yet know if Wyatt's here for that. It could just be an extra,' Ramsey replied, looking at the plate of half-eaten burger in front of Ellie. 'Look at it like this, Elisa. You ordered a burger, but you got French fries and a pickle. You didn't ask for them, you wanted the burger, but that won't stop you from eating them. Wyatt is exactly the same.'

'That's what I love about you,' Tinker grinned. 'You can compare the sale of hundreds of thousands of dollars' worth of antiquities to a burger and chips.'

Ramsey smiled and clapped his hands twice.

'I believe in fairies,' he said.

'So where's the painting?' Casey was tapping on his tablet. 'Maybe we should ask Christian Wyatt that.'

There was movement at the door to the diner, and Robert walked through, quickly making his way over to the booth.

'Go home, have a shower, change your clothes and be back as soon as you can,' he said. 'We just had a call from Christian Wyatt.'

'Wyatt called?' Ellie frowned. 'Why?'

'I left my business card at the hotel,' Robert replied. 'He returned, heard we'd come by and knew we were talking shite about the "sting" we were doing, as he knows the vase is real. But it's shaken him, he's probably heard our names in relation to the painting and he's coming to the office to chat.'

'We've less than two hours before Nicky Simpson calls his debt in, so this might be our last chance to find the location of the painting,' Tinker shifted out of the booth so Ellie could leave. 'Go. I'll cover the food.'

Scooting across, Ellie nodded.

'Keep looking for anything that can help us,' she said as she snaffled a handful of french fries from her plate. 'And find out if Danny's doing any other last-minute fire sales to raise the money, or whether he's running.'

'He mentioned a yacht,' Tinker remembered. 'Chantelle has a friend. Maybe he's heading to the coast?'

'Maybe it's time to call the police,' Robert suggested. 'As much as I don't want to say it, we can't do anything more, and we sure as hell can't arrest them, no matter what your instincts cry out.'

Ellie sighed, nodding.

'I'll call Whitehouse,' she said. 'But not until we speak to Wyatt.'

Smiling, she looked over at Ramsey.

'Can I borrow your car?' she asked. However, before Ramsey could reply, Tinker tossed her Land Rover Defender keys across.

'It's downstairs,' she replied. 'Don't break it.'

Holding the keys up triumphantly, Ellie turned and left the diner. A moment later, nodding to the others, Robert followed her.

Stealing some of Ellie's French fries, Casey looked up from the tablet.

'Um, I might have something else,' he said. 'Chantelle has

no money, right? And if Danny was to be arrested, she'd get nothing?'

'Prenup,' Tinker nodded. 'Why?'

'I'm still going through the data I stole from Simpson's health clubs,' Casey explained. 'People direct debit their fees on, and I realised I could reverse a transaction to Chantelle's account, the one she used when she was a member, and gave the details to a friend in Russian tech support.'

'I have no idea what you're talking about,' Ramsey muttered. 'What, may I ask, is a Russian tech support?'

'Russian hackers are super organised,' Casey explained. 'So much so that the sledgehammer apps they have to break through encryptions come with a tech support advisor. One owed me after I modded his *Fortnite* avatar, so I got him to use the app on her current account.'

'Again, remind me never to mock you,' Ramsey replied.

'Too late, old man,' Casey grinned. 'Anyway, he just sent me a snapshot of her current account worth, and I'm curious —how does an apparently broke woman have just under *five million pounds* in her account?'

ELLIE WAS IN THE CAR PARK, LIMPING TO TINKER'S CAR, WHEN Ramsey caught up with her.

'Following me now?' she asked with a smile. 'Should I be flattered by your concern or should I be a little worried?'

'Look, you don't have to go all the way back home,' Ramsey replied as he moved towards his own car. 'I have clothes in the boot of my car you can use, and last time I checked, there's a shower up in the Finders executive toilets.'

'You check showers much, do you?'

'Oh behave, Elisa,' walking over to his Rover, Ramsey opened the trunk, pulling out an overnight bag, 'I'm trying to help you.'

'Why do you have women's clothes ready to go?' Ellie frowned.

'They're my mother's,' Ramsey replied. 'I meant to drop them off to her at the home, but haven't had a chance to. They're about your size; a couple of skirts, a pair of trousers, a jumper or two, I'm sure you can find something wearable in them.'

'Your mum's almost ninety, right?' Ellie took the bag cautiously. 'I think they might be a little out of date.'

'Ellie, these are clothes she's kept from the seventies, eighties and nineties,' Ramsey replied icily. 'Not only are they in fashion again, they're actual vintage, barely used. You should thank me for changing up your style.'

'Thank you,' Ellie said as she rummaged through the bag, nodding. 'Yeah, they look my size. And I can definitely put something together here.'

She looked up from the bag.

'So, why don't you tell me why you really came down here?' she asked.

Ramsey rubbed at the back of his neck, looking away.

'I may have messed things up rather spectacularly,' he said.

'I know that,' Ellie fired back. 'Robert told me—'

'I don't mean about Somerville,' Ramsey interrupted, holding a hand up. 'I—I've been lying to you.'

Ellie paused, and then nodded.

'I know,' she said. 'I'd be a shit investigator if I didn't know about your deal with Nicky Simpson.'

'You *knew?*' Ramsey seemed appalled at this. 'Does everyone know?'

'Just me and Robert,' Ellie replied. 'And possibly Casey, as he said to not trust you. And Tinker probably suspects because she's not stupid. So, yeah, let's go with *everyone knows*.'

She placed the bag over her shoulder, wincing a little as she did so.

'I heard what you needed to do for your mum,' she said. 'I also trust you, believe it or not. I know you wouldn't deliberately screw me over, or compromise us.'

'I haven't,' Ramsey replied. 'He wants to know about the favours, but I couldn't answer him, because I didn't know.'

'And that's by design,' Ellie placed a hand on Ramsey's shoulder. 'Plausible deniability. It's not that I don't trust you, it's the same as putting a bottle in front of an alcoholic. I don't want you to be in a situation where you have to lie.'

'You think I can't lie?'

'I think Nicky Simpson can tell,' Ellie smiled. 'And I wanted you to at least get your feet under his stupid, glass-topped table before we let you into what's going on.'

'You're okay with this?' Ramsey was confused now. As a response, Ellie laughed.

'Of course I am,' she said, turning back to the car park entrance now. 'You're going to be my man inside.'

'But everyone knows, according to you!'

'No,' Ellie winked. 'Everyone *suspects*. Far different thing.'

With that, Ellie left the car park, heading towards the elevators that would take her to the executive levels and the showers.

Ramsey stood alone, fuming.

He'd been used, he'd been lied to, and he'd risked his life

for someone who wanted him to be in hock to Nicky Simpson.

But, at the same time, it impressed him. Ellie trusted him enough to know he'd do his best for her.

'Well played, Reckless, well played,' he muttered as he walked back to the diner.

22

BILLIONAIRE BUYS CLUB

ELLIE NOT ONLY FOUND A COLLECTION OF CLOTHES FROM THE bag that weren't too badly out of style, but also found they fit her pretty well; Ramsey Allen definitely had an eye for sizing. And, after a hot shower in the Finders executive bathroom, one where she could check her wounds, she removed the bandage around her head, wincing as she touched the seven stitches in her forehead, deciding to keep the wound open though, rather than covering it again. Letting the air get to it was a better plan right now, and to be honest, it was close enough to the hair line not to garner too much attention.

She laughed at this thought; with the stitches, the black eye and the bruises, even makeup wouldn't hide this. Instead of even trying, Ellie leant into the situation more, placing a minimum of makeup over, before heading down to the boardroom.

Casey was waiting for her; she'd texted him to attend the meeting as well, as he was the one who'd found the dark web conversations from Wyatt and Speer, and there was a chance he might pick up something she missed. As he saw her emerge from the elevators, his eyes widened a little.

'That bad?' she asked, forcing a smile, even though it hurt her temples.

'Well, there's a bit of Frankenstein's monster here, but I—' Casey stopped himself, searching for words. 'The bandage hid it. I didn't realise how bad it was.'

Ellie nodded. Casey had been the only one not at the hospital; it was natural for him to be surprised.

'It's not as bad as it looks,' she lied in reassurance. 'I'm more worried about the clothing.'

'Did you raid an *Oxfam?*'

'Ramsey's mum.'

'Well, she's got taste,' Casey grinned. 'You look okay.'

Taking this as a compliment, Ellie nodded for Casey to follow her, and walked into the same boardroom where, two days earlier, she'd sat down with Danny Flynn and his wife.

Now, there was a single man in there; Christian Wyatt. He was wearing a leather jacket over a T-shirt, dark blue jeans just visible before the table blocked his view. He was relaxed, and even smiled as he recognised Casey.

'Boy from the hotel,' he nodded. 'So you're part of this, too. Makes me wonder how much of this is about a vase.'

Ellie sat down on a chair, Casey moving to another one a couple of chairs down. As they did this, Robert walked in. He gave a slight double take at Ellie's clothes and then sat on the other side of Wyatt.

'Now, Mister Wyatt has come here of his own volition,' he stated carefully. 'He's not a suspect, nor are you a police officer.'

'Anymore,' Wyatt added in a southern drawl, smiling at Ellie. 'Oh, I know all about you, Miss Reckless.'

Ellie forced herself to smile back. She knew this was a power move on his part.

'It makes sense that a man as rich as yourself has a couple of private investigators on retainer,' she replied. 'I'd expect nothing less.'

'I have a couple of *firms*,' Wyatt relaxed in the chair. 'I know about you, why you were arrested, I even know about the affair with Bryan Noyce.'

Ellie didn't look, but she could almost feel Casey freeze at this line. Glaring at Wyatt, she went to reply, but he grinned wider, completely unconcerned as he made a mock shocked expression, glancing at Casey.

'Oh, wait, you're the son,' he breezed. 'Probably should have given you a warning on that one.'

'I hope you're not here to talk about the past,' Ellie snapped, bringing his attention back to her. 'Because that's not what I wanted to talk to you about.'

'No, you want to talk about a vase,' Wyatt almost yawned. 'And remember, I came here, not the other way around.'

Ellie smiled darkly, resting her elbows on the table, steepling her fingers together as she leant closer.

'Actually, I wanted to talk about three dead bodies and a stolen painting you own,' she said.

Christian Wyatt stopped smiling.

'Dead bodies?'

'Oh, yes,' Ellie replied. 'Actually, we should add Sebastian LaFleur to that list. And the attempted murder of myself and my colleague, Tinker Jones.'

As if finally seeing the bruises and scars on Ellie's face, Wyatt looked over at Robert.

'Do I need my lawyer here?' he asked.

Robert shrugged.

'As I said, we're not police and we're just having a chat,' he said. 'But at the same time, there's no client solicitor privilege here, and we do occasionally work with the authorities.'

'But not in this case,' Ellie added. 'I think you're okay for the moment. How do you know Sebastian LaFleur?'

'I don't.'

'Oh, yeah, you told us that,' Ellie didn't want to, but she glanced over at Casey. 'What did he say?'

'That he didn't know the name,' Casey's tone was robotic, emotionless, staring at his tablet as he typed on a bluetooth keyboard.

Ellie pulled out her phone, bringing up the image of Wyatt and LaFleur Casey had sent her.

'Let's try that again,' she said, showing Wyatt the photo. 'Sebastian LaFleur.'

'Okay, I know him,' Wyatt sighed. 'I have some of his work.'

'Forgeries?'

'Bit of both,' Wyatt made a weak smile at this. 'A couple of years back, I bought a Banksy at auction. Learned later it was a forgery, by LaFleur. This started me down a rabbit hole, and I followed his work with interest. Met him in person a year ago—'

'To get revenge?'

Wyatt laughed at this.

'*Caveat emptor,*' he stated. 'Let the buyer beware. It was my fault, I didn't check thoroughly. I learned about his likes and dislikes, saw he loved doing Turner forgeries. I asked him for an original.'

'An original Turner?'

'Kinda,' Wyatt replied. 'I said I'd pay him six figures if he created me a completely original painting, in Turner's style, that could only be from the man himself. Not to claim I'd found a new one, but to see if he could do it. And he did. I have it hanging in my Dallas penthouse.'

'How did you meet Chantelle Flynn?'

'Have I met—'

'Please,' Ellie sighed. 'Give me some respect here, yeah? If I'm asking something like this, take it as read I know.'

'Also, you gave her five million pounds,' Casey said, looking up. 'I mean, it was through five companies, but it came from you.'

'Okay, how much to hire the kid?' Wyatt asked, looking back. 'No deal? Okay, sure. I know Chantelle Flynn. We met at a party. But I'm not saying anything.'

'Then let me say it,' Ellie smiled. 'And just tell me if I'm wrong, okay? You've been looking for a particular painting, Vermeer's *The Concert,* for a while. Both you and Hugo Speer have chased around the world for it, since the damn thing was stolen in the nineties.'

'Guilty,' Wyatt waved a hand.

'Now, you've got investigators working for you, and I'm guessing you've known that Essex gangster and thief Arthur Flynn was likely involved.'

'Never proven, but suspected.'

'So, hoping he had the painting, over the years you've made offers, but never had a reply or refusal. Maybe you even wondered if it existed in the Flynn family.'

'You're fishing.'

'Not really,' Ellie moved off the table now, leaning back, relaxing into this. 'You would have tried to steal it a lot earlier if you believed it was actually there.'

Wyatt didn't reply; instead, he bobbed his head slightly.

'You still hunt for details on the painting, unsure where it is, but thinking the Flynns might have it. During this time, you meet Sebastian LaFleur, work with him, and get close to him.'

Ellie showed the image on the phone again.

'Close enough to be like this with him,' she said. 'When was this party?'

'New Year,' Wyatt replied. 'So about eight months back?'

'Do you remember whose party?'

'Some influencer,' Wyatt shrugged. 'Gave me a tip that the Vermeer owner would be there.'

Ellie nodded. Chantelle had a previous life as a reality star; there was every chance she'd know people still in the industry.

'Now, at this party, you also meet Danny and Chantelle Flynn,' Ellie tapped the image, pointing at Chantelle, behind the two men. 'Or maybe it's just Chantelle. Either way, you mention a painting you've been after. Maybe even show an image of it. And, to your delight, Chantelle tells you she not only knows the painting, but it's hanging up in her living room.'

Ellie's temple was aching now; looking at her hand, she saw it trembling. Reaching to the middle of the boardroom table, she took a pitcher of water and a glass, filling it before returning to her seat. Taking a moment to drink a couple of mouthfuls, she willed herself to relax.

'Sorry, dry throat,' she placed the now empty glass down. 'Now here's the part I'm not completely sure about. At some point, you make a deal with Chantelle for the painting; she's happy to sell it, as she gets nothing from her prenup and wants to leave Danny. She fakes a theft, sells it to you, you give her the money—'

'I'm going to stop you there,' Wyatt raised a hand. 'It's

obvious you're not a hundred percent, fitness wise, but I need to point out you're way off the mark. You see, I bought that painting, and I bought it from Chantelle Flynn. But I bought it for five-point-two million, over six months ago, not now.'

Ellie stopped, staring at Wyatt as her head spun a little. Looking at Casey, she saw him look up, nodding.

'The money went into the account in early January,' he said. 'Sebastian died in March.'

'Sorry,' Ellie rose shakily. 'I'm not—that is, I need a moment.'

She half staggered out of the room, waving off Robert's half-rise of concern, stumbling into the women's bathroom, and collapsing in a cubicle, throwing up parts of a half-digested cheeseburger into the bowl.

How did you get it so wrong, the voice in her head cried out. *You thought you had it—*

No, she replied to the voice, more determined. *I had it. And now this makes sense.*

Standing up, walking to the sink, washing out and wiping her mouth with a paper napkin, Ellie stared at herself in the mirror. She really was a state, right now; but, with just over an hour to go before the deadline ran out, she finally had all the pieces she'd needed.

She now knew the truth about the painting.

Taking a deep breath, she straightened, leaving the bathroom and walking back into the boardroom.

'I'd offer to do this later,' Wyatt said, concern clear in his voice, 'but I leave today.'

'I don't have any flights booked for you,' Casey looked up, confused.

'I'm going to Cannes,' Wyatt replied. 'I have a boat at St Katherine's Docks.'

'No, I'm fine,' Ellie said, sitting in the chair once more. 'To be honest, you've explained everything and answered a question I had.'

'Glad to help,' Wyatt shifted in his seat. 'Can I ask how?'

'The timing,' Ellie continued. 'If Chantelle gave you the painting six months ago, that means she's had a painting on the wall for six months that's a forgery, and that fits everything we've heard. I'm guessing she offers to sell it back in January, but explains she can't; Danny would notice. That's fine though, as you know this awesome forger who paints a copy. But to make it identical, he'll need to look at it, so he visits the house when Danny's away.'

'I couldn't possibly confirm or deny that,' Wyatt smiled.

'But here's where things get complicated, and problems kick in,' Ellie was on a role now. 'Two, in fact. First, after they swapped the paintings, Chantelle now worries that LaFleur will tell her husband what he did. He needs to disappear.'

'She was lucky, then,' Wyatt replied. 'His death helped her.'

'You knew about the death?'

'I was at the funeral.'

'Then you were at the funeral for his murder,' Ellie continued, waiting for Wyatt to realise. 'Ricardo, her driver hacked his car in the same way he hacked mine yesterday. However, Sebastian wasn't as lucky, and crashed into a transport lorry at speed.'

'His death *wasn't* accidental?' Wyatt leant forward now, anger rising.

'I'm sorry,' Ellie replied. 'But no. It looks like he was a loose end Chantelle needed to remove.'

Wyatt sat back, his mouth half open in disbelief.

'And with LaFleur gone, everything was fine,' Ellie continued. 'Chantelle waited for a suitable moment to leave. She was in love with Ricardo, you see, but didn't realise a rival gangster placed him in the house, looking for a way to gain Danny's Boston contacts instead of a loan he owed. Ricardo tells the rival the painting was sold, and that Danny didn't get the money; the rival, realising Danny can't pay the loan, calls it in, about a month back.'

'That's when Hugo started mouthing off he had a sale opportunity,' Wyatt nodded. 'Danny must have gone straight to him. I'd heard he was looking to sell, and I laughed.'

'Because you owned the original,' Ellie nodded. 'But Danny didn't realise this. He was happy to sell to Hugo, but Hugo wanted to independently examine it, and Chantelle knew they'd discover the forgery to be as such. So, she arranged for it to be stolen, in the process building a death toll that included the two thieves, arranged by Ricardo and from a gang she was once close to...'

She stopped.

'She got Natalie to hide the gun,' she said.

There was a long, awkward moment as Ellie realised everyone was waiting for her to continue.

'Basically, Chantelle killed Sebastian and his grand-daughter because people were about to realise she'd sold a stolen painting to you, and is about to leave her husband high and dry as she runs with...' she trailed off. 'You're taking her on your yacht, aren't you?'

'Why would you think that?'

'Because you're leaving this evening on one, and it seems real convenient,' Ellie smiled.

'I was,' Wyatt admitted. 'But not if she killed my friend.'

'It's more than that,' Ellie rose now. 'It's not a forgery case anymore. It's murder. Attempted murder. Probably other things. And you're smack bang in the middle of it. The police will stop you from leaving town.'

Now Wyatt rose to face Ellie.

'That would be an inconvenience,' he said. 'What can I do to help you, that would stop my name from being involved in this?'

He looked down at Robert.

'After all, this isn't a police interview, it's just friends having a chat, right?'

Ellie looked at Robert too; after a moment, he nodded at her.

'We have a couple of favours we'd like of you,' Ellie smiled. 'And then you'll never hear from us again.'

'Deal,' Wyatt held out a hand to be shaken. 'And what deal have I made with the devil this time?'

Ellie told him.

23

REVELATIONS

After leaving the office, Ellie had made a call to Tinker; although it was gone five in the afternoon now, with less than an hour to go, she needed something done fast. Tinker agreed to head over to Hoxton, meet someone and revisit the art studio, and Ellie was about to enter the elevator when Casey walked up beside her, quietly.

He hadn't spoken since the meeting had ended.

'I know you have questions,' she said, turning right as they walked through the sliding doors of the elevator. 'And I should have told you. But it was—well...'

'Yeah, I get it,' Casey said. 'No worries.'

Ellie risked a quick glimpse across at the teenager; his jaw was set, his hands clenching and unclenching.

He really didn't want to be there.

'Just say it,' she said.

'I'm fine.'

'*Dammit, Casey, you're not!*' Ellie shouted as the doors closed and the elevator started downwards. 'Look at you? You're more coiled than a spring!'

Casey looked back at Ellie.

'My mum can tell me that,' he said. 'You're not my mum, whatever you *wanted* to be.'

Ellie felt all the air come out of her as he spoke.

'I never wanted to replace your mum,' she said. 'I never wanted... hell, Casey. I didn't even want this in the first place. It just...'

She trailed off once more, unable to find the words.

At this, Casey leapt forward, slamming the emergency stop on the elevator. As the car jerked to a halt, Ellie looked shocked at him.

'We have less than an hour—'

'How did it start?' Casey asked.

'Look, it wasn't—'

'I said *how did it start,*' Casey hissed, the anger clear in his voice. 'And before you lie to me again, know I'll find the truth out. And if you do lie, I'll destroy your life.'

'Like my life's not destroyed already?' Ellie snapped back, immediately regretting it. 'How much do you know about what your dad did?' she asked now, leaning against the wall of the elevator car.

'He was an accountant,' Casey replied. 'Self employed, worked for about six or seven companies.'

'Yes and no,' Ellie sighed. She didn't want to tell him this, but he deserved to know. 'He was an accountant, and he worked for the companies, but they were all owned by the same person. Nicky Simpson.'

'He was Simpson's accountant?'

'Yeah,' Ellie replied. 'He'd been Max Simpson's accountant before Max retired from the business, and was grandfathered into Nicky's new empire. At the start he only did the legitimate entities, but Nicky didn't want those on his books, and so he started removing them. The only legitimate entities *he* wanted were the health clubs and his own brand. And because of this, Bryan found himself peeking behind the curtain, and not liking what he saw.'

'So he came to you?'

'He came to my then-boss, Alex Monroe,' Ellie continued. 'Monroe had a connection to gangs, and had known people in Mile End. He'd known Max too, had nicked him a couple of times, nothing that stuck. And, when Max came down with Parkinsons, Monroe was the only copper that sent him a sympathy card. Bryan thought Monroe might be able to give advice. And, in the process, after they spoke, they brought in me.'

'When was this?'

'About five years back,' Ellie counted off her fingers. 'I was waiting for my bump to Detective Inspector, and only just arrived at Vauxhall from Mile End. At the start, I was brought in to handle Bryan as an asset; he wanted witness protection, a way to get out with you and your mum, and he thought he had enough on Nicky to do it. But he didn't. Nicky was clever, and none of the paperwork your dad had on him was enough to give us an arrest. And so we—*I*—pressured him to stay, and to get in deeper.'

'A double agent.'

'Yeah,' Ellie nodded. 'And he did. He was doing it for you and your mum, but he couldn't say anything. This caused cracks in his marriage and the only person he could speak to about it was me. We would meet up clandestinely to discuss it. And, over time, we got closer.'

Casey stared at the mirrored wall of the elevator, his eyes unfocused, staring through his own reflection for a moment.

Then, with a curt not, he pressed the ground floor button, starting the elevator once more.

'I remember him being distant around then,' he said. 'This was about three years back, yeah?'

Ellie nodded.

'It wasn't supposed to happen,' she breathed softly, letting the pent-up worries of revealing this leave her as she spoke. 'But we were each other's anchors, our rocks, you know? I was going through problems in my own marriage, and Bryan—'

She stopped, before deciding to continue.

'Look, your parents weren't saints,' she said. 'They had their problems. And with the two of us in dark places where we couldn't speak to others, we kind of, well, just fell into each other's arms.'

'Did you love him?'

'At the start, I liked him,' Ellie admitted. 'He made me laugh, we were on the same wavelength. And, over time, that grew. Yeah, by the end? I loved him.'

'And did he love you?' Casey wouldn't look at Ellie as he asked.

'I don't think so,' Ellie replied as the doors opened. 'I mean, he acted like it, and he told me he did, but his life was more complicated. He loved you more.'

Casey kept quiet as they walked through the office corridors, heading to the car park.

'We need to get to St Katherine's Dock,' Ellie continued as they entered the underground car park. 'If you don't want to—'

'I'll finish this,' Casey stated as he walked over to Robert's car. 'We've got fifty minutes.'

Ellie nodded, clicking the remote. She wasn't sure if Robert even realised she had the remote, but that didn't matter right now.

Getting into the car, she looked at Casey, already placing his seatbelt on.

'I'm sorry he died,' she said.

'When we first spoke, you told me he'd had an affair,' Casey looked up at her now.

'No, you told me he had,' Ellie started the engine. 'You'd hacked his records. I just gave confirmation.'

'You said that he ended it with *the woman*,' Casey considered this. 'Now I know you're the woman, was what you said true?'

'Yes,' Ellie pulled the car out of the bay. 'And I did drunkenly punch him, bloodying his nose.'

I'm sorry, Ellie. I can't do this. I'll lose my son.

'He loved you,' she added, shuddering at the memory. 'He broke it off because your mum suspected. She'd told him if he was having an affair, she'd take you from him. He couldn't have that. His last words to me were to break up, saying he couldn't do it anymore, as he knew he'd lose you.'

'Sorry.'

'No,' Ellie stopped the car in the car park, looking at Casey. 'He was right. If he'd carried on, if he'd lost you, he'd never get past it. He'd blame me for the loss, or blame you for not wanting to see him. He did the right thing, and I over-reacted.'

'So what happened then?'

'Nicky Simpson had a mole in the police,' Ellie drove towards the barrier. 'They told him Bryan was informing. Nicky met with him the night of our row, and then two days later, they found his body. He'd been beaten, and shot.'

Casey swallowed as he nodded.

'Do you know who did it?' he asked. 'Who grassed you up, set you for the fall?'

'I have my suspicions, but I—'

'Delgado? She hates you.'

'A lot of coppers hate me,' Ellie said as they pulled out of the parking garage. 'Doesn't mean—'

'Thank god,' Ramsey said, opening the rear passenger door and sliding in. 'Tinker left without me. I thought I was going to have to go to the docks alone. What do we have?'

He stared at Casey and Ellie.

'Did I miss something?'

As Ellie brought Ramsey up to speed on what Christian Wyatt had said to them, Casey pulled his tablet out once more, typing into it. And, by the time Ellie had finished her explanation, they were heading out of the City and towards Tower Hill.

The traffic was heavy, however; five in the evening was the start of rush hour, and the roads were nose-to-tail solid with cars.

'I've found something,' Casey said suddenly, looking up from the screen. 'On the video. The second one.'

'The one on the SD card?'

Casey nodded.

'About two-fifteen am, the Bentley leaves Danny's house,' he said. 'Looks like two people in it, but I can't be sure. Then, around six-thirty am, it comes back.'

'Cutting it close,' Ramsey commented. 'That's what, an hour and a half driving to London, meet Molloy and Cornell around four in the morning, shoot them, take the painting and come back before Danny wakes up?'

'That's if they kept the painting,' Ellie replied. 'They could have arranged for Natalie to meet them, and then give it to her.'

'She had a bad arm,' Ramsey shook his head. 'She'd have to have help getting it into the studio.'

'They could have torn it out, rolled it up,' Ellie suggested. 'We know the painting was in a frame, but that doesn't mean it was still in it when they passed it on.'

'And a frame is easy to toss away,' Casey said. 'It's definitely Chantelle and Ricardo, you see them on the way back, as the morning's lighter.'

'This is why June kept the SD hidden,' Ellie considered. 'She knew this was damning. Chantelle claimed she was there all night while they drove off. But surely ANPR would have—'

'You're thinking like police now,' Ramsey said. 'Why would the police look? Danny said only jewels had been stolen, and the police weren't looking at them, just a red car. One that appeared the next day.'

'I should get the police to look at it,' Ellie nodded. 'When I call them.'

'Whitehouse and Delgado won't help you,' Ramsey sat back on the rear seat, looking at the screen. 'Sat Nav says we won't make it, by the way.'

'Sat Nav says we're only *just* not making it,' Ellie growled, trying to overtake a bicycle courier on the left. 'And I drive faster than it realises.'

'Not right now,' Ramsey replied. 'And besides, when we get there, what do we do? Certainly, we know Chantelle is guilty, and sure, we can get some police to turn up, but that's not what Danny hired us for.'

Ellie nodded as she cut left down a side road.

'I know,' she said, wincing as she almost clipped a parked car's wing mirror as she sped past. 'Danny needs to pay his debt. But how can—'

'So why don't we pay it?' Casey suggested. 'When you met Nicky, he said "Danny can pay me in any of my accounts", remember?'

Ellie nodded. 'And?'

'And so I have the health club membership account details for direct debits,' Casey smiled. 'It's how I found Chantelle's account. I could just take the five million and pay it across.'

'You could do that?' Ramsey was surprised at this. 'Just pay five million like that?'

'It's not as easy as it sounds, but banks? The higher the amount, the less it's checked. Chantelle doesn't have it in a high street bank, it's Swiss. You need the right details to access it, but when you do? Only a passcode is needed to send any amount.'

Casey grinned.

'And I got those from Mister Wyatt when he showed me the transfer he made to Chantelle six months ago.'

'Do it,' Ramsey said, but Ellie held up a hand.

'Hold on,' she said. 'We need—'

'We need to stop thinking like coppers, Elisa,' Ramsey snapped. 'You're not solving the murders, or the thefts. That's the police's job, and you're not police. Your job here is only to get a favour from Danny Flynn, by making sure he can pay his debt to Simpson.'

'Can't I do both?' Ellie asked as she sped across a busy crossing without stopping, cars on either side hammering their horns at her.

'Yes,' Ramsey held onto the handle above the rear window for dear life. 'But you have to decide which one is the most important to you right now.'

'*Dammit!*' Ellie cried out. 'I don't want Simpson winning!'

'I get that,' Ramsey replied. 'But if he doesn't, then Danny Flynn loses. And to be honest, we don't even know if Danny's still alive right now; there's no way they'll be taking him to St Katherine's Docks with them.'

'They might,' Casey looked up. 'I'm in the health club files, and I have Nicky's day planner. He has from five until seven booked out, "event at Tower Bridge" in it.'

'Which is next to St Katherine's Docks,' Ellie now hammered into Crosswalk, accelerating as she headed towards Minories. 'He's there.'

'If it helps,' Casey tried his best to look innocent, 'I think I know how Nicky Simpson can win, but still get stung.'

'Do it,' Ellie sighed. 'Let's just hope everything comes together in time.'

Casey went to reply but instead squeaked a yelp as Ellie slammed the brakes on while approaching Tower Bridge, skipping through the narrowest of openings between cars on the left and skidding into St Katherine's Way, running parallel to the bridge but heading downwards.

After a hundred yards, she screeched to a stop on double yellow lines; beside her were stairs heading down to St Katherine's Dock.

'See?' she smiled, tapping the screen. 'Two minutes to go.'

And with this she leapt out of the car, ignoring the

annoyed driver behind who had to also stop for her, waving for Ramsey and Casey to follow.

'I think I'm going to be sick,' Ramsey muttered as he climbed warily out.

24

DOCKED LANDS

Danny Flynn hadn't had a particularly good afternoon.

It had started when Chantelle, his beautiful wife of ten years had claimed she needed to "show him something in the garage", which then turned out to be a gun, held by Chantelle as she sat in the back of the Bentley, Danny beside her and Ricardo driving.

He'd *never* liked Ricardo.

During the drive, a two-hour journey to London, Chantelle had tried to play it down; she claimed this was for his own good, that he needed to man up and face his own demons, but at the end, Danny knew what was happening. He wasn't stupid, no matter what his wife currently claimed.

She was leaving him for the driver, had likely stolen the painting herself, and was about to run away with the profits while dumping Danny on Nicky Simpson's lap.

He had to admire her for it; the ruthlessness she showed here was how he should have been playing things from the very start.

They'd spent much of the journey in silence, Chantelle

refusing to answer any of Danny's questions, followed by a rather excessive amount of histrionics at him when he not only asked whether she'd been involved in Natalie Myles' death, but also when he noticed that the bracelet she was wearing, a diamond swan, was one of the items believed stolen a couple of days earlier.

He also wondered whether this had been bought by Ricardo; he didn't remember buying her such an item. When he challenged her on this, Chantelle had snapped, pistol-whipping his temple, knocking him back into the seat and clutching at his head, a small trickle of blood slipping through his fingers.

He decided not to speak any more after that.

It was around five-forty when they reached Tower Bridge; Danny knew Chantelle had a friend, an industrialist who'd promised them a route out, if they needed it, on his yacht, and wondered for a moment whether he'd read her wrong— maybe she was just scared, and blamed Danny for this.

But, when they stopped in a car park beside St Katherine's Docks, Danny quickly realised he wasn't getting on any yacht, as the only luggage they had was their own bags.

Ricardo and Chantelle would take this trip alone, it seemed.

And so Danny kept quiet as Chantelle sat in the back of the car, checking her phone repeatedly for a message, getting visibly angrier with every passing minute without one.

At five minutes to six, however, the phone buzzed. Chantelle read the message, nodded, and showed Danny the screen of the phone; he could see the end of whatever conversation she'd been having with an unknown number.

Bring him to me

We have a boat waiting at St Katherine's Docks

We'll give you him there

What time

Six

Okay I'll see you there. Happy holidays.

I'm here.

Danny felt a trickle of fear slide down between his shoulder blades.

'You're giving me to Simpson?' he asked.

'You owe him a debt,' Chantelle was pulling her luggage out of the back of the car as she spoke. A wheeled cabin case, she pulled out the handle as Ricardo removed a Gucci overnight bag.

'That's my bag!' Danny exclaimed in anger. 'You're stealing my bloody stuff now?'

'Mate, she's been stealing your stuff for years,' Ricardo grinned, and Danny realised that his Italian accent seemed to have dropped considerably, giving him more of a South London tone.

He felt the uncomfortable poke of a gun in his back as Chantelle walked up behind him.

'Come on, don't make this harder than it is,' she whispered.

'How could it be harder?' Danny snapped back, pausing when Ricardo placed a muscled hand on his shoulder.

'I could break your arm,' he said matter-of-factly, as if

throwing the idea out in a conversation between friends. 'I could do it in a way that never heals properly. That'd make it harder for you, yeah?'

Now they were walking into St Katherine's Docks, crossing Thomas More street and entering through a metal gate. It was early evening, and the offices were closing, the employees arriving at the bars and restaurants for after-work drinks and food, and the place was heaving.

'Don't worry about getting a table,' Chantelle smiled. 'We won't be dining tonight.'

Danny stopped, spinning to face her.

'Shoot me,' he said, tears welling up. 'If you're leaving me, I'm dead anyway. You were my soulmate!'

'And you were mine,' Chantelle replied with a hint of sadness. 'But then you—you *compromised*. You didn't care about hustling anymore. You didn't make an effort to keep me in the style I was accustomed to.'

'Style you were accustomed to?' Danny shook his head in disbelief. 'You lived in a shared flat in Loughton when we met! The only thing you had of worth was that sodding necklace and the pennies you still had from TOWIE! I gave you a mansion!'

'You wanted babies!' Chantelle snapped back. 'I'm in my twenties! I need to spread my wings! Have fun!'

'You're *thirty-three*,' Danny muttered, and in return received a sharp prod in the ribs from the gun.

'My IMDB and talent agency pages both say I'm in my late twenties!' she almost screamed. 'I will not have alternative facts like that thrown in my face!'

'You're mad,' Danny sadly turned away as Chantelle pushed him towards the boardwalk beside the marina.

'Yeah? Well, at least I'm not the one about to be turned

into dog food by a pissed off gangster,' she hissed. 'Maybe you should have been nicer to me. All I was to you was *tits and teeth*.'

'And I bought those for you because you demanded them,' Danny replied sullenly.

'I *deserved* them!' Chantelle angrily replied.

'Then why are you using them against me?'

Chantelle stopped.

'Look,' she said. 'This is sad times, yeah? I don't want to see you fall. I really don't. But between you and Ricky, there's no choice. And you'd admit you've been a bit of a disappointment to your dad, wouldn't you?'

Across the boardwalk, Danny saw the muscled figure of Nicky Simpson, standing in a black suit and white-collared shirt, *Ray Ban* glasses not really hiding his identity as his bodyguard Saleh stood beside him, glaring at anyone who even considered walking over and asking for a selfie or autograph.

'Please,' Danny said to Chantelle, and he didn't need to continue. She knew what he meant with that one terrified word.

'Sorry,' she said, her voice more uncertain as they carried on. 'You need to pay your debt.'

Walking over to Simpson, Chantelle stopped, glancing at Danny before continuing.

'Here you go,' she said. 'As promised.'

Simpson smiled at Danny now; the smile of a shark about to munch down on their prey.

'Glad you didn't run from me,' he said, glancing at his watch. 'And right on time. Six pm. You have my money?'

'What?' Danny, terrified, half mumbled in reply.

'My five million,' Simpson said nonchalantly. 'The money you had until, oh, right now to pay. You have it, right?'

He nodded to Saleh, who moved in, patting Danny down.

'Maybe it's in crypto?' Simpson suggested. 'You have a small wallet we can attach? Or is it being transferred as we speak?'

'I don't have it,' Danny whispered.

'Sorry, could you speak up?' Simpson, enjoying the moment, cupped a hand to an ear.

'I said I don't have it,' Danny said more forcefully now, glaring back at Simpson. 'And you know it. You made sure I wouldn't.'

'Don't blame me if you welch on deals,' Simpson's face darkened now. 'You went into the contract with open eyes.'

'You knew it wouldn't happen!' Danny, exasperated, replied. 'You knew because your developers told you!'

'And yet I trusted *you*,' Simpson smiled wider now, aware that he was being watched by over a dozen people from their tables at the restaurants. No matter what he may want to do right now, he had to be all smiles as he did it. 'I went with my gut to help the son of my father's friend, and he screwed me.'

'My dad *hated* your dad,' Danny, realising he had no escape, had become more brazen in his replies. 'Max was always sniffing for dad's Boston connections. And he never gave him them.'

'Imagine how he must feel, now his own flesh and blood is about to give them, freely, to me.'

'If I give them to you, what do I get out of it?' Danny asked.

'Your life?' Simpson suggested. 'The ability to still walk? You'll be broke and be nothing, but you'll have a nice cardboard box to live in.'

Danny looked away, bitterly biting his lip as Simpson leant in close.

'Hear that rumbling?' Simpson whispered. 'That's Arthur Flynn, screaming, spinning in his own grave.'

Before Danny could reply, Simpson stepped back.

'Well, this has been fun,' he said to Chantelle and Ricardo, 'but I assume you have a boat to catch. I'll look after your husband, and I won't break him—well, not at the start, anyway. He'll work to pay off—'

'Ah, there you are!' Another voice spoke now, and Nicky Simpson spun around to see Ellie Reckless, her gait a mixture of limping and striding as she walked towards him, Ramsey and Casey following. 'We looked everywhere for you.'

'And yet you seem to have found me,' Simpson replied, but stopped as Ellie glared at him.

'Not you,' she stated, pushing past him, walking to Danny. 'I was talking to my *client*.'

'Your client hired you to help find a painting, so he could sell it by a particular deadline,' Simpson looked at his watch. 'The deadline has passed.'

'No, Nicky,' Ellie waggled a finger. 'We were hired to help him *pay* you.'

'My *friends* call me Nicky,' Simpson hissed. 'You can call me Mister Simpson.'

'No, I'm not really feeling that,' Ellie considered the suggestion. 'How about Nicholas? Bit of a compromise?'

'What do you want?' Simpson asked, his anger rising.

'My client,' Ellie smiled. 'You see, *Nicholas*, we were tasked with paying you the five million owed before the deadline, which was six pm, right?'

'Yes.'

'And we did it,' Ellie smiled. 'You had a bank transfer of five million pounds into your account, a minute before the deadline.'

She looked over at Danny now.

'Your debt is cleared,' she said.

'No, this is bullshit,' Simpson snapped. 'I would have had a message. And I never gave my private account details to you.'

'Oh, were we supposed to use the *private* account?' Casey looked horrified. 'I didn't realise that.'

'No,' Ellie smiled at Casey, patting him on the shoulder. 'I remember exactly what Nicholas here said to us in his office.'

She looked back at Nicky Simpson.

'He said "Danny can pay me in *any* of my accounts".'

Simpson paled.

'What account did you use?'

Casey pulled out his tablet, tapping on the screen and spinning it around to show Simpson.

'Your health club membership one,' he said. 'It was the only one we had to use.'

'You placed *five million pounds* into my health club account?' Simpson was apoplectic with rage. 'I'll have to declare it! I'll lose almost half in tax!'

'True, but "almost half" means you won't be at a loss, will you?' Ellie replied. 'You still make more than the two and a half million you paid, and Danny's debt to you is sorted.'

There was a long moment of awkward silence on the dock now, and Ellie knew Simpson was trying to work out how to stay on top here.

'You won,' she said softly. 'You don't look bad, you had a debt, it was paid, and you can fold the millions you'll lose in tax into some kind of family-friendly PR stunt, I'm sure.'

'You did this deliberately to screw me over,' Simpson hissed.

'Now, why would I do that?' Ellie asked innocently. 'It's not like you had your man there punch me, or order him to kill me or anything, is it?'

She stepped back now.

'Anyway,' she finished. 'Our client is paid off, and the only debt left is a favour he owes me, at a time and date of my choosing.'

'Wait,' Chantelle spoke now. 'This ain't right! How did he have the money to pay the debt?'

'Oh, he didn't,' Ramsey replied. 'We took it from the money you were paid by Christian Wyatt for the painting. After the money you'd spent out on various expenses, you had just over five million in there. Money taken from the sale of Danny's painting, so technically Danny's. Although you probably knew that already.'

Chantelle's face purpled.

'I'm going to kill you,' she hissed.

'In fairness, you weren't going to spend it,' Ellie added. 'Nicky—sorry, *Nicholas* here was going to have his man take it from you.'

'His man?' Chantelle was floundering now.

'Oh yes, his man Richard, here,' Ellie nodded at Ricardo. 'Would you like to know how?'

Chantelle didn't reply, but Danny did.

'I'd like to know,' he said, glaring at his wife. 'I'd like to know everything.'

'It's quite simple,' Ellie replied, looking back at Nicky Simpson. 'And it all starts with *you*.'

25

LEGACIES

'You see, Nicholas here has wanted Danny's Boston details for a while now,' Ellie explained. 'His father, Max, wanted them back when Arthur Flynn ran the firm, and when Danny took over, Nicholas assumed he'd get hold of them. But then Danny moved west, left London with his trophy wife, and allowed his more illegal side to bubble away in the background.'

'I wanted to go legit for Chantelle,' Danny admitted.

'That's admirable,' Ellie half-mocked. 'But you still kept all the Boston money.'

'It's not technically illegal if it comes from abroad,' Danny shrugged. 'It's like eating someone else's dessert.'

There was a moment of confusion as everyone stared at him.

'You know, how the calories don't count if it's from someone else's plate?'

Ellie sighed.

'Anyway, that aside, you looked to find other ways to fund

your empire,' she continued. 'Including a land deal you'd heard about.'

Now she turned back to Simpson.

'One you knew about and had been told to stay away from, as it was folly.'

'My developers may have offered concern,' Simpson admitted.

'Yet still you loaned the money,' Ellie nodded, 'At a steep interest rate.'

'I believed him,' Danny snapped. 'He told me I was gonna make ten times the investment.'

'And of course it failed, and Nicholas here now had you by the short and curlies. But he needed you to give him something more important than money; he needed you to be so broke you had no other choice. So, he held off from calling the loan in, knowing you'd somehow screw up.'

'I thought he was being a gent,' Danny moaned.

'At this time, he looked for other ways to get one over on you,' Ellie continued. 'Chantelle was attending his health club, and her personal trainer, "Ricardo", or more accurately Richard, was getting close. He had a mechanical background, her driver was retiring, and it was suggested Ricardo move across.'

'Hearsay,' Simpson interrupted. 'Whatever my staff does when they leave my employment isn't up to me.'

'Either way, Ricardo here still kept you in the loop,' Ellie smiled back at the health-club-guru-turned-gangster. 'And one night, maybe during pillow talk, she mentions the painting. Danny's dad's greatest achievement. Vermeer's *The Concert*. And he tells you.'

'I may have heard about it in passing.'

Ellie turned back to Danny now, seeing the anger rising on his face.

'On Nicholas' orders, Ricardo lays it on thick, suggests that perhaps Chantelle should sell the painting and escape,' she carried on. 'He knows about the prenup, and his boss—sorry, ex-boss, would be more than happy to see it disappear. And so, Ricardo does some checking and finds two billionaires hunting for it. One of them, Christian Wyatt, is even in the country later in the year, and has a friend who's a forger, someone who can help the situation. All you have to do is meet.'

'And how did they do that?' Simpson asked. 'Exciting as the bedtime story is, I really need to move on.'

'It was at your New Year's bash last December,' Casey spoke now.

'We didn't go to a New Year's bash,' Danny frowned. 'No, wait, I had stomach pains and stayed in—'

'While Chantelle and her driver went in your absence,' Ellie nodded. 'Yeah, the photo we showed of Chantelle at a party? This was the party. And there, Chantelle made the deal with Wyatt, sold your painting for five-point-two million, and agreed to work with LaFleur on creating a double. After all, she couldn't just take it. You'd notice.'

'What people do at my parties—' Simpson started, but stopped as Ellie cut him off.

'I know,' she said irritably. 'We all know. And to be honest, you're not really a part of this bit. So shush for a moment.'

She could see that Nicky Simpson was furious at being spoken to like this, but was also banking that the crowded location would assist her.

'In fairness to Chantelle, she probably didn't realise you had plans to take everything,' she added. 'She probably thought Danny would never sell the painting, so he'd never know the painting was fake.'

Chantelle didn't speak, glowering at Ellie.

'But now the problems start,' Ellie rubbed at the scar on her temple, feeling the headache returning. 'LaFleur knows the painting, but to create a forgery needs to be close to it. Needs to see *everything*. And so, when Danny goes off to Boston for a couple of days, or any time Chantelle's left alone, LaFleur arrives with his assistant, Natalie, and takes notes. Which would be fine, if not for your neighbour.'

'Hudson?' Danny shook his head. 'She's involved?'

'By circumstance,' Ellie nodded. 'You see, many years ago, she had a child out of wedlock, something that caused a family to split down the line. Natalie, the assistant, was June's granddaughter. They hadn't spoken for five years, ever since Natalie's father learned his true heritage. And, at some point, father told daughter, and daughter likely sought grandfather, taking a role as his assistant, but never telling him.'

'A family business,' Ramsey spoke now, avoiding Nicky Simpson's gaze. 'But one June hadn't been informed of. And, watching out of her window, a productive member of the Neighbourhood Watch, she sees granddaughter Natalie and her unaware granddad Sebastian, repeatedly appearing at the house.'

'We don't know when she confronts him, but we think June intercepted Sebastian shortly after he finished the forgery,' Ellie explained. 'They had swapped the painting, Christian had his original, and Chantelle had the money. But now, Sebastian LaFleur is a loose end. And now he knows he's unwillingly brought his own flesh and blood into his criminal life, he confronts Chantelle and Ricardo, maybe even in the house, probably demanding more money, maybe trying to secure a deal for her. Before he leaves, Ricardo fixes his car to make sure the cruise control goes crazy. And, that day, driving home, Sebastian LaFleur dies.'

'He wasn't looking out for her at all!' Chantelle snapped. 'He wanted more money when he heard I'd sold it for five million. We'd agreed forty grand for the job and he wanted double. And we knew he was coming to us, because Natalie had called ahead to warn us! She wasn't trying to reconnect with her granddaddy! She was pissed he'd walked out on them, and she wanted to screw him over!'

'You gave her the money, didn't you?' Casey said. 'The studio space is worth about two grand a month, and she paid eighteen months in advance.'

'We gave her independence,' Chantelle hissed. 'Just as I'd gained my own.'

'But you couldn't leave just yet, could you?' Ellie turned to her. 'Your paramour there was suggesting you wait a little longer, while getting his orders from his boss. And with Sebastian dead, you're worried someone might put everything together. But then Nicholas here calls in the loan.'

'As is my right.'

'Absolutely,' Ellie nodded. 'And rather well timed, making sure Danny had nothing to pay it with. But now Chantelle here has a problem, because she knows the only thing Danny has to pay it off is a forgery, and the moment Hugo Spears, the new buyer authenticates it, Danny'll learn it's fake, will know she stole it, and go after her. She can't lose the money.'

She patted the furious Chantelle on the shoulder.

'And so she fakes a robbery,' she continued. 'She gets Ricardo to set up a couple of Loughton kids to retrieve the painting from the house one night, as well as a few jewels to make it look legit. She keeps her own special ones on her person and goes to dinner. Having dropped them off at the golf club, Ricardo returns, opens the gates and turns off the alarm before leaving. The two thieves arrive in a red Peugeot 308, 2010 plate, load up and leave.'

'That's remarkably well informed,' Simpson glanced at Ramsey. 'How did you know this?'

'A returning character,' Ellie moved in between Simpson and Ramsey, diverting his gaze. 'June Hudson, now suspicious of Chantelle after LaFleur's death, had taken to watching the house. She also filmed it with a small camera in the front bedroom. She witnessed everything. And she was the one that called the police.'

'But the following day, she changed her story,' Casey spoke now. 'Instead of telling them she saw a champagne coloured car open the gates, now it was black.'

'Maybe she made a mistake,' Chantelle suggested.

'No,' Casey insisted. 'She had a camera on the house all night. Not only did it show Ricardo here open the door for the thieves, it also showed you drive off that night.'

Chantelle glared at Casey.

'Little boys should be seen and not heard,' she growled.

'Little *bitches* should know when they're *beaten*,' Casey snapped back. 'So now we have June Hudson with actual proof you disappeared that night—'

'Wait,' Danny was rubbing his eyes now. 'The night after the theft? She was gone?'

'You were asleep, zonked out on sleeping tablets,' Ramsey said. 'The video shows Chantelle and Ricardo disappear for a good few hours, arriving back before you woke up.'

'Enough time to drive to London, meet with the thieves, and kill them,' Ellie added. 'They weren't expecting to be double-crossed, so the headshots are fast. Maybe not

Chantelle, more Ricardo's forté. But now they have jewels returned, a painting to get rid of and a gun to hide. They're in London, and they're in a hurry. It's almost four in the morning now. They drive quickly to the only person who owes them, and who they knew works nights a lot —Natalie.'

'She's working on a sculpture,' Ramsey added to Chantelle. 'Which is handy. She takes the gun, promising to get rid of it, and agrees to burn the forgery in the incinerator, too, probably because you threatened to reveal her part in the forging.'

'But as you get back home, you get another call from her,' Ellie said. 'She'd just heard from her estranged grandmother, warning her to stay away from you. The call doesn't go well.'

'And how would you know that?'

'June told us, we just didn't realise it was Natalie she was talking about,' Ellie replied. 'And Natalie's phone had a call from a Chipping Norton number that morning. But now you need to fix *this* problem, and so before heading to bed, you pop across the road, have a chat with June, maybe threaten Natalie's health, and give her a bracelet as a sweetener. In return, she changes the story, but you don't realise she has an SD card with video, which she hides.'

'Bitch,' Chantelle muttered, before paling as she realised she'd spoken aloud. 'All she cared about was getting that sodding bracelet. Wasn't even worth much.'

'You get back into bed just as Danny wakes, and then come all the way back to London when he hires me,' Ellie looked back at her. 'After that, you know you're on borrowed time. You're paranoid now, probably think Natalie can't be trusted, and so you go back to London the following day and fake her suicide.'

'And how do you know that?' for the first time that day, it was Ricardo who spoke.

'Because you faked a handwritten suicide note for a woman with a broken wrist, and made a theatrical pig's ear of the scene,' Ramsey snapped back. 'She was on your bloody side! She made her grandmother lie for you! You didn't have to kill her!'

'You looked for the murder weapon, but you didn't know where she'd hidden it,' Ellie snapped. 'Majorly stressed, you get back home, only to find I'm speaking to June. So, you decide to get rid of her as well. Which gets you your bracelet back.'

She pointed at the bracelet on Chantelle's wrist.

'That swan one, in fact. The one you claimed wasn't worth much.'

'You've got nothing,' Chantelle sneered. 'You've got lies and stories. I didn't kill no one. Natalie committed suicide. June probably died falling down the stairs. She's pretty old and feeble.'

'Oh, didn't I mention?' Ellie asked. 'June's not dead.'

Chantelle glanced guiltily at Ricardo at this.

'Yeah, she survived your attack, just like me and Tinker did,' Ellie continued. 'And we found the code Ricardo placed in my Ford Focus. What do you reckon will happen when we check Sebastian LaFleur's old car? We know you could hack it; we had an expert check. And I'm sure it's still around somewhere.'

'This is bullshit!' Chantelle screamed now, clutching at her handbag; Ellie was guessing now there was a gun inside it. 'You have no proof!'

'We have a video of Ricardo opening the door for the thieves, and the two of you leaving in the middle of the night.'

'Then arrest Ricardo!' Chantelle fired back. 'Oh, you can't because you're not the police! And you don't have a murder weapon!'

'Actually, we might have an update on that,' Ellie smiled as she nodded past the group where, walking casually towards them with a smile on her face was Tinker Jones, hands in the pockets of her olive ex-army jacket, still spattered with blood.

'Did you get it?' Ellie asked.

Tinker nodded.

'Glock 17, real one, welded onto a sculpture of fakes,' she replied. 'As LaFleur always said, apparently, hide in plain sight.'

Ramsey nodded at this.

'What's to bet your fingerprints are still on it?' Ellie returned her attention to Chantelle. 'You seem stupid enough not to wipe them.'

'You planted it there,' she pouted. 'The police won't know fu—'

'Actually, the police were the ones who found it,' Tinker interrupted, grinning wider now. 'Old friends of Ellie's.'

Ellie noticed a twitch from Nicky Simpson at this and wondered whether he was trying to work out if his mole was involved in this revelation.

'DCI Alex Monroe and DI Declan Walsh of Temple Inn,' she said, looking back at him. 'I believe you've met both before?'

Simpson said nothing.

'Anyway, they found the gun easily, and they've got forensics on it already,' Tinker finished.

'Well, my time here is over,' Simpson said suddenly,

nodding at Saleh. 'I'm not part of this triple murder, so I'll be on my way. I have a gala to attend.'

He looked at Ellie, his eyes dark and hooded.

'I'll not forget what you did for me,' he threatened.

'I got your money back, when you claimed it was impossible, I placed it into an account you said was alright to do so, and I saved your life,' Ellie smiled back. 'Who knows what might have happened to you later? These two are killers, so you're welcome.'

She looked back at Chantelle.

'Oh, and the police are surrounding you,' she said conversationally. 'I called some other old colleagues too.'

Ricardo grabbed Simpson's arm.

'Boss?'

Simpson pulled himself away as he stared dispassionately at his employee.

'You left my employ a year ago,' he said.

'Boss!'

'I suggest you plan your story well,' Simpson said as he patted Ricardo's shoulder. 'It'll make a real difference to how you're treated in prison.'

With this, Nicky Simpson and Saleh walked away from the group, smiling and waving at some diners who shouted out at them.

Chantelle opened and shut her mouth a couple of times before looking back at Danny, Ellie, Tinker, Ramsey, and Casey.

'Let the police come,' she said defiantly, thrusting her chin out. 'You think you're so clever. Wait until I tell them about the painting!'

Ellie frowned.

'What painting?' she asked. 'I don't know about any painting.'

She looked over at Danny.

'Do you?'

Realising what was happening and smiling for the first time, Danny shook his head.

'Nope,' he replied. 'A mystery to me.'

'You burned the only evidence of the theft, remember?' Tinker said. 'And Mister Wyatt won't be admitting he bought stolen goods soon. But the police do have you on three counts of murder, and three of *attempted* murder, if you include June. So that's gonna be fun—'

She stopped as Chantelle dropped her purse, the gun in her hand now wavering as she aimed at each of them in turn.

'Two cripples, an OAP, a kid and my ex,' she hissed. 'Against me and Ricky. I don't see it being much of a problem.'

The docks erupted into noise now as some of the closer diners saw the brandished weapon, and Chantelle laughed.

'We're grabbing a boat and getting out of here,' she hissed. 'The only question is which of you I take as hostages, and which of you I shoot here and now?'

She aimed the gun directly at Ellie's face.

'I'm thinking the latter for you, bitch,' she said as she pulled the trigger.

26

SLAPPY ENDINGS

ELLIE HAD BEEN SO CONFIDENT THAT CHANTELLE WOULDN'T fire the gun in a public location, she hadn't even considered the fact Chantelle might have been pushed to a level past normality, and it was only Ramsey, charging into the onetime reality TV star, and knocking the gun to the side that saved Ellie's life in that moment.

As the shot fired, the screams started; St Katherine's Dock was now filled with terror, as diners and evening drinkers ran for cover. And it was understandable, as London had lived under the threat of terrorism for many years; the sound of a gun was enough to send people scurrying for safety.

It was also enough to bring in armed police, Ellie realised as she now charged into Chantelle, taking her to the floor as, across the promenade, Tinker ran at Ricardo. The Tower of London was on the other side of Tower Bridge, easily accessible by a path along the north bank. And, more importantly, not only were the Beefeaters, the colourful Yeoman Guard of the Tower ex-soldiers, but there were also armed officers, usually patrolling places of national interest, such as both the

Tower and the Bridge; screaming civilians and a gunshot were definitely likely to bring them running.

All Ellie had to do was secure Chantelle and Ricardo until the police turned up. Whether it was the *right* police was up for grabs.

But Chantelle had other plans and, having dropped the gun in the scuffle, was now running for the marina, looking to escape on one of the yachts. Wincing at the reopened gash on her thigh, Ellie hobbled after her, Danny in quick pursuit after his wife.

WITH DANNY AND ELLIE NOW DISAPPEARING AROUND THE Docks, Tinker turned her attention to Ricardo, standing alone and realising his options were increasingly limited. However, he was fast, desperate, and she still had bruised ribs to deal with. Besides this, although Ramsey and Casey were both still next to her, Ricardo had pulled a wicked-looking box knife out of his pocket, and was swinging it wildly at them; the last thing Tinker wanted was for people to learn that she, Tinkerbelle Jones, had let an old man and a child get hurt on her watch, and so she pushed them behind her as she squared up against the wild-eyed driver.

'You should have died in the car, bitch!' he snarled as he lunged forward, slashing with the blade, missing by inches as Tinker pulled backwards, *bullet time* style, rocking back on her feet and then springing back upright.

'You should have done a better job then,' she snapped back as she leant in on Ricardo's next wild swing, moving within his reach before he could finish it and grabbing the arm, slamming it down onto her knee, the pain causing

Ricardo to scream out, his hand jerking open, the knife falling.

Now with Ramsey's reluctant help, Tinker restrained Ricardo, slamming him bodily, face down, onto the wooden dock, his good arm pinned behind his back as Tinker now sat on him, screaming out to anyone listening that *his arm was broken and he was going to sue.*

'Get the gun,' she shouted to Casey, standing still, watching her with what looked to be awe. 'Use a pencil to pick it up. We need Chantelle's fingerprints if we're going to have her down for this.'

'I think enough people were filming it,' Casey said as he looked at the dock, frowning. And, with a look of horror, he looked up at the yachts, and the now distant Ellie and Danny.

'Ellie!' Casey shouted. 'She's still got the gun!'

But, with the noise of the crowd behind him, Casey realised there was no way Ellie could have heard, and so, dropping his bag, he started to run.

AT THE YACHTS, ELLIE CAUGHT UP WITH CHANTELLE, GRABBING the back of her coat as she tried to clamber onto the deck of the vessel beside her, swinging her around and slamming her head into the railing running along the side of the deck.

As Chantelle staggered back from this, blood streaming from her face, Ellie threw a solid right hander, a punch she'd practised so many times against various sparring partners, a punch she'd wanted to place on Chantelle for a while now, and a solid blow that connected with a wicked-sounding *crunch* on Chantelle's jaw, actively sending her off the ground for a split second, as her momentum sent her tumbling to the edge of the dock and over the side, tumbling aimlessly into the icy waters of the Thames.

'My hair!' was all she could shout at this.

Ellie, standing at the side of the dock, watching Chantelle spluttering in the water, laughed.

'If that's all you're worried about, then bitch? You've got problems,' she wheezed, doubling over, forcing herself not to throw up from the wave of pain now thrusting through her skull as the head wound, overloaded with blood flow from the brief workout, screamed at her.

There was the sound of running from far away, and the shouting of her name, and Ellie heard Casey's voice.

'She's got the gun!'

At this, Ellie looked back at Chantelle, catching her breath as she did so—and frowned.

If Chantelle still held the gun, this would have been a far shorter fight, and one that would have ended differently.

Looking back at Casey, about to ask what he meant by this, Ellie stopped as she saw Danny, staring down at his waterlogged wife.

With Chantelle's gun in his hand, currently aiming at her.

Casey had been mistaken when he saw the gun was missing; it wasn't Chantelle that had taken it, but her rejected, battered, kidnapped and abused husband, now touching gently at his own head wound, the clotted blood showing it to be an injury he must have gained earlier that day, and probably caused by the woman in the water, now staring up at him in shock.

'You said you loved me,' he whispered.

'Danny,' Ellie went to move closer. 'We need—'

'*Stay away from me!*' Danny screamed, the gun wavering

for a moment before aiming back at Chantelle. 'You said you loved me! You said we'd be together forever!'

He looked back at Tinker, still sitting on the crying Ricardo across the dock, Ramsey standing beside her.

'And you'd leave me for *him?*' he hissed in disbelief. 'That whining piece of crap?'

In the water, Chantelle glared up at him.

'Well, go on then! Pull the trigger!' she shouted back at Danny. 'You ain't got the sauce! You've *never* had the sauce!'

'And *he's* got the sauce?' Danny shook his head in disbelief. 'Don't look like it to me.'

'Danny...' Ellie tried again, but stopped as Danny, his eyes narrowing, placed pressure on the trigger, his index finger trembling as he kept shaking his head sadly at his wife.

'Danny.'

Ellie repeated the name, this time with the harshness of a schoolteacher. It seemed to break the spell, and Danny looked up at Ellie now, tears running down his face.

'She used me, Reckless!' he said. 'She never loved me, she was screwing the driver, and she stole my dad's painting!'

'Which, in fairness, your dad stole too,' Ellie tried a faint smile. 'She's also killed people and tried to kill others. If you shoot her, if you *kill* her, you'll just save her a long and uncomfortable prison sentence.'

'She won't go to prison,' Danny hissed. 'She'll get off. Get away with it. She *always* gets away with things. But not this time.'

His shaking hand calmed, and his body relaxed as he committed himself to the moment.

'I'm Danny friggin' Flynn,' he muttered. 'And I don't take shit from anyone, even my—'

'*I'm calling in my favour!*'

Danny paused, frowning as he looked back at Ellie, hands on hips, puffing as she straightened.

"What?'

'I found your painting, and I paid off your debt,' Ellie reminded him. 'You owe me a favour. Given at a time of my choosing, and you agreed to honour it, no matter what it was. We made a deal. You signed the contract.'

Danny's arm lowered slightly as he shook his head.

'I know,' he replied, confused. 'But you—'

'*Any time of my choosing,*' Ellie repeated, emphasising the words strongly. 'And I choose now. I'm calling in my chit. Put the gun down. That's my favour. *Leave her to the police, and put the gun down.*'

Danny looked from Ellie to Chantelle, now climbing out of the water, drenched and bedraggled, and then back to Ellie again.

'You got all this from her,' he said, nodding with his head at Ellie's injuries, 'you were almost killed, you suffered all of these things so I'd owe you a favour, and now you want to burn it on *this bitch?*'

'Not really,' Ellie shrugged. 'But I also don't want her killed, and you put away for murder, so this is my only way to get through to you, it seems.'

Danny nodded, his arm lowering, the gun still in his hand, but no longer aimed at his wife.

'Hah!' Chantelle, standing waterlogged on the dock, and only a matter of feet away from Danny, crowed as she saw this. 'I knew you were a puss—'

She stopped as Ellie punched her a second time, square in the face, sending her slumping into a sitting position, blood streaming down her face as, in the distance, they could hear the sound of police cars.

'You're under arrest, bitch,' Ellie smiled.

'You can't arrest me,' Chantelle whined, clutching her nose. 'You're not police.'

Ellie thought about this for a moment.

'Yeah, and you know? I'm actually good with that,' she said as she pulled Chantelle to her feet, dragging her back to the dining area of St Katherine's docks, where Tinker still sat on Ricardo. 'I'll let the *real* police do it.'

THE REAL POLICE TURNED OUT TO BE DI WHITEHOUSE AND DS Delgado, a score of officers having arrived behind them. Ellie hadn't been surprised to see them; after all, it'd been Ellie who gave Mark Whitehouse the tip that something big was about to happen at the docks. Of course, she'd done it by text as she'd left Robert's car, just to make sure they weren't interrupted too early, and from the look on Whitehouse's face, this hadn't been appreciated.

Probably didn't help that the whole confrontation was all over social media, as diners and drinkers had been filming the crazy woman with the gun, Ellie smiled as she considered this. *They were likely assuming she'd been some kind of stalker, trying to kill YouTube celebrity Nicky Simpson, before his security got him away.*

As the uniforms took Chantelle and Ricardo into custody, Whitehouse paused them, watching Chantelle carefully as he spoke.

'Chantelle Flynn, Richard Vieceli, I'm arresting you both for the murders of Sebastian LaFleur, Victor Cornell, Keith Molloy and Natalie Myles,' he said.

'Don't forget they tried to kill us,' Tinker added. Delgado, standing uncomfortably to the side, went to reply to this but thought better of it, staying silent, only coming to life when Whitehouse indicated for her to take the two in custody and stick them in a waiting car.

As Delgado grudgingly did so, Whitehouse looked at Danny Flynn.

'You'll have to come in too,' he said. 'Make a statement.'

'Of course,' Danny replied, looking back at Ellie before moving. 'Thank you.'

'Part of the job,' Ellie forced a smile, even if she wasn't happy.

'It wasn't part of your job to burn that favour,' Danny said, looking back at his wife as they bundled her into the back of a squad car. 'But in burning it, you stopped me from doing something I'd regret for the rest of my life.'

'Exactly,' Ellie nodded. 'At best, you'd have been taken out by a police sniper.'

Danny grinned sheepishly at this.

'You saved my life,' he said. 'I *owe* you, Ellie Reckless. You understand?'

'I think I do,' Ellie shook Danny's outstretched hand as he allowed another uniformed officer to escort him to a nearby car. 'And I will collect, one day.'

'I heard Nicky Simpson was here,' Whitehouse said, now the two of them were alone.

'Was he?' Ellie looked around innocently, as if searching for him. 'Didn't notice.'

'He's all over social media, and there's a dozen pap shots from phones,' Whitehouse looked over to the dock, where Ellie had confronted Simpson earlier. 'Right there, in fact. In a crowd of people. One of whom looked remarkably like you.'

'I have one of those faces,' Ellie shrugged.

'Delgado's gonna be pissed at this,' Whitehouse chuckled. 'She was hoping we'd get to arrest you as well, but from what we've seen on the videos, you and your team stopped a mad gunman from causing a massive terrorist attack. That's good work. *Old* Ellie Reckless levels of good work.'

Ellie didn't reply; to hear Mark Whitehouse even consider that meant the world to her.

'For what it's worth, I've said it before, but I'll say it again. I believe you,' he added. 'You loved Bryan. We all saw that. And maybe that was your problem; you were too visible. Someone saw this and was able to use it against you.'

'Do you have any ideas about who that someone could be?' Ellie asked.

In response, Whitehouse looked back at Delgado.

'Only concerns,' he said, turning back and shaking Ellie's hand. 'You did good. Almost police like. Monroe would have been proud of you.'

'I think only *he* can say that, laddie,' a gruff Scottish voice spoke, and Ellie and Whitehouse turned to see DCI Alex Monroe crossing the dock from the south side. 'Sorry to interrupt, but I wanted to make sure Tinker Jones got the information about the Glock across to you.'

'You were checking up, you mean,' Ellie chuckled, but stopped, wincing as her head pounded again. In return, Monroe raised his shoulders in a "you got me" shrug.

'Good to see you both talking,' he said, glancing at Whitehouse as he spoke. 'And it's good to see you're on the same side finally.'

'You believe her too, Guv?' Whitehouse asked.

'I didn't, but she proved herself to me a little while back,' Monroe smiled. 'She does that a lot.'

Ellie was about to reply when Delgado suddenly stormed

back to them, a police officer beside her, and a triumphant expression on her face.

'Search her,' she said, pointing at Ellie. 'Check the pockets.' However, as she did this, she finally saw Monroe, paling as she did so. Like Whitehouse, she too had worked briefly under him before he was transferred from Vauxhall to the City of London police.

'Guv,' she said. 'Isn't this a bit outside your remit? City boundaries stop before the Tower.'

'Aye, but they're a damn sight closer than Vauxhall,' Monroe replied lightly. 'I had an urge for a wee dram in the bar over there. Complete shock to me this was going on.'

Delgado obviously wanted to reply to this, but amazingly held her tongue. Smiling at her expression, Monroe looked back at Ellie.

'But before I go, what's the lassie supposed to have taken?'

'A bracelet, silver, with a diamond swan on it,' Delgado replied. 'Stolen from Chantelle Flynn's wrist during the fight.'

As the officer reluctantly searched Ellie's pockets, Ellie smiled.

'Swan bracelet? I'm sure that was on the list of items Chantelle claimed were stolen,' she said.

'Are you saying I stole an item that she'd already *had* stolen?'

Delgado frowned.

'All I know—'

'And to be honest, *Detective Sergeant*, she was flailing around in the Thames for a good while,' Ellie pointed into the water. 'You know, *after* I stopped her from killing civilians, or causing an act of domestic terrorism. Might be best to grab a scuba team.'

'She's clean,' the officer stepped back.

'She's never been clean,' Delgado hissed, glaring at Ellie before storming off, aware that everyone was watching her.

Whitehouse sighed.

'I ought to follow up with her, make sure she doesn't do something stupid,' he replied, nodding to Monroe. 'Guv.'

With that, Whitehouse called out after Delgado, running to catch up with her. Now left with Ellie alone on the dock, Monroe looked up to the sky, taking in a breath.

'Love this place,' he said. 'Did you know it used to be a medieval church and hospital? Lasted from the eleven hundreds until the mid-nineteenth century.'

'That must have been nice for you,' Ellie smiled. 'That you were alive to see it before they demolished the place.'

Monroe went to reply, but then chuckled.

'I spoke to your friend Tinker,' he said. 'When we checked for the gun. She said you're poking Nicky Simpson's cage.'

'I only have one go at it, and one stick,' Ellie said as they walked back to the others. 'If I don't try—'

'Aye, I know, and I'm canny enough to know you won't stop,' Monroe replied. 'Just be careful, aye? The laddie with you there's Bryan Noyce's son. He's seen enough death already.'

'I'll be careful,' Ellie smiled. 'And if I can't be, I'll call you.'

'Och, I'd rather you didn't,' Monroe smiled. 'Young Declan's rightly annoyed that you demoted him to DS.'

Ellie shook her head, laughing.

'Tinker Jones can't keep a damned secret,' she said. 'None whatsoever.'

Monroe patted Ellie on the shoulder, nodded to the others, and then walked off into the crowds that still watched from the bars and restaurants, before they, realising the show was over, began returning to their dining.

'You burned the favour,' Ramsey muttered.

'He gave us a new one,' Ellie replied, and Ramsey raised an eyebrow.

'Danny Flynn does something honourable?' he asked. 'Wonders never cease.'

He looked at his watch.

'Anyone want a drink?' he asked. 'I really need one.'

'I'll join you,' Casey smiled.

'Anyone *grown up* want a drink?' Ramsey altered his question to a glare from Casey.

'We can't,' Ellie tapped her watch. 'We have one more thing to do. Or don't you *want* a payday?'

Ramsey grinned.

'I thought you'd never get around to it,' he said, as they headed back to St Katherine's Way, and Robert's car.

Which, hopefully, hadn't been towed away.

27

SWAN BRACELETS

CHRISTIAN WYATT HAD BEEN GOOD TO HIS WORD. HE'D arranged a final meeting with Marcus Somerville "before he left London", while still sitting in the Finders offices, arranging the purchase of the Ming vase for three hundred grand in cash that very night.

Of course, Wyatt hadn't arrived for the meeting; his part in the performance was already over, and, guaranteed that he wouldn't be brought into any murder enquiries by the staff of Finders, in particular Ellie and her team, he'd returned to his yacht, conveniently *after* Chantelle and Ricardo had been arrested, and left for Cannes as soon as he could.

And, at seven pm, once again at the Sea Containers Hotel, Marcus Somerville had arrived to find not only Ellie and Ramsey waiting for him but also the other members of his immediate family, who, after a short and intense conversation with the wayward eldest son, retrieved the Ming vase into their own collection, thanked Ellie for her sterling efforts and left the hotel with their antique, while Marcus ranted and bitched at Ellie until she threatened to break his arm off and feed it down his throat.

This, added to her current bruised and battered look, was enough to stop Marcus in his tracks, and send him running after his family, promising to clean up as long as they didn't disown him, or cut him out of the will.

This done, Ellie had promised to dry clean Ramsey's mother's clothes, waved goodbye and called a cab.

However, as nothing was arriving for at least twenty minutes, she reluctantly agreed to buy Ramsey a celebratory drink. Sitting down at a table by the window, Ellie raised a glass to him.

'Thanks,' she said. 'I owe you for this.'

'I'll be handing in my notice as soon as the Somerville cheque clears,' Ramsey said as he sipped at his gin, watching out of the window. 'I think you should have someone who you can trust on the team, instead of me.'

'I *can* trust you,' Ellie smiled. 'I owe you my life now, remember?'

Ramsey shuddered as he recalled charging Chantelle.

'That was reckless of me, pardon the pun,' he muttered. 'I could have died.'

'Well, you didn't, you proved your worth on this case, and it all turned out okay.'

'Apart from the fact I'm now your spy inside Simpson's office,' Ramsey moaned.

'I don't need a spy in there,' Ellie shook her head. 'We don't need to know what Nicky's up to, as we already know it. What I need is interference. When Nicky Simpson wants to know what I'm up to, tell him. But tell him what *we* decide. I want him convinced he has the advantage, right up to the moment he doesn't.'

'Why the hatred of Simpson?' Ramsey asked. 'I know you have a past and issues, but do you really believe he killed your boyfriend?'

Ellie pondered the question for a long moment.

'I haven't told you everything,' she said. 'The full story isn't out there about Bryan Noyce. And for a year, I've held it in by myself. Only Robert knows.'

She let out a breath, staring at the ceiling.

'Tomorrow,' she decided. 'Tomorrow, at Caesar's, I'll tell you all everything.'

'Why not tonight?'

Ellie looked around.

'Tinker's meeting her old army mates for dinner, Casey's got homework, I suppose, and my cab's in ten minutes,' she replied. 'And believe me, it'll take longer than that.'

Ramsey nodded at this.

'Fair enough,' he said. 'Oh, I have something to show you.'

Pulling out his phone, he opened up a picture, showing it to Ellie. It was a charcoal sketch of a young woman posing gracefully for the picture. The woman was familiar, from a photo Ellie had seen; it was a young June Hudson.

'Where did you find this?' Ellie asked, surprised.

'Rajesh,' Ramsey explained. 'He texted me last night, but I totally forgot about it with all the... well, all the *stuff* that happened. It was sketched on the back of the painting I gave him.'

'The one you bought and tested?'

Ramsey nodded.

'His last piece,' he said. 'Natalie said he'd used an old canvas to paint the forgery on, and I think he didn't realise.

Either that or he didn't care. But Raj got them to date the charcoal, and it's over twenty years old, so way before this.'

'A picture within a painting, left against a wall in a studio for two decades or more, possibly sketched when they were together,' Ellie stared at the image. 'It's beautiful. We should give it to June when she wakes.'

'Look closer,' Ramsey smiled, tapping the image. 'Zoom in.'

Ellie did, scanning around the image—until she stopped.

'She's wearing the bracelet,' she said. 'The swan.'

'Yes,' Ramsey took the phone back. 'Do you have the photo? The one with the SD card?'

Ellie nodded, pulling out the photo they'd found of the young Sebastian LaFleur and June Hudson.

'She's wearing it there,' Ramsey said, zooming in. 'It's small, but you can just make it out.'

'Maybe,' Ellie replied, unconvinced. 'But how—'

Now, Ramsey showed the image of Wyatt and LaFleur at the party, zooming in on the arm LaFleur had around Wyatt, the silver glint of a bracelet showing.

'I think she gave it to him,' he said, 'When she called it off. And he never took it off.'

'Until Chantelle got hold of it,' Ellie nodded. 'Possibly the day he drove off.'

'He could have dropped it, had it stolen, maybe even Natalie gave it to her, we'll never know,' Ramsey replied. 'But when Chantelle offered it to June as a payment to shut up, she knew they had killed Seb. That's why she knew she could be next, and kept the SD card safe.'

'It's a shame it fell into the Thames,' Ellie mused, and was unsurprised to see Ramsey reach into his pocket, pulling a rather familiar silver bracelet out.

'It fell into my hand when I grappled for the gun,' he said, with a mixture of nonchalance and bravado. 'I thought maybe June would like it back.'

'She's lost everything else,' Ellie nodded, taking it.

'And when you give them to her, tell her Natalie died trying to avenge her grandfather,' Ramsey suggested. 'Don't tell her the truth. People never like to hear the truth.'

'Thanks again, Ramsey,' Ellie placed the bracelet safely in her pocket. 'You know, you're really not how you portray yourself.'

'Nobody is,' Ramsey pointed with his glass at the window. 'And your cab's here.'

Ellie rose.

'Caesar's, ten am,' she said. 'Pass it around. I'll explain everything tomorrow.'

'You'd better,' Ramsey smiled as he raised his gin at her in a toast. 'Stay safe, Reckless.'

'You too, Allen,' Ellie said as she walked out into the night, nodding to the cab and climbing in.

As the cab drove off, Ramsey watched it for a moment before picking the phone up once more, dialling a number from memory and holding it to his ear.

'Mother,' he said. 'I thought I'd call, see how you're doing.'

And, settling into the hotel bar chair, gin in hand, Ramsey Allen settled comfortably into his role as dutiful son to his sick mother.

ELLIE WAS EXHAUSTED BY THE TIME THE CAB DROPPED HER OFF at her apartment, and the only thing she wanted was a warm bath, followed by a long sleep.

However, as she saw Nathan standing beside his car, she knew this wouldn't be happening for a while.

'Really, not the time,' she muttered, stopping as she reached him. 'Come shout at me tomorrow, or maybe even next week, yeah?'

'I was at the hospital,' Nathan replied calmly.

'I know,' Ellie sighed. 'We spoke. You threatened to have Millie put down.'

Nathan frowned.

'Well, that explains one thing,' he said. 'I was there five minutes. You groaned and muttered something about Millie and, realising you were dreaming and not in a coma, I left you alone.'

'You didn't talk to me?'

'No.'

'You didn't see Nicky Simpson?'

'The YouTube guy? No,' Nathan smiled. 'What drugs did they have you on?'

'All of them, I think,' Ellie rubbed at her head wound. 'So why are you here?'

'I saw you on TV,' Nathan replied. 'They haven't named you, but I saw you stop that girl from TOWIE shooting up a tourist area. You saved a lot of lives today.'

'Not as many as you think,' Ellie forced an embarrassed smile.

'Anyway, with you almost dying yesterday and charging at people with guns today, I realised you're broken,' Nathan continued. 'You've got nothing to live for, have you?'

Ellie went to snap back, to shout at Nathan at this, but stopped.

Nathan was right.

'It's been a bad year,' she mumbled.

'Too much drink, too little self care,' Nathan nodded. 'So I've found a way to help you.'

He walked to his car and opened the back door. Even before it was fully open, Ellie heard the yelp of joy as a golden-brown Cocker Spaniel leapt out, running over to Ellie, leaping up at her, sniffing her face as she crouched, hugging the dog, tears running down her cheeks.

'You were right, I've not been the best of owners, and you need her more than I do,' Nathan placed a lead beside the couple. 'So take good care of her, yeah?'

Ellie looked up.

'You sure?'

Nathan shrugged.

'I'm guessing, going on the last couple of days, that you'll still kill yourself soon,' he said. 'So, this is more *loaning* than giving back to you.'

'And her stuff?'

'Oh, that's all staying with me,' Nathan replied. 'You can buy your own stuff. I didn't say I don't want to see her again, I still want to have the occasional weekend with her for doggie snuggles.'

Ellie chuckled.

'Deal,' she said as Nathan closed the door and walked over to the driver's side.

'Try not to die,' he said as he opened the driver's door now. 'I might not be your biggest fan, but you seem to be trying to do the right thing. It'd be a shame to get Millie back at your funeral, yeah?'

And, this morose final warning given, Nathan clambered into his car and, with a beep of the horn, drove off into the London traffic.

Ellie kept Millie close for a minute longer, hugging her, all thoughts of baths and beds now gone. She needed to go shopping for dog beds, and dog food, and dog toys, and—

Ellie rose, attaching the lead to Millie as she frowned, looking down the street. The Ford Focus was still a write-off, Ramsey and Tinker were in the wind, and likely drunk by now, and Robert was finishing the Somerville case. She could call another cab, but often they didn't like dogs in their cars—

Eventually, weighing up her options, Ellie pulled her phone out, scrolling through her numbers. There was one she could call, a small fry she hadn't spoken to in months. Nodding, she dialled it.

'Hi, Jayston?' she said as the call answered. 'Ellie Reckless. You remember you owe me a favour, at a time or place of my choosing, for when I helped your sister get into drama school?'

She waited, crouching back down and ruffling Millie's head.

'Excellent,' she said, standing back up. 'I need you, or someone who works for you, to go to *Pets at Home*, pick up some things and bring them to me right now. I'll cover the cost, and I'll send you a list of what I need.'

She laughed as she listened to the reply.

'I know,' she said. 'But needs must and all that. Thanks.'

Disconnecting the call, she walked to the door to her apartment block. She'd send the list in a moment, and then she'd have a nap, likely with a Cocker Spaniel snuggled against her.

She needed the sleep, because tomorrow was going to be a long day; especially if she was telling everyone the truth.

She stopped, the door half open. *I wonder if Caesar's is pet friendly?*

'Come on, good girl,' she said to Millie, shaking the thought away, mentally filing it as something that could wait until the morning. 'Welcome home.'

Ellie Reckless and her team
will return in their second thriller

STEAL
THE —
GOLD

Buy now on Amazon:
mybook.to/stealthegold

Released November 13th 2022

Gain up-to-the-moment information on the release by
signing up to the Jack Gatland VIP Reader's Club!

Join at www.subscribepage.com/jackgatland

ACKNOWLEDGEMENTS

When you write a series of books, you find that there are a ton of people out there who help you, sometimes without even realising, and so I wanted to do a little acknowledgement to some of them.

There are people I need to thank, and they know who they are. People who patiently gave advice when I started writing under this pen name back in 2020, the people on various Facebook groups who encouraged me when I didn't know if I could even do this; the designers who gave advice on cover design and on book formatting, all the way to my friends and family, who saw what I was doing, not as mad folly, but as something good, including my brother Chris Lee, who I truly believe could make a fortune as a post-retirement copy editor, if not start a solid writing career of his own; and Jacqueline Beard MBE, who has copy-edited all my books so far (including the prequel), line by line for me, and deserves *way more* than our agreed fee.

Also, I couldn't have done this without my growing army of ARC readers, who not only show me where I falter, but also raise awareness of me in the social media world, ensuring that other people learn of my books.

But mainly, I tip my hat and thank you. *The reader.* Who took a chance on me within a pile of Kindle books, and thought you'd give my stories a go.

I write Ellie Reckless for you. She (and her team) gains favours for you. And with luck, she'll keep on gaining these favours for a very long time.

Jack Gatland / Tony Lee,
 London, April 2022

ABOUT THE AUTHOR

Jack Gatland is the pen name of *#1 New York Times Bestselling Author* Tony Lee, who has been writing in all media for thirty-five years, including comics, graphic novels, middle grade books, audio drama, TV and film for *DC Comics, Marvel, BBC, ITV, Random House, Penguin USA, Hachette* and a ton of other publishers and broadcasters.

These have included licenses such as ***Doctor Who, Spider Man, X-Men, Star Trek, Battlestar Galactica, MacGyver,*** BBC's ***Doctors, Wallace and Gromit*** and ***Shrek***, as well as work created with musicians such as ***Ozzy Osbourne, Joe Satriani, Beartooth*** and ***Megadeth.***

As Tony, he's toured the world talking to reluctant readers with his 'Change The Channel' school tours, and lectures on screenwriting and comic scripting for *Raindance* in London.

As ***Jack Gatland***, he's written ten books so far in the *DI Declan Walsh* procedural crime series, and one book in the *Damian Lucas* adventure thrillers series. He doesn't intend to stop any time soon.

An introvert West Londoner by heart, he lives with his wife Tracy and dog Fosco, just outside London.

Locations / Items In The Book

The locations and items I use in my books are often real, if altered slightly for dramatic intent. Here's some more information about a few of them...

Although Danny's house in **Chipping Norton** doesn't exist, the area does, and the *Chipping Norton Set* includes celebrities including Jeremy Clarkson, Alex James from *Blur*, ex-Prime Minister David Cameron and Rebekah Brooks.

And yes, there is a *Soho House* there.

The Boxing Club near Meath Gardens in which Ellie spars doesn't exist, and neither does Johnny Lucas - but the location used is the current **Globe Town Social Club**, within **Green Lens Studios**, a community centre formerly known as Eastbourne House, that I would pass occasionally in my 20s.

Vermeer's "The Concert" is a real painting, and was stolen during the Gardner Heist. In the early morning hours of March 18, 1990, thirteen works of art were stolen from the Isabella Stewart Gardner Museum in Boston. Guards admitted two men posing as police officers responding to a disturbance call, and the thieves tied the guards up and looted the museum over the next hour. The case is unsolved; no arrests have been made and no works have been recovered. The stolen works have been valued at hundreds of millions of dollars by the FBI and art dealers. The museum is offering a

$10 million reward for information leading to the art's recovery, the largest bounty ever offered by a private institution.

The stolen works were originally procured by art collector Isabella Stewart Gardner (1840–1924) and intended for permanent display at the museum with the rest of her collection. Among them was *The Concert*, one of only 34 known paintings by Johannes Vermeer and thought to be the most valuable unrecovered painting in the world. Also missing is *The Storm on the Sea of Galilee*, Rembrandt's only seascape. Other paintings and sketches by Rembrandt, Edgar Degas, Édouard Manet, and Govert Flinck were stolen, along with a relatively valueless eagle finial and Chinese *gu*.

Experts were puzzled by the choice of artwork, since more valuable works were left untouched. The collection and its layout are permanent, so empty frames remain hanging both in homage to the missing works and as placeholders for their return.

Finally, **St Katherine Docks** is exactly as Monroe describes; they took their name from the former hospital of *St Katharine's by the Tower*, built in the 12th century, which stood on the site. An intensely built-up 23-acre site was earmarked for redevelopment by an Act of Parliament in 1825, with construction commencing in May 1827. Some 1,250 houses were demolished, together with the medieval hospital of St. Katharine. Around 11,300 inhabitants, mostly port workers crammed into unsanitary slums, lost their homes; only the property owners received compensation.

The docks were officially opened on 25 October 1828 and although well used, they were not a great commercial success and were unable to accommodate large ships. They were badly damaged by German bombing during the Second World War. All the warehouses around the eastern basin were destroyed, and the site remained derelict until the 1960s. Rebuilt in the last twenty years, the area now features offices, public and private housing, a large hotel, shops and restaurants, a pub (*The Dickens Inn*, a former brewery dating back to the 18th century), a yachting marina and other recreational facilities.

It remains a popular leisure destination.

If you're interested in seeing what the *real* locations look like, I post 'behind the scenes' location images on my Instagram feed. This will continue through all the books, and I suggest you follow it.

www.jackgatland.com
www.hoodemanmedia.com

Subscribe to my Readers List:
www.subscribepage.com/jackgatland

www.facebook.com/jackgatlandbooks
www.twitter.com/jackgatlandbook
ww.instagram.com/jackgatland

Want more books by Jack Gatland? Turn the page...

LETTER FROM THE DEAD

"BY THE TIME YOU READ THIS, I WILL BE DEAD..."

A TWENTY YEAR OLD MURDER...
A PRIME MINISTER LEADERSHIP BATTLE...
A PARANOID, HOMELESS EX-MINISTER...
AN EVANGELICAL PREACHER WITH A SECRET...

DI DECLAN WALSH HAS HAD BETTER FIRST DAYS...

AVAILABLE ON AMAZON / KINDLEUNLIMITED

EIGHT PEOPLE. EIGHT SECRETS.
ONE SNIPER.

THE
B⊕ARD
ROOM

HOW FAR WOULD YOU GO TO GAIN JUSTICE?

NEW YORK TIMES #1 BESTSELLER TONY LEE WRITING AS

JACK GATLAND

A NEW STANDALONE THRILLER WITH
A TWIST - FROM THE CREATOR OF THE
BESTSELLING 'DI DECLAN WALSH' SERIES

AVAILABLE ON AMAZON / KINDLE UNLIMITED

THEY TRIED TO KILL HIM...
NOW HE'S OUT FOR **REVENGE.**

NEW YORK TIMES #1 BESTSELLER **TONY LEE** WRITING AS

JACK GATLAND

THE MURDER OF AN **MI5 AGENT**...
A BURNED SPY **ON THE RUN** FROM HIS OWN PEOPLE...
AN ENEMY OUT TO **STOP HIM** AT ANY COST...
AND A **PRESIDENT** ABOUT TO BE **ASSASSINATED**...

SLEEPING SOLDIERS

A **TOM MARLOWE** THRILLER

BOOK 1 IN A NEW SERIES OF THRILLERS IN THE STYLE OF
JASON BOURNE, JOHN MILTON OR **BURN NOTICE,** AND
SPINNING OUT OF THE **DECLAN WALSH** SERIES OF BOOKS

AVAILABLE ON AMAZON / KINDLE UNLIMITED

JACK GATLAND

THE
LIONHEART
CURSE

HUNT THE GREATEST TREASURES
PAY THE GREATEST PRICE

BOOK 1 IN A NEW SERIES OF ADVENTURES
IN THE STYLE OF 'THE DA VINCI CODE'
FROM THE CREATOR OF DECLAN WALSH

AVAILABLE ON AMAZON / KINDLEUNLIMITED

Printed in Great Britain
by Amazon

19236526R00198